Ruben da Silva

ABSENCE
OF
EVIDENCE

Trust with your heart,
believe what you see

First published by Herberto Camara, 2021

Copyright © 2021 Herberto Camara

ISBN: 978-0-620-96147-9 (print)
ISBN: 978-0-620-96148-6 (e-book)

Cover and interior crafted with love by the team at:
www.myebook.online

ACKNOWLEDGMENTS

We are, in part, the accumulation of positive and negative past events. In my case, many of these resulted in me conceiving and writing this story. It would therefore be excessive for me to acknowledge everything and everyone that lead to this and I'm probably not even aware of many of the influences.

I would, however, like to make special thanks to Virgilio Goncalves, who mentored and critiqued my novel. His generosity was as heartfelt as it was needed. As a first-time author, the process of writing has been long and grueling at times, an endeavor more complex and nuanced than I initially estimated. In the end, I shall look back fondly at creating this story and the imprint of Virgilio's kindness will forever resonate with me.

The story was practically fully-fledged before I began writing. I knew I wanted the main character to be a professor and decided he would specialize in philosophy and religious studies. Even I was surprised at how well the philosophy interlaced with my preconceived thoughts. I undertook in an online philosophy course from the University of Edinburgh, called "Introduction to Philosophy", to better understand the subject matter. It proved enlightening.

At its core, the novel was born from a concept and the resulting thoughts that manifested for me many years ago. I hope the story will resonate with some readers and conceptualize the subject matter in ways that I hadn't considered.

CHAPTER ONE

'Why are we here? Who or what created us? These questions have plagued mankind since the birth of our consciousness and will arguably remain until our demise.' George lent towards the precipice of his lecture room pulpit, his second-year students listening intently to his lecture. Some were writing key points, others formulated ideas in their heads.

'Over the centuries, cultures have devised many different plausible theories as a solution. Many of them took aspects of older cultures and evolved them, while others concluded completely altered philosophies. Cultures of bygone eras tended to be spiritual. More recent explanations are far more practical.

'The unexamined life is not worth living. Those were the words of Socrates over two thousand years ago and they will remain just as applicable for millennia to come. Our inquisitive minds are what make us what we are. Science is playing a larger part in explaining our existence. The problem from a scientific perspective is even if we were to determine what happened at year zero, the birth date of existence, we would still not have answers as to what came before it and who or what caused it as well as why.'

George took the moment to take a gulp from a water bottle he had readily available. He did this to ease his throat, as well as to make the thought resonate with the students.

'While in certain respects, quantum physics has become the religion of our age, broadening our awareness beyond what it was, the understanding of time and space and how they occur will only take us so far. In many cases, science is still a theoretical rule book for the universe. I say theoretical because the rules are always being amended. Determining what is a fact is questionable when science is constantly redrafting what was regarded as a fact yesterday. For example, some scientists are now questioning the validity of the Big Bang. Certain Albert Einstein theories have been disputed and some of Stephen Hawking's theories will lose their validity in the future.

'Science is, however, currently limited to this universe and is therefore limited. For instance, our dreams are another form of reality. Is our awake state any more real than the other? Therefore, is one state of being more valid than another? Our minds can create a whole new plane of existence. A universe unto its own if you will. Consequently, these dream universes don't necessarily follow the same rules of nature and science as are present in our awake state. Whether it be lack of gravity, time, light et cetera, these are oddities we have experienced when asleep. Therefore, the rules being devised by scientists are truly just a rulebook of our current existence. Granted, it will allow further insight into parallel universes and other realizations we have not even considered as of yet.

'Now imagine if reality, all forms of reality, could be explained in a single state. For the purposes of this example, the state is sight. Would anyone like to attempt to explain the concept of sight to the class?'

The room remained still for a moment before a few hands started to rise.

'Professor, I would say that it's the ability to distinguish shapes and... stuff,' said a student.

'True, but is it not even more than that? Does anyone else have anything further to add?'

'Color. Being able to see in different colors,' guessed another student.

'Very good, but it's still so much more. From a human perspective, there is also being able to gauge the depth and distance of objects. This is, however, merely limiting sight to the human experience. Is it any more a valid form of sight than the sonar of bats, or if I'm not mistaken, that snakes can see in infrared? Is that any more valid than smell? Sight is merely a form of being able to assess one's surroundings - arguably the primary way humans process surrounding information. Perhaps an evolved sense of smell can do just as well. So why limit the concept of sight to our rudimentary viewpoint? There are undoubtedly other senses we are not even aware of yet. Therefore, there is far more to existence than we can perceive or consider. Perhaps there is more to the occult and the supernatural than meets the eye. Pun intended.'

The lecture room with its seventy students smiled in appreciation.

'The point I'm trying to make is that our view of reality and existence is still limited. It will evolve, but will likely always remain limited. Even if humanity becomes so advanced - to the point we are one day able to create our own realities and I'm not simply talking about virtual reality but actual tangible forms of reality - it will however still not answer the question, why are we here? Did something create us? Was it this almighty benevolent being or was it nothing but reactions within matter with no entity behind it? Where they multiple beings rather than a singular entity? Should any of these be true, it still leads to the question: what in turn created the event or entity responsible for creating the universe? For example, an almighty God is a possible solution to the creation of everything we are aware of. The problem with this is whether it's a sufficient enough answer?

'Surely something, in turn, must have created the creator. Why do so many regard it as an acceptable solution and why not question what happened before creation? The Big Bang is not a sufficient starting point for us because if true, a cause must have ignited it. In God, why are we less willing to question the concept of the creator? Excuse my statement. What I mean to put across is the God of the primary religions is and was so powerful that he is now, was then and ever shall be. Why are so many people willing to accept a statement like this as a starting point, but not a conclusion like the Big Bang? With religion, we don't question what came before, but with science we do. Humans cannot conceptualize a commencement without a cause or a creator.

Our minds and understanding are too limited to truly understand and accept that somehow everything must at some point have been created from nothing, but in turn, what created the creator? Eventually, one would run out of creators and suffer from the same initial hurdle of what created it all. Something that has always existed and created itself is too unfathomable to wrap our heads around. I don't know if it's a question that science will ever be able to answer.'

George gulped down more water.

'When I was at school, I read a book about a group of entities responsible for creating the universe. Unfortunately, I can't recall the title or the author. The book tracked the progression of humanity through the ages and into the future until humanity became so enlightened that they, in turn, created a new universe. As it turns out the group of entities responsible for creating the initial universe were also humans. In this book, the universes were in a perpetual circle of creation. Where humanity kept on creating the next universe and humans were therefore always responsible for creating the last. Thus producing a paradox of what came first, similar to the chicken or the egg.

George recognized some students were struggling with his explanation. He opted to clarify.

'This is one potential solution to the starting point of existence and God - an endless loop creating itself over and over again. The Almighty might have been created by the god before him, who in turn was created by the god before that, with the initial god being the final god in an endless loop because the starting point and finishing point is all relative. A loop of Alphas and the Omegas if you will. However, while the loop potentially negates the need for a starting point, what created the perpetual circle, to begin with? It's merely as strong as an argument as a singular creator being the loop in its singularity. If you recall from our class two weeks ago, this is known as a causal loop. A causal loop, being where an event is the cause of another event, which is in turn the cause of the first-mentioned event. This can even be found in ancient cultures like Egypt where they depict a snake eating its tail. It's known as an Ouroboros symbol and depicts an endless cycle of renewal which is inspired by life, death and rebirth. There are no easy solutions. We clearly don't have the knowledge and ability at this stage to solve the puzzle. Perhaps we never shall. Perhaps we are better off with our limited insight.'

The bell tower sounded in the distance to signal the end of the hour.

'Before you leave, your assignment for next week is to accumulate your thoughts on year zero and these concepts. There are no limitations of scope. You may focus on a specific category or create your own argument or solution. You can be highly practical or creative. My intention is for you to expand your consciousness, rather than researching. I'll send out an email to you all later today with further guidance. I look forward to reading your thoughts. Have a good weekend.'

CHAPTER TWO

George was relieved to be home. It had been a long day at university due to the volume of papers needing to be marked. Having to do his weekly shopping to boot, left him more exhausted than usual on his arrival home. He shifted his weight to place the burdening groceries on the kitchen countertop and began packing the contents in the fridge, freezer and cupboards before he stepped towards his wine rack. It was not elaborate by any means, but he did enjoy a glass of wine on occasion. George was not particular when it came to wine and did not go out of his way to collect older vintages. No bottle could be considered subpar, nor were there any vintages of repute.

He selected one of his better Cabernets and, wine in hand, switched on his vinyl turntable. The needle began caressing Al Green's Greatest Hits. George had an appreciation for timeless music.

'Aah, that's better,' said George as he took a few moments to sit in his favorite listening chair.

George loved his job, but there were aspects of it which he found more tedious than others. Marking papers was one of the more monotonous features. Viewing an expression of interest in his students' eyes and knowing he was imparting knowledge to others made it all worthwhile. Beyond worthwhile. Lecturing enabled him to be in charge of his work environment, while at the same time interacting with young adults. This enabled him to remain young at heart to some degree. George was in his early forties. The onset of a new decade made him start to take more care of his health. His thirties had been a rough period for him. These stresses had taken their toll on his body so he had recently taken up running during the week before work. He was also attempting to lower his sugar intake.

A few songs later he rose to prepare a simple meal of spaghetti bolognese. George lived alone which meant that simple was often the best adjective to describe the meals he prepared. He was, however, able to concoct a tasty meal when the need arose. Trial and error as well as late-night cooking shows had allowed him to progress beyond amateur proficiency. George was not one to entertain, but cooking was an activity he seemed to have a flair for and he found it to be a pleasant distraction. His sister, Lila, had tried to convince him to take cooking classes, but he preferred undertakings tasks at his own pace and in his own time. It saddened Lila that George had been single for so long and she thought cooking classes would be a great way to meet new people. To her, these classes would be as successful a method to meet a single lady as any other. He actually agreed with this theory and preferred the idea of meeting someone in a class atmosphere rather than in a bar or club. He had left the clubbing and bar hopping behind for his younger self.

George was an attractive looking man. He was not magazine-cover handsome, but he had a neutrality which many women found pleasing. If he were to go on a blind date and put effort into his appearance, the woman would no doubt be be proud to be seen with him. Since he had commenced his running routine, he had lost a few pounds and began to cast a similar silhouette to when he was in his twenties. During the last few years, however, grooming had not been high on his priority list. George was a very clean person, but his hair was often scruffy and his beard unkempt. He would invariably only shave once a week and went for a haircut once every two months if not three. His disheveled appearance made him look as though he had rolled out of bed, but this had its allure.

He did, however, have a certain charm to him. He was quite a light-hearted person despite the seriousness which had established itself with being a university professor and was very learned. His horn-rimmed spectacles added to his intellectual appearance. This in turn almost complemented his unkempt appearance.

As a lecturer, he was required to command a room and present himself to his students in such a way which allowed him to maintain people's interest. This skill had taken him years to perfect, but he was now regarded as one of the more entertaining and interesting lecturers in his faculty. These were, of course, skills that translated well with interacting with people one on one as well as in small groups. George was, however, a forthright man. He didn't believe in playing a part or manipulating people. What you saw was what you got. People who knew him appreciated this aspect of his personality. He was grounded and consistent in his disposition. Not purposefully trying to be the center of attention meant he did not stand out at first impression and, for the most part, he was confident in his own skin. However, generally speaking, he found meeting new people tedious.

Politics and religion were two immeasurably divisive topics. George was well aware of this and realized the subject of much of his work was a gateway to argumentative topics of conversation. To negate this he spoke about the subject matter from a historical standpoint. George preferred to veer away from continuous frames of reference and stick to interesting facts about the history of religion and philosophy. Unfortunately, there was often no viewpoint that could be agreed upon for much of the subject matter that he taught.

He lost his train of thought and the meat was about to sear. He turned down the stove and added the tomato sauce. George tested the spaghetti. It was al dente so he dipped it into a colander and went back to stir the bolognese. Once it was ready, he placed his creation on a freshly washed plate. He collected a tray from the cupboard as well as cutlery. George took another sip of wine. The Cabernet was full and aromatic. The smell and taste of a cigar box were the most dominant for him. He topped up his glass of wine and placed everything on the tray before switching off the record player and sitting in front of the television. George didn't believe in replacing items if they were still functioning, but his previous television was old and the picture quality had tested his patience. He had therefore recently taken some money from his investments to buy a new flat-screen television. He flicked through the streaming categories for a while before settling on a wildlife documentary.

His mother had loved nature. She always tried to impart her love of the outdoors onto Lila and George with the aim of making them more well-rounded and more appreciative of nature. She wanted them to see as much of the beauty in nature as possible. He had loved their family camping trips when he was young. Lila preferred the concrete jungle rather than the natural one when she was younger. George had not been on a camp for years. He did, however, go on hikes on a regular basis during the more temperate months. Living in a town rather than a city enabled him to appreciate this endeavor. There was much flora and fauna to appreciate within a stone's throw. He was fortunate to be living in a region with a diverse topography of generous amounts of mountains, valleys, hills and rivers on the outskirts of town. He loved to go out by himself to clear his head and just inhale the fresh air.

This particular nature episode was about the wildebeests' migration across the Serengeti in Tanzania, Africa. It was quite a sight to watch more than a million antelopes crossing the plains of central Africa for the change in season. With this came a primary feeding time for lions and crocodiles. Picking off on their prey as opportunities arose created powerful imagery. Parts of Earth could still be tremendously primal and ferocious he thought to himself.

He continued watching for another hour before losing interest. He had seen similar footage a month earlier. Living by himself in an apartment was uninspiring at the best of times. George switched the television off, washed and dried the dishes before placing them in their allocated places.

He sauntered to the window and looked outside at the neighborhood below. It was a pleasant area to live in and was relatively quiet, but with a sufficient amount of life and many residents who were quick to offer a smile. He hadn't altered much over the past few years in the two-bedroom apartment. To his eye, the space was sufficiently furnished and did not require a refresh. Decor was not something he was passionate about and the look had remained neutral since its inception. The size of the space was manageable and he had always liked this area. One of the positive aspects of this neighborhood was its close proximity to the university which enabled him to save thirty minutes in traffic had he lived in the more affordable outskirts of town. Having a prestigious tertiary institute and a growing commercial industry resulted in the town's vibrancy.

He closed the curtains with a sluggish tug and prepared for bed. He was looking forward to a good night's sleep.

CHAPTER THREE

George strained to open his eyes as he awoke to the sound of birds twittering outside his window and a car engine lightly revving past. Not one to waste time in the morning, he rose from the bed and stretched with pleasure. George held the position for a moment and squeezed every last drop of indulgence out of extension. He walked over to the kitchen to gulp down a glass of water and eat an apricot yogurt. He then went to brush his teeth and put on his running clothes. His shoes were starting to look worn out. He had only taken up running two months earlier and hadn't realized it was time to buy a new pair. He decided to look for another pair online when he returned. He was curious to research what was available and designed for running, rather than a generic athletic shoe. George was aware that running was resulting in extra wear and tear on his knees and since he seemed to be keeping up with his new routine, it was time to find a pair of more appropriate footwear.

Before leaving, he went through the motions of a few basic stretches to limber himself up. He performed a few lunges, hip circles then stretched out his limbs purposefully and methodically. Grabbing his apartment keys he returned towards his bed pedestal to take his cellular phone and earphones. Showering, making his bed and eating a proper breakfast would wait for later.

George jogged with leisure down his street. He still felt sluggish from the night before. Running at dawn was his preference. Not only was it cooler and therefore easier to run, but it was also quieter. Most of the residents in the area were sleeping or still preparing for their day. The solitude resulted in fewer distractions and enabled him to clear his head. He liked the quietness this early in the morning. It was rejuvenating. At times, he wouldn't see another person for a couple of minutes. It was as though he was gliding through life. Partly so, yet not. There were lights on in a few apartments and he could hear the odd person in the distance, but because there were no faces to be seen it seemed almost dreamlike. The sky was slightly dabbed with illumination as the sun hadn't risen yet.

The trees were full and green. The inception of summer had arrived the week before and it made the streets look inviting and vibrant. George turned right towards the park and began to pick up pace. The park was popular for runners because of its many lanes and trails which were canopied by large, aged trees. None of the runners, however, were to be seen at this hour. The park was similar to New York's Central Park, but on a much smaller magnitude. It was a rectangular, green belt that was quarantined by some of the more expensive residential homes in the town. Many aspects of the town were on a lesser scale but it was not tiny. It bustled with life during the day. Quaint yet energetic, was how many travel journalists referred to it. This was in part due to the local university which brought the energy of youth with it. Only the locals knew of the sleepier recesses of its streets.

George climbed three steps to enter the park at the nearest entrance towards a narrow lane skirted by large oaks. Their shade made joggers' journeys much easier during the summer months. He inserted his earphones before adjusting his selection to random on his cellular phone's music track selector. The Rolling Stones' *Wild Horses* filled his ears. It instantly enabled his mind to trail away as he disengaged his consciousness.

CHAPTER FOUR

'Coming!' Lila yelled after George knocked on the front door. George stared through the pained glass window, waiting for his loving sister to open the door. Lila and her husband, Joe, had lived there for nearly four years. It was a spacious, middle-class house with a welcoming quality like a favored quilted blanket embracing a bed. George was a regular visitor due to his sister's warm and caring nature despite her often coarse delivery. He was also fortunate he and Joe got along so well. There was a ten-year age gap between the two men yet they interacted as though they had known each other from birth. Lila and Joe's two children, Julia and Noah, were six and three respectively. A growing family had meant they had to find a more spacious home with a back yard in which the kids could run around in.

The latch unlocked and the door swung open. His sister's beaming smile stared back at him.

'Good to see you, Bro,' said Lila as she kissed him on the cheek.

'Happy birthday Lila,' said George as he handed her a fresh bouquet of flowers.

'Thank you! They are beautiful!'

'I see you managed to remove the stains from the driveway,' said

George. 'I don't know where you find the time and energy. A mother of two, running a hair salon, plus maintaining a home.'

'All in a good day's work. I managed to borrow a high-pressure hose from one of my clients. You know these fucking hands can do more than cut hair, you asshole.'

'Charming,' said George to his sister's eloquent tongue. It was one of the quirks about her that he had always found amusing.

'Now get the fuck inside before the hubby starts joking about me neglecting the kitchen!'

As George stepped into the house, Julia and Noah burst around the corner as fast as their diminutive legs could carry them.

'Uncle George, Uncle George!' they screeched.

'Hi kids. My oh my, are the two of you taller than the last time I was here? I'm sure you're bigger than when I saw you three weeks ago. One of these days you are going to be the same height as me.'

Giggling and tickling followed before they ran off and performed another act of terrorism in another room as their mother termed it.

'This is another beautiful day we are having,' George said as the summer light streamed in through the large French windows. It was one of the main reasons Lila and Joe loved the house. The sizeable windows made an immense difference to the light intake and the sense of spaciousness of the home.

'Joe is out back getting the fish ready. Why don't you go greet him so I can do my....duties in the kitchen?' Lila joked. She had a dichotomized personality. She was loving and friendly yet her choice of words was often abrasive or rude which people either loved or hated. She was always herself though and never backed down to appease societal stereotypes. Those close to her always appreciated her honesty and forthright nature.

George fondly rested his hands on Lila's shoulders as he stepped past her into the spacious yet unorganized living area. Joe was the neater member of the family, but having two young children had meant he had reduced his standards. The space did, however, look lived in and comfortable, in an endearing way with its explosions of color everywhere. He skirted around the room and through the French doors towards their green back yard with a children's slide and swing in the center as well as a small splash pool.

'Great to see you, George. How have you been?'

'Well, thanks, Joe. It certainly helps when the days are as beautiful as this.'

'Excuse my hands, I'd rather not shake yours,' Joe said as oil dripped onto the countertop.

'No problem.'

Joe looked ungainly as he prepared the sardines. His six foot four frame was far too large to be handling the diminutive fish without looking clown-like. Despite his size and military-like haircut, Joe was a quiet, unassuming and approachable man. He came across as the polar opposite to his wife, who was half his size yet twice as loud and jovial. It was a case of opposites complementing one another as they were the happiest couple George knew. This was partly due to their nonchalant attitude to one another. They could often be seen mocking each other to test the boundaries of each other's sense of humor. It was one of the parts of their recipe which resulted in a functional marriage.

'I'll put them on the grill in a minute. They seem super fresh. Let's hope they taste as good as they look,' Joe said in his burly voice. 'I know these little guys are annoying to eat, but they are so tasty when they are fresh.'

'Two cold ones for my two favorite men,' Lila interjected, as she walked onto the patio before exiting back into the house, her long, bright red hair trailing behind her.

'Thanks, honey!' said Joe.

'Thanks, honey!' said George. 'How is the mechanic industry treating you, Joe? This is your busy season, isn't it?'

'Yeah, it is. Right before the school holidays. The car owners want their vehicles to be reliable before they go on their long holiday trips. It suits me fine. The more business the better. Having two young kids to take care of definitely changes your financial position. Suddenly preparing for school and college or varsity becomes a necessity. You better be able to get our kids a special deal when they are older,' Joe said.

'I may be able to pull some strings,' said George.

'Julia wants to become a doctor. I think she was a slight crush on her pediatrician, Doctor Jones. God help me. Six years old and she has a crush on an older man. How am I going to be able to control her when she is a teenager? Or should I say how am I going to control the boys? Maybe she will become a hermit or better yet a lesbian. Yes, maybe she will become a lesbian and I don't have to worry about pregnancy and STDs!' A laughing Joe chugged down a third of his beer.

'I'm pretty sure lesbians still get STDs. Also, even if she is a lesbian, it wouldn't stop the pedophiles from circling,' mocked George.

'Okay, I know I started this weird joke, but Georgie, you're crossing a line here. You see this?' Joe pointed to the ground and moved it from left to right to signify a line on the ground. 'This is a line. You just crossed it. In fact, you just jumped over it! Lesbians are fair game, but those pedophiles, hell no!'

George laughed. 'The interesting aspect about this is most of the viewpoints of taboo topics like these are heavily based on society.'

'Okay, I'll hear you out. Enlighten me Professor, you know I'm just a blue-collared worker.'

'I'm not condoning pedophilia, certainly not. All I'm saying is what is right and wrong is often based on society. Let's take the gay disposition for example. It was an orientation which was kept secret years ago; in fact, it was considered a sin by many religions. Now it's considered acceptable and, in a generation from now, it will be inconsequential what one's sexual orientation is. This also depends on cultures. Transgenders are still not accepted here if you ignore people's obligations to be politically correct, yet in Thailand, it's considered as a genuine sexual orientation.'

'I get what you are saying. You may have a point,' said Joe.

'Okay let's look at this from a different perspective. Medical breakthroughs. Scientists are knocking on the door of cloning and even brain transplants. It's just a matter of time before they perfect it, but one of the facets holding it back is society being morally repulsed. It's still seen as being against nature and brings into question talk on the origin of the human soul. Yet decades ago, the same battles were being fought over heart transplants and artificial insemination. Heart transplants are seen as a medical marvel now and while artificial insemination isn't considered entirely without hostility in some circles, it's moving in a more acceptable direction. It's just a case of will society accept it, in which case it will be acceptable. Another example is…'

Joe raised his hand. 'How about we talk about something more savory?' he said as he looked down towards the fish, 'You see what I did there?'

'You Sir are a genius. This grill looks as though it needs to get fired up!' said George. Joe waddled towards the grill like a penguin with a toothy smile. George and Joe lived different lives, but they always seemed to enjoy each other best when they acted like children.

CHAPTER FIVE

'I'm ready when you are, lovey,' said Lila stepping once more onto the patio.

'That was fast. How did you ever manage to marry such a capable wife?' said Joe.

'More importantly, how were you so lucky to end up with such a capable human being like me!' laughed Lila. Joe looked towards George and shrugged his shoulders.

'Since you are so capable, would you mind fetching us another beer? I would be eternally grateful,' Joe said after a moment, realizing he could take advantage of the situation. Half the fun was to see how she would respond to his playful prods.

'Back to the fucking kitchen with me then. You're lucky my brother is here. So I have to behave better!' she shouted as she walked away towards the fridge.

'Behave better?' queried George, smiling.

'I heard that ass wipe!' exclaimed Lila.

'Mommy, what's a ass wipe?' asked Julia.

'Someone who makes stupid comments like your uncle,' answered Lila, followed by giggles from the children. 'You see the trouble you guys get me into,' Lila said as she handed over the beers in exchange for further laughter by the adult contingent. 'Sometimes I need to be more careful about what I say when the kids are around. They have the hearing of dogs. I'm not the best role model in that regard.'

George smiled and confirmed, 'While you do need to be careful what you say around the kids, as they are very impressionable, I think the two of you are terrific parents. You give Julia and Noah a lot of love and attention. That is all that children really want and it's more than many receive. Plus look at everything you have done for me. I'd like to think I turned out all right so in many ways I'm a reflection of your love.'

'Thanks, bro. That's sweet.'

'It's sweet because it's true. I owe so much to you.' A large part of George's world revolved around his sister and her family. She almost never failed him and was always expedient to provide help when it was needed. He was immensely loyal to his sister and they got along surprisingly well despite their personalities being so different. He loved to visit as often as he could without feeling like he was imposing. George was refined while Lila was brash. He enjoyed pushing himself intellectually while she preferred to just have fun. Despite being a lecturer, he tended towards introversion while Lila was an out-and-out extrovert. Notwithstanding their many differences, they had shared a lot of hardship together over the years and they always seemed to find each other in the middle ground. George always found the conversations he had in the neutral territory with Lila to be the most enjoyable - almost as entertaining as the bizarre things Lila and Joe's two children did and said. He affectionately referred to babysitting them as the most important job he had. It was a role which he was thankful to enjoy.

'Whaaa! Mommy!'

'What's wrong Noah? Come to Mommy so she can make it better.' Noah came sniffling outside, his face flushed and feeling very sorry for himself.

'Julia pull Noah's hair.'

'Noah wouldn't let go of my doll! It's my doll!' shouted Julia as she ran to join them. She idolized her uncle and did not want to be seen as the misbehaving one in his eyes as well as her parents. 'Please don't be cross with me. I'm sorry.'

Joe wiped his hands and picked his daughter up. 'It's okay, sweetie. Noah is still very small. He doesn't understand how to share yet. You are the big sister and you need to show him how to share. And no more pulling your brother's hair.'

'Okay, Daddy. You smell of fish,' giggled Julia. 'Come Noah. Let's go play on the slide!' The two scurried away towards the other end of the yard.

'Sharing is caring,' Lila said.

'Isn't that from *Care Bears* or something?' asked George.

'Yip.'

'I've no idea how I knew that reference and, as a grown man, I'm a little ashamed to admit that I remembered it.'

'You should be ashamed of yourself Georgie. *Care Bears*...' Joe laughed. 'You should only refer to cartoons like *Ninja Turtles* and *He-man*. That's what the cool the boys used to watch.'

'Don't forget *BraveStarr* and *Thundercats*.'

'Right and you so-called cool boys back in the day have only grown up to remain boys. You just upgraded from He-man to *Game of Thrones*. You're still kids at heart.'

Joe stopped turning the near perfectly seared sardines on the grill. 'You know I love you Lila, but don't you put down *Game of Thrones*. That show is legendary. Plus it's very mature. Look at all the blood and nudity. It's way too grown up for kids to watch. Back me up here Georgie.'

'I'm afraid I haven't watched the show, Joe. You'll have to look for support elsewhere.'

'You haven't watched Game of Thrones! You know, Georgie, sometimes I think you need to read less.'

'Don't try and move the focus onto my brother. I'm not finished fucking belittling you. You've never thought about the fact that the show is just about a bunch of guys fighting for a throne with their armies. They are all fighting one another with swords and shields with a sprinkling of magic and dragons thrown in for good effect. Doesn't this sound like an excellent premise for a kid's cartoon?'

Joe looked at George and then back at his wife. 'Um, okay, it's a valid point. Noted. You loved that show too though.'

'Noted,' said Lila.

'The students at varsity loved the show. I heard one lecturer even threatened the class once that he had read all the books and if they didn't want him to give away any spoilers, they should keep quiet and focus. Apparently, the class was dead quiet for the remainder of the period.'

'That's pretty clever. Ruthless, but clever,' said Joe.

'I believe a lot of the story is based on actual historic events which occurred in Britain and they have merely been placed into a fantasy world.'

'Leave it to you to intellectualize a fantasy TV show, bro.'

'The fish is ready people. Lila, would you mind getting the little ones. I'm starving,' said Joe. As usual, he had gone overboard by grilling twice as many sardines as they were likely to eat.

'I can't blame you. The fish looks great,' said George. 'I think everyone is starting to salivate. Let the feasting begin.'

CHAPTER SIX

The extended family of five sat around the patio dining table with the steaming food placed in the center drawing them in. Before taking any food, they sang happy birthday to Lila. Most of the gusto was generated by Julia and Noah. Thereafter, they all clamored for the food.

'So how is the new semester goingGeorge?' asked Lila

'It's going quite well actually. The new students seem bright and eager to learn. Enthusiasm makes all the difference. Lecturing the same topic every year can get monotonous. It requires student involvement to make it more interesting and invigorating. Their energy helps me a lot to bring my A-game.'

'Not too many slackers then, hey?' asked Joe.

'Not really. They do, however, need to have a thirst for knowledge and a questioning mindset. If they are not there to learn, they are merely wasting their own time and their parents' money. Unfortunately, many of them only realize this years later. Philosophy or religious studies are a bit on the periphery though. They are certainly not the first subjects that come to mind when deciding what to study. The science, commerce and art fields are far more popular. This is why many of the students couple this degree with another such as psychology or politics. Certain religious groups tend to be stauncher and their religion is more at the forefront of their lives. However, they tend to receive adequate learning from their churches, synagogues or temples. However, I try to expose their minds to new thoughts. On the philosophy side, it's often about thinking about the subject matter from an alternative viewpoint and to reassess validity where necessary. It can be quite difficult at times because the students all come from different backgrounds and beliefs and knowing how to term topics without alienating anyone can be challenging. Sometimes I think it would be easier to be lecturing one of the other primary degrees. Lecturing philosophy and religious studies can be tricky at times, but I like having diverse subject matter.'

'So, by periphery subjects are you saying your position is becoming obsolete?' asked Lila.

'As long as humanity queries its existence and wants to understand how different cultures interpret their being, I shall have a job. Simply put, my position isn't going anywhere soon. It tends to work in cycles. Every year society is moving the yardstick of what is acceptable, but it becomes more apparent when viewing it in decades or generations. For example, the famous line, 'Frankly my dear, I don't give a damn,' from *Gone with the Wind* was considered cursing at the time and not proper vocabulary for a gentleman. These days, that phrase would almost be considered posh.'

George was finding his rhythm.

'As these shifts in etiquette perpetuate, so does humanity become more and more godless. Cursing does not have anything to do with morality, it's more about etiquette, but in this sense, the two usually work hand in hand. Humanity is at a point where it's further away from spirituality than it has ever been. There are so many stimuli available to people which results in religion being pushed further and further into the background. The cycle tends to correct itself with tragedy rears its head. Especially tragedy on a mass scale. A world war or a tsunami and suddenly religion moves back to the forefront as thoughts of Armageddon return into focus. Needless to say, our continued self-awareness will always necessitate a need for philosophy.'

'Uncle George, can we go for a swim after we finish eating? It's so hot today,' asked Julia.

'Sure, sweetheart. I think cooling down is a great idea. I left my swimming trunks in the car just in case. When the weather is this good, I have to take advantage and swim with my niece and nephew. Right?'

'Right, Uncle George,' Julia laughed.

'As long as you eat all your vegetables, kids. I need you to grow up big and strong. And don't interrupt Uncle George when he is talking. It's rude,' Lila said.

'Yes, Mommy.' The weight of the world resided in Julia's tone and posture.

'It's just as well Julia interrupted me. Let's rather change the topic. We were hardly having the best birthday conversation,' said George. 'Mmm. I must say, these sardines are delicious.'

'I'm glad you are enjoying them, Georgie. There is plenty so feel free to take a big plate of seconds,' said Joe, pleased his chef skills were acknowledged.

'Can I try one, Daddy?' asked Noah.

'Sorry Noah, you are too small. The sardines have a lot of bones and we don't want you to choke,' replied Joe.

'Talking about a lighter note, I have a new client who I think would be great for you, George,' said Lila. 'I'd like to set her up with you. She is smart, funny and so down to earth. I hit it off with her and I can see the two of you clicking. Chloe is her name. She even has a great head of hair. Some people have it all.'

'Thanks, sis, but you know I'm not fond of blind dates. It can be so difficult to find your feet and is so awkward. They end up being so trivial.'

'Oh, come on. What have you got to lose?' asked Lila.

'As much as the great head of hair sounds, I'm going to have to take a rain check.'

CHAPTER SEVEN

'Red solid in side pocket,' announced Mr. Yang brazenly before sinking the red ball as stated.

'Nice shot,' confirmed George.

It was the last Thursday of the month and it had been a standing ritual between the two to meet at the local pool bar on a regular basis on this day of the month. Mr. Yang was a history professor at the university. His office was on the same floor as George's and the pair had become friends over the past three years. All the other faculty members referred to him as Mr. Yang. Not out of intimidation. Quite the contrary, Mr. Yang had a laid-back disposition. Nor was he senior to many of the other lecturers based on age. He was in his late forties and had only recently shown signs of grey hair. Mr. Yang did, however, join the university with an impeccable record as well as a catalogue of recommendations. His surname rolled off the tongue and his colleagues had referred to him by it ever since he joined the university years prior. In fact, not many lecturers knew what his first name was. George referred to him affectionately as Yang. Even though Mr. Yang had an intellect far exceeding other members of his faculty, he tended to be inappropriate when he was drunk. Inappropriateness was not a trait that bothered George because he found the idiosyncrasy amusing.

The pool bar was a modest one, but with modesty came a lot of character. It had been around for fifty years, mostly as a bar and diner at first. Mr. Yang and George where just two of many regular custodians.

'Can I get you another beer, Yang?' asked George.

'Sure. Why not. My classes only start at ten 'o clock.'

'The benefits of being a university lecturer.'

'Living the dream my friend, living the dream. I never understood why people are okay with an eight-hour day office job with the same fixed hours day in and day out. Such high levels of rigidity are definitely not for me.'

'Well, office jobs certainly are not for everyone. However, public speaking is one of the largest fears people have, so what we do isn't for everyone either. If I'm not mistaken, many people are more terrified by public speaking than death.'

'I've had a couple of instances where it felt like death. There are a couple of topics in the syllabus that can bore the students to an early grave and the lack of feedback feels like death for me. Either that or this generation has no appreciation for fucking culture,' said Mr. Yang.

'I know what you mean.'

'Really? I've heard that your lectures are engaging and the students respond well to you.'

'Ah, my reputation precedes me,' George said. 'I guess I try to conceptualize thoughts in a way that would interest me and focus on the subjects that intrigue me. Right now, what intrigues me is another beer. I'll be right back.'

'Cheers,' said George on his return as he handed Mr. Yang his draft.

'Cheers.'

'Is it my turn?' asked George. 'You didn't sink another ball, did you?'

'Go for it. Do students hit on you often?'

'What? Why in the world would you ask me such a question?'

'Oh, just curious George. Your students like your classes and you are a handsome man. I hear your classes are always well attended.'

'You think I'm handsome?' George asked, as he struggled to hold back a laugh while chalking his cue.

'Not that handsome. My interests are curvier in nature. Preferably shorter than me. Don't change the subject. Do students sometimes hit on you?'

'I'm not young anymore,' said George, taking a moment to deliberate a response so as not to be misinterpreted in any way. Although it was against the university's charter of conduct and ethics, it wasn't unheard of for a newly qualified lecturer to have a brief relationship with one of their students. This was especially true of the male lecturers. The allure of the young students was too much for some even though it was a taboo. In my case, it used to happen more when I was younger,' he added. 'The fact I was in a relationship didn't seem to faze them. I guess some of them saw it as a conquest. Plus, they had all the power to have me fired or suspended if I had gone through with it and I suppose it made the experience empowering for them. I can't say it still happens exceptionally often that I get the impression one of my students is interested in me. The age gap is getting quite large now. I'm not sure when the age differential reared its head, but it did materialize without me realizing it. Just the other day I was one of them, thinking that adulthood was far away.'

'That's interesting since a cornerstone of what you teach revolves around morality. You never indulged one of them?' asked Mr. Yang.

'Where are these questions coming from? No, I never dipped my toe in this pond. Have you Yang?'

'Me! Hahaha. No. This belly is a major babe repellant,' he added while stroking his inflated midriff. 'My marriage might have had its rough patches over the years, but we are loyal to one another. My wife and I both know that neither of us is going to find someone better at this stage in our life.'

'What do you mean at this stage in your life? You make it sound like you're old. You are middle-aged. You still have decades ahead of you.'

'You think I should get a divorce and hook up with a young student?'

'Oh God. Yang, you are hopeless.'

CHAPTER EIGHT

'Another beer?' asked George.

'No, no, no. I have had enough for tonight. I can't handle my alcohol as well as you. What is with all the beer tonight? Are the self-loathing levels especially high tonight?' queried Mr. Yang.

George had changed over the period Mr. Yang had known him. Adversity had made him retreat from people to a large extent, despite being well-liked and enjoyable to be around by those who knew him. He still saw a lot of his sister and her family and enjoyed being around Mr. Yang but, for the most part, social gatherings were becoming rare for George. He did have these regular pool nights as well as bowling nights, but he started doing them because of the pressure to join, although he had to admit he enjoyed these nights once he was in the swing of them. He generally kept up the same pleasant disposition, but repeated hardships were eroding his once outgoing nature. George tended to internalize his emotions much more now.

Mr. Yang realized this and almost poked fun at it in the hope it would redirect the raft that George was traveling on. Mr. Yang understood that having a light-hearted disposition about the subject would help George more than ignoring it or over-sympathizing with him. Ignoring the subject would not do anyone any good.

'Self-loathing levels? Is that the way it seemed? Stop psychoanalyzing me, Yang. I'm a beacon of fortitude!'

'No doubt, George, just make sure your beacon is not built from a foundation of empty beer bottles.'

'One should never question what another man's beacon is made from,' replied George.

'Hahaha. Fair enough. Fair enough.'

'I'm doing fine, Yang. All the running I'm doing has definitely helped my health and cleared my head. I suppose I'm feeling a tiny bit lonely at times, but other than that I'm fine. Comfortably numb if you will.'

'A wise man once said: "Life must be shared with someone to call it life",' mimicked Mr. Yang.

'I don't suppose by any chance you are that wise man?'

'That is not important, but now that you mention it, I'm a very wise man.'

'Self-affirmation does not make it true, but yes you are a wise man.'

'Stroking my ego will not distract me. Neither will all these beers I've had.'

'I noticed.'

'What about Beth? She has always been interested in you. Plus, there is the added benefit that she looks as though she is into some kinky shit,' said Mr. Yang, referring to another lecturer who had an office in the same building as theirs.

'Oh, wow. I might have to retract my wise man comment. You know I'm not interested in Beth. She seems like a nice enough person, but I'm not attracted to anything about her. Plus, that lazy eye of hers is extremely distracting.'

'I think the lazy eye is charming,' said Mr. Yang.

'Great. Then you have an affair with her. I'm sure your loving wife won't mind.'

'Oh hell, no. My wife will divorce me for everything I have. What would I do without the ample university pension fund that I have managed to amass over all these years?'

'I know. It's amazing how engorged a tertiary education pension can get,' said George. 'Tell me though, how exactly does a kinky looking person look? You do know that she is a devout Jew? I sincerely doubt that she is kinky. In fact, she comes across quite prudish if you ask me.'

'Oh. I didn't even know that she was Jewish. Now that you mention it, I guess she does come across prudish.' Mr. Yang did not bother trying to defend the statement he had made as he knew there was no substance to it.

'Let's be honest, you fantasize that everyone is kinky. I don't even want to know what that says about you, Yang. Or is it all because of her lazy eye?'

'What, a man can't find a lazy eye attractive?'

'I suspect you find every aspect of a person attractive, as long as it's on a person with curves.'

'What can I say, I'm a lover, not a hater. I don't discriminate,' said Mr. Yang.

'Your poor wife, I don't know how she puts up with you.'

CHAPTER NINE

Sitting in his office the next morning, George realized he had overdone the drinking the night before. He always enjoyed his time with Mr. Yang. The regression into more adolescent behavior was Mr. Yang's forte. George wondered how Mr. Yang would behave when he was in his eighties. It was a strange juxtaposition for such a learned man.

The day progressed expediently for George. There was a spring in his step for most of the day despite the mild hangover. His lectures went by without incident. He preferred his students to question and challenge him but, on that day, he was merely a shepherd herding sheep. Even though, much of what he lectured on the subject of religious studies was historical and not his own thoughts and beliefs, he always thought it was important to question, irrespective of the topic.

The weather was beautiful and he chose to eat his lunch in one of the university's quasi park areas. He had bought two hot dogs from the cafeteria. The onion heaped inside battled to be contained as he bit into the bun. The slight breeze blowing in his face was invigorating and helped quench the rising midday temperature. Many students had also been drawn to bask outside. It was a simple pleasure but, for him, it was somewhat tainted by the array of phones that were being used to post and tweet while on the grass. George wondered how this generation would turn out. Their form of communication and, in a way, existence was evolving in a contrasting fashion to those generations before them. To him, it all seemed a little soulless but, then again, previous generations had probably said the same about television, phones and emails. It was a sad dichotomy for him that these young adults were connected to everything, yet not truly connected with anyone. In his mind, he couldn't help but find it sad. He wondered to what extent they lived in the moment and felt a more tangible reaction to the world rather than via the conduit of their phones. Despite all of this, he did think they seemed happy and carefree lying on the grass.

The afternoon lectures mirrored those of the morning. Before George knew it, it was six o'clock and he was home again. This was one of his favorite times of the week. Arriving home on a Friday afternoon with the week's work behind him and sitting back on his most comfortable chair, listening to his record collection, always gave him joy. He chose to play an orchestral record in the background to lift his mood while he read. He was currently reading Carl Jung's *The Archetypes and The Collective Unconscious.*

An hour later he felt the need to be more productive, so he sat behind his desk to write some ideas down for a story. He found in the past he was most effective when writing at night. A year ago, he had written and published a novel about some of the topics he discussed in his lectures as well as life in general and human interaction, but all set in the distant future. It had been well received even though it had been his first attempt at writing a novel. With the profits, he was able to pay off the final installments on his flat. While it had certainly not made him wealthy, it did make him more financially stable. George had been perplexed that people had enjoyed reading his book as he was not sure whether he could write such a extensive piece of material and keep it interesting. Public interest had made him consider writing a second related book. He was finding this one far harder to conceptualize because it was not fully fleshed out beforehand like the story before.

After an hour of theorizing and not gaining any quality ideas, George's mind wandered to other thoughts. Some of his students had suggested he start filming portions of his lectures and uploading them onto YouTube. George found the idea intriguing and had recently started considering what sort of topics he would upload without conflicting with university policy. In the end, he decided it might be better to keep it organic and film whole lectures, then edit them afterward if he felt there were portions worthy of being uploaded. Knowing beforehand what topics were going to be uploaded might impede him in some way. A more nonchalant approach would in all probability be easier for him and might be better received. He decided to discuss it with his senior, Professor Daedalus, some time. He was aware the university was planning on starting online courses and did not want any YouTube uploads to conflict with the university's plans.

After a further hour, he realized his energy levels were depleted and decided to call it a night.

CHAPTER TEN

George shifted his weight onto his left side as he began to waken. To his astonishment, the sun was already up. He had overslept, but the urge for fluid had woken him. His throat was so dry it almost felt raw. He had been remained dormant throughout the night. On most occasions he was a restless sleeper, yet the comfort of a bed was one of his favorite places. He stretched expediently and rose to drink a glass of water. He was frustrated with himself because now his morning run was going to have to be far more arduous. He was usually back from his run by the time the park got busy and the fact that it was a Saturday only made matters worse. To add to his misery, he was already perspiring profusely and the sun's rays baking down on him were going to make the run much more grueling. He much preferred his early runs, not only for the isolation, but also because the dawn's temperature was so much easier for running. Nonetheless, he put his running gear on, brushed his teeth and rinsed his face, sacrificed a bite to eat in order to get going, grabbed his cellular phone with its earphones and hit the road at pace putting on Nina Simone's *Feeling Good* to put extra energy in his step. At times, he preferred a more slug-gish pace for longer distances, but today he was aiming for an intensi-fied pace in exchange for a shorter distance.

Despite the heat and needing to be more aware of not running into pedestrians or other runners, he started at a good pace. Perhaps the energy of the people around him fueled his run; perhaps it was because he had slept so well. His energy levels were dialed to maximum and he suspected he was going to be pleased with his performance today. George was often a relatively methodical person but, when it came to running, he didn't track his distances nor his times, but rather the experience and how his body felt afterward. In a way, this made it harder to stay motivated as he was never aware of how well he performed on any given run and therefore was never able to push himself further as most people doing physical activities were inspired to do. It did, however, allow him to just keep his process simple. As someone with an intellectual profession, he appreciated keeping something less psychological.

His surroundings were far more chaotic than usual. The warm air had brought the residents out in their numbers. George chose to remove his earphones so he could take in the sounds of the families playing with their children in the park, the sound of owners walking their dogs, and ducks quacking in adjacent ponds. Traffic murmured in the far distance. Observing the people outside made George remember the accumulation of small pleasures in life was invariably what made people happy. As he glanced at the residents, they exuded genuine content simply by being outside with their families, taking in the fresh air and warm sunshine. He remembered a past when he, too, had loved and been loved. He pushed harder and took a detour up a flight of steps. He focused on his breathing to distract himself. It was not very healthy, but not dealing with his problems was the way he managed them. He had lived a life of pain for large parts of his life. Distraction was his coping mechanism.

George started to feel a degree of light-headiness. He slowed down and took a moment to take a rest on a park bench in front of a pond. He was frustrated with himself for unnecessarily pushing so much harder than usual because it required him to compose himself. He took the moment to gather his thoughts and regulate his breathing. In front of him, a young boy was playing by the side of the pond. His father was on the other side of the pond reading from his tablet. Every once in a while the father would raise his eye towards the boy but, for the most part, he was engrossed in what he was reading. Like most fathers he was giving his son plenty of room to tend to himself, which was far more than a mother would have appreciated. Not that the boy was in any danger, but the pond did have rocks in it and had the boy fallen in, he would more than likely - hurt himself, and got wet, which would immediately set off alarm bells when they return home. George didn't particularly have any issue with this. He agreed with the code that kids learn from making mistakes and getting hurt. What did sadden George was the father seemed to take no interest in what his son was doing. In all likelihood, they would spend a miniscule amount of time together during the week as the father in all probability worked elongated hours which only left evenings and weekends to spend time together. The weekends would be the best time for him to bond with his son and, because it was just the two of them, made it even more important. George realized that perhaps he shouldn't be too judgmental as he certainly couldn't assess their circumstances and people were often too quick to judge.

George lost his train of thought when the boy giggled. He was playing with a remote-controlled yacht and he had flustered a duck as the yacht came at the bird at the speed of slow. The duck would have nothing of it and flew away, no doubt towards one of the other ponds in the park. The yacht continued to cruise around the pond. George couldn't help but dream he was sailing in the open sea somewhere half a world away.

The brief pit stop had done him good. He walked over to a drinking basin, gulped down a few mouthfuls of water and stretched back with his hands on his hips. George set off once more, feeling rejuvenated. Having taken the break at the pond, he decided to take the longer way home as he was sure he could now manage a greater distance. The light-headedness had dissipated and was now a distant memory. George moved through the remainder of the park at a favorable pace. He then circled back towards the heart of the park in the direction of his apartment.

His mind drifted towards work and a lesson he had lectured the day before. He appreciated it when his students were engrossed in one of his lectures and the day before had been one of those days. He was currently operating in autopilot, his mind reliving the lecture from the prior day when a female voice to his left stated: 'I haven't seen you around here before.'

'Huh, oh, um yes,' said George aware of his surroundings again. Being ripped from his thoughtful inebriation without warning jarred him.

'You in a hurry? You look as though you are running as if your life depended on it,' she asked.

'Sorry about that,' said George, slowing his pace. 'I was in another world for a moment there.'

'Somewhere nice I hope.'

'Kinda. Nothing too exciting. I was thinking of my day at work yesterday. I'm a lecturer at the university.'

'Oh really! How interesting. I hear the university has a very good reputation. What is it you lecture?'

'Philosophy and religious studies,' he said as they wrapped around a bend. George was not used to running and talking at the same time which was resulting in a diminished lung capacity.

'You don't seem like you would be a philosopher. I would have pictured you in more of a desk job or perhaps a doctor, no wait, a dentist.'

'Heavens no! I would never be able to sit behind a desk all day. I would get too fidgety and for some reason, biology never appealed to me much.'

'How long have you been running for?'

'If you are referring to today, I have been running for about half an hour, but if you mean before this, it's been about three months now. You?'

'I used to run track and field at school. Since then I just run once or twice a week just to keep the fitness levels up. Once in a while, I'll run in a half marathon competition.'

'Half marathons? Ah, so you are a legitimate runner. That explains how effortlessly you move. You make it look easy. You're quite impressive.'

She frowned and looked at George, 'Are you checking me out?'

'I was just noticing the way you move; I wasn't trying to objectify you. Is that the way it sounded?'

'Oh....so you think I'm not worthy of being objectified,' she suggested.

George slowed down to a standstill, both to gather his breath as well as to better take in who was running next to him. What stood before him was the most gorgeous woman he had ever seen in his life. Instead of regaining his breath, he felt the air in his lungs lose its way, as for a moment he lost sense of feeling in his torso. She was tall, brunette and had an athletic build while still remaining curvy. Even with what many would consider unfetching running clothes, her attire looked magnificent on her and only accentuated her graceful yet feminine physique. Her physical beauty was, however, nothing compared to her large brown eyes. They were beautiful teleports to another world. An elegant nose and lush lips completed the figure which had George entranced.

'Are you trying to mess with me?'

'In as polite a way as possible,' she grinned.

Feeling confident, George responded, 'I see. Well, I suppose when someone is as attractive as you, they have so much confidence they can say whatever they want to a stranger and said stranger would be completely enthralled by it.'

'I'll take it as a compliment, Mister.'

'It certainly was meant as one.'

'I'm an air hostess, so talking to complete strangers is what I do on a daily basis. It's so ingrained in me now and I don't even realize that it might be somewhat unusual.'

'Well, you undoubtedly are talented at approaching random people. I'm sure your passengers would tend to agree.'

'Hmm...it's different at work. Most passengers are pleasant, but you find as soon as people are paying large amounts for your services, they feel they can take ownership of you and objectify you,' she replied while stretching to keep muscles warm and limber.

George thought her statement and posturing quite ironic since she would most definitely be objectified by most men and it had nothing to do with a work dynamic. Many women possibly objectified her as well and would be tempted into experimentation if the opportunity arose.

'What! Objectify you. Noooo! How could that be?'

'Are you saying I invite the objectification?' she asked. 'I suppose it's the nature of the job to some degree.'

George could not tell if she was being modest or if she genuinely did not realize people's reactions to her had more to do with the way she looked and carried herself. She was poised despite the circum-stances and her voice eloquent for someone who, at face value, did not come from an ivy-league background. She was responsive and every-thing she said was done with so much warmth that he instantly felt at ease and drawn to her.

CHAPTER ELEVEN

'Could I entice you with some frozen yogurt?' asked George. 'I know a great spot around the corner.'

'That sounds super. I'd love to. I have a sudden craving for something sweet.'

'Do you live here or are you only passing through for business?' asked George as they moved towards the frozen yogurt shop.

'No, I don't live here. I love the tranquility and unpretentiousness of this place and I thought I'd take a break from work and spend a few days here. I'm loving the pace of this town. I'm so used to doing everything at a hundred miles an hour, so it's nice to slow down and take the time to appreciate life more.'

'You do know it's a little ironic you decided to become an air hostess if you like the slower pace.'

'I know. I like balance though. I couldn't stay in the same place the whole time. It would be the death of me. There is so much to see in the world. Don't you agree?'

'It's true. There is a lot to see and experience out there. For some reason, it hasn't seduced me of late. I like the simplicity of living in a town like this. I suppose I'm quite simple in that regard.'

'So, a simple intellectual?'

'Hahaha. Something like that. I'm glad you are enjoying your stay here. It's always pleasant to hear an outsider say they like our humble town.'

'I never imagined it to be this beautiful. There is still so much vegetation everywhere. I'm so used to seeing concrete and steel, so when I do fly somewhere more quaint or rural, I find it quite revitalizing.'

'We certainly don't have towering buildings here. To be honest, I doubt people would want them.'

'I noticed, but I love just walking along these charming streets and taking it all in. I love the architecture here and you have so many beautiful parks like these.'

'I suppose we take it for granted. I'm sorry, I haven't even asked your name. Mine is George.'

'Beatrice.'

CHAPTER TWELVE

They stopped outside the frozen yogurt shop to look at the sign of flavors the store had on offer.

'Do you have money on you?' asked Beatrice. 'I don't carry any on me when I'm running.'

'Yes. I keep some cash on me in case of emergencies. You never know what might happen.'

'You are an incredibly cautious person, aren't you? You probably take all outcomes into account wherever you are. Do you have a nuclear bunker where you live? I assume you also look for the nearest exit whenever you enter a new environment.'

'True. I also take into account what objects in the vicinity can be used as a weapon. Plus, I sort my music collection in alphabetical order in case, God forbid, I'm struggling to find what I'm looking for.'

'Nice. A practical man I see.'

'Exactly. Any particular flavor interest you? I think I'm going to go with the mango.'

'Hmm… Let me try the blueberry. Is it any good?'

'I'm not sure. I've never tried it, but I'm sure it's great. This place is extremely popular so most of the flavors should be good.'

'Blueberry it is then!'

They walked into the shop to pay for the yogurts. A few tables and chairs where placed inside for those who wanted to eat on the premises. The shop was cramped because of this, and the queue of four people was about as much as could be managed.

'One blueberry and one mango please,' requested George as he placed the money on the counter.

'Coming right up!' said the shop owner. 'Here you are,' he said as he handed over two large bright frozen yogurts.

'Oh wow, these look amazing,' Beatrice said.

'I think we'll eat these outside,' said George.

'Okay.....' said the owner.

'Maybe we can sit on one of the park benches,' suggested George.

'That sounds great,' agreed Beatrice.

'Whatever suits you,' said the shop owner.

George and Beatrice found a bench sheltered by a canopy of foliage on the outskirts of the park which was situated near the shop.

'Mmm, this is yummy. I'm glad you suggested frozen yogurt. It isn't something I have that often.'

'I suppose that it's sort of the less thrilling version of its cousin, ice cream.'

'I don't care what the temperature is or what the time of day is, I'm always happy to eat some ice cream.'

'Are you aware ice cream is apparently a natural antidepressant?'

'No I didn't,' responded Beatrice. 'Maybe that is why I enjoy it so much when I'm traveling. It helps diminish the impact of the troublesome passengers. I'm glad we went with the frozen yogurt though. It's a nice change. How is the mango?'

'Summery.'

'Hahaha. Mango is a very summery fruit, isn't it? Even the color is overpoweringly warm. Luminous summer.'

'It's interesting now that you mention it. Mine looks like summer, while yours is wintery - cold and dark,' said George.

'You make a valid analysis. It tastes divine though.'

'I'm glad you are enjoying it. How long are you in town for?'

'Just a couple more days, but if I like it, I'll be back again.'

'Challenge accepted!'

'Ah, a confident man I see. Okay. We shall see how effective you are Mr. George. I'm not so easily entertained. I'm very raspberry blue after all!' Beatrice said.

'Well blue happens to be my favorite color.'

'Well played.'

'Honestly, there is something about you. You have me completely transfixed. I can't quite put my finger on what it is.'

'That's sweet… I think. It's kinda a strange choice of words.'

'Oh sorry. I was a bit too much in my head there wasn't I? It was a compliment. I find you to be completely and utterly captivating. Your essence. It's enthralling.'

Beatrice brushed off the compliment. 'My essence? Are you referring to the roll-on deodorant, My Essence? I'm afraid that my roll-on wore off ages ago. My essence is nothing but perspiration now.'

'Touché.'

Beatrice's tone became more serious. 'No one has called me enthralling before. I'm not sure how to respond. You barely know me.'

'Am I coming across too strong? I haven't done this for a while. Not with conviction anyway. I haven't felt like this for some time.'

'That must be one amazing mango frozen yogurt.' She said becoming playful. George was mesmerized by her as he felt the bonds around his heart strain.

'Best frozen yogurt I have had for many, many days,' George said.

'I know what you mean though,' said Beatrice, looking into the distance. 'I noticed you running earlier and for some reason, I couldn't help catching up to you. I feel really… alive right now,' she said. 'The way you look at me…'

George smiled and gently placed his hand on hers.

CHAPTER THIRTEEN

'What are you doing today?' asked George.

'Today? You move quickly.'

'As you said, you are only here for a couple more days.'

'I don't have anything in particular planned today. I only arrived the night before last so I was planning on just walking around to see what I find. The idea for this getaway was to just unwind. What did you have in mind?'

'Would you like to join me for lunch? I know a great French restaurant around the corner from here.'

'Hahaha. Is everything around the corner here?'

'Basically. There are a lot of great places to see within arm's reach.

'I don't think it would be appropriate to walk into a restaurant in my present sweaty state. I'm pretty sure the garcon will not approve. Also, that was quite a lot of frozen yogurt on top of the large breakfast I already had. I'll be fine for the next few hours. Why don't we rather save it for later? Maybe at your place? I spend so much of my time around people, so sometimes I prefer the quiet.'

'I can appreciate what you're saying. How about seven o'clock?'

'Perfect.'

'Super. Seven o'clock should give me more than enough time to make my place look presentable and buy groceries. Do you have any dietary requirements?'

'No. I'm pretty easy. You don't need to fuss too much over me. You can make whatever works for you.'

George took her empty container and threw the both into a bin near the bench like a basketball player.

'Three pointer!' Beatrice cheered.

'Ah, you are a sports lover?' George asked.

'I believe you will find that I'm a lady full of surprises. A good knowledge of sports perhaps is one of the more surprising characteristics about me.'

'Impressive. I look forward to discovering further revelations.' George stood up gradually, never taking his eyes off of Beatrice. Her spell on him had circumvented all his defenses. She rose to meet him, her smile as wide as the grand canyon.

'I bid you adieu, Mademoiselle,' George said as he kissed her on the cheek.

CHAPTER FOURTEEN

George wandered the lanes of the supermarket, deciding what to buy for his date later in the evening. Shopping for groceries midday on a Saturday after payday proved to be a frenetic process. George bought most of his shopping on the way home from work during the week, so he was not used to the chaotic level of hustle and bustle. He was however battling to focus. Who was this remarkable woman entering his life? He hadn't felt this alive for years. Not since before those dark days. The world seemed to move more effortlessly and irritations that might have flustered him the day before were now mere distractions which he handled nonchalantly. The music playing in the recesses of George's mind was almost loud enough for him to confuse with music being played through the supermarket's loudspeakers. George couldn't help but draw the comparison that it was almost like living in a movie, with delicate duets playing in the background.

After browsing the aisles for a few minutes to decide what he was going to cook, he settled on fish. Somehow, it seemed like a more sophisticated option to him.

'Two medium-sized tuna steaks and thirty mussels please,' George asked the staff member behind the refrigerated counter. All of those hours watching the cooking channel had made him more adventurous in the kitchen. This would be the perfect opportunity to try out the mussel soup.

The staff member behind the counter took the two steaks he had pointed towards and prepared, weighed and packaged the tuna and mussels.

George moved over to the fruit and vegetable section to purchase sweet potatoes, tomatoes, lettuce and lemons. His last acquisitions were a meringue pie and a French loaf of bread from the bakery section.

He then glanced over the signage above the aisles to determine if there was anything he had forgotten. Nothing else came to mind other than a bottle of white wine which he would purchase from the liquor store afterward. George then moved over to the till to pay for what he had chosen, the music still playing in his mind.

CHAPTER FIFTEEN

After returning home and packing away the groceries, George began straightening up the flat. Work-related paperwork and mail tended to pile up without him otherwise noticing. Thankfully, for him he maintained his residence in a tidy fashion. Within half-an-hour, the space looked presentable for a visitor.

The next step George decided to take on was seeing to the dining room table. He placed a white linen table cloth followed by placemats on the table as well as napkins. Then he proceeded to take out his better crockery and cutlery. He always used the cheaper utensils when he ate by himself, therefore his better cutlery hadn't been used in a while and needed some buffing. He also managed to find some old crystal wine glasses. Candles! He almost forgot about candles. He scrounged around in a dining room drawer and was relieved to discover he still had two. He certainly did not want to go back to the shop just for candles. He placed them in two graceful glass candlestick holders and took a step back to make sure everything was in place.

Next, he moved over to the kitchen to start preparing the food, but not before putting on a Roy Orbison vinyl to set the mood for himself. George always found cooking more enjoyable if there was music playing. Most of the food would be quick to cook so he decided to cut and peel the sweet potatoes for now, while the tuna would not need marinating as the lemon, pepper and olive oil would be added while he fried it. The mussel soup was, however, another story and he thought it best to commence cooking of the soup. He took out the recipe he had scribbled on a piece of paper a few weeks earlier and commenced inserting the oil, tomatoes, white wine and other ingredients at the appropriate times.

There was still an hour to go before seven o'clock, but he had no idea how punctual a person she was, so he went to the bathroom to have another shower, shave and brush his teeth. He wasn't sure what to wear and sifted through his limited wardrobe. He settled on navy trousers and a white collared shirt. Simple, but effective, he thought as he looked in the mirror. He still had charm when he needed it, he thought as he started doing a subtle dance before becoming self-aware and realizing how ridiculous he looked.

George chose a new record to play before moving back to the kitchen to see how the soup was coming along and add a few more condiments according to his palate. As he closed the pot, the doorbell rang. Perfect timing.

CHAPTER SIXTEEN

'Welcome!' George smiled as he stepped aside from the entrance door to let Beatrice in.

'Thank you,' said Beatrice kissing him on the cheek. She was wearing a simple, short yet elegant, black dress. George was almost taken aback. She was even more gorgeous than what stood before him a few hours prior. Beatrice was a naturally beautiful woman who did not require makeup, but now that she was wearing some, it only accentuated her best features.

'I wasn't sure what to bring so I thought I'd bring a bottle of wine. I hope you like Shiraz.'

'Perfect,' said George as he took the bottle from her hands. 'Although this wasn't necessary, it's greatly appreciated.'

'My pleasure. I didn't want to arrive empty-handed. Where can I put my shawl?'

'Let me take it,' he said, draping it on his coat stand. The burnt apricot-colored silk fabric with its floral print instantly feminized his entranceway. 'You smell wonderful. I thought you were mesmerizing before, but now...' he said in an unashamed manner that even surprised him. Her hair was no longer tied up, but lengthy and draped softly on her shoulders. It was lush and immaculate, glistening against the well-lit hallway in the background. Her red lipstick was her final flourish. She looked as vibrant as a blossoming flower.

'Thank you. It's amazing what a little makeup can do,' said Beatrice to downplay the compliment, but her prodigious smile reinforced her appreciation. She stepped into the living area and glanced around to take in the environment. 'This place is nice. It looks homey and inviting.'

'Well, it's nothing exceedingly fancy, but it's home.'

'That's what I like about it. When you are on the road all the time and effectively live your life in hotels, you realize how cold and stale they can be. They lack the warmth and personality of a home. This space is nice and cozy.'

'Thank you for the backhanded compliment.'

'Hahaha. I'm sorry. Did it come across that way? It wasn't my intention. Let me change the topic, fast. This music is nice. It sounds very organic. Is it Brazilian?'

'Yes. The artist's name is Joao Gilberto. He is from the fifties and sixties if I recall correctly. It has an uncomplicated, comforting sound, doesn't it?'

'Wow, this is a huge record collection you have. How many are there? It looks like you must have over a thousand records.'

'I can't say I have ever counted, but over a thousand sounds about right. I've been collecting them for years now. I invariably buy myself at least one record a month.'

'Mind if I take a look?'

'Go ahead.'

Beatrice strolled towards his record collection without George being able to take his eyes off of her. Beatrice ran her index finger across the titles as she read them at first, before taking out the odd album that piqued her interest. A few years prior, George had managed to buy a large bookshelf unit with adjustable shelves that he had repurposed for his record collection.

'This is quite an eclectic range of genres. Some of these are very old. How old are you again?' asked Beatrice as she half-turned back to him, smiling.

'Young enough to also call some of this music old. I suppose I prefer music from a few decades ago because it feels less commercial. More human perhaps. I can't say I gravitate towards much of the current music. It has a lot to do with the corporate aspect and how record companies don't want to take risks on outlying artists which in turn means music starts to sound one-note and innocuous. It has been a while since music took risks. I don't know what happened to melodies. It's no wonder youths seem to be gravitating more and more towards bygone eras. When I was a kid, I certainly did not want to listen to my parents' music. There was more than enough current music at the time, to keep me satisfied. To make matters worse, the same can unfortunately be said for the film industry. When last have you seen a blockbuster movie that wasn't a sequel or based on another source material with a bankable following? Indie filmmakers are creating the most innovative material at the moment from what I can tell.'

Beatrice stared at the ground in thought before looking up. 'You are probably right. I can't think of a good example. I guess it has all become excessively safe.'

'Exactly! Who wants their life to be safe the whole time? Sometimes you want to jump off a cliff and experience what is out there. Can I offer you some of the wine you brought?' asked George as he raised the bottle Beatrice had brought into the air. George was putting up somewhat of a façade. Of late, he had led a predictable, safe life. The woman standing before him was, however, making him edge closer towards the cliff. Perhaps it was time for him to take more chances in life before they passed him by.

CHAPTER SEVENTEEN

'Wow, these mussels look delicious!' Beatrice said as George brought the starter to the table.

'Thank you. I made them in a creamy wine sauce. I hope you like them. I don't work with mussels very often so they aren't my forte, but I've wanted to try this recipe for some time now and this seemed like as opportune a time as any. I'm also curious to see how it tastes. The ingredients are relatively standard so it should be tasty.'

Beatrice waited for George to sit down before sampling the first mussel. 'Mmm. This is so tasty. You've done a great job. You can't go wrong with fresh seafood. Mmm. So good.'

'It certainly helps when seafood is fresh. Then there is hardly any need for additional flavors.'

'I agree. It goes great with this wine despite it being red,' said Beatrice before taking a sip of her Shiraz. 'I obviously didn't realize you were making seafood. So other than running and cooking for damsels, you were saying earlier that you lecture at the university?'

'Yes,' responded George. 'I'm a professor of philosophy and religious studies.'

'Ah, a deep, learned man.'

'Something like that. I try to extend the knowledge I know to others. It's somewhat of a mixed bag with the students. Some of them merely do the course for the credits for a semester or two before it starts becoming more challenging. It can however become quite interesting for many and they tend to stay longer. The art of thinking can be quite liberating in its own way.'

'I'm sure, but hopefully not at the expense of experiencing. Life is meant to be lived after all.'

'Yes of course.'

'I'd love to hear some of the subject matter sometime. Preferably the easier topics, please. I'm not yet experienced in the way of the world to over-analyze philosophical facets.'

'Sure. I'd love to share some subject matter with you.'

'Please don't do it now. I don't want this evening to feel like work for you.'

'Fair enough,' smiled George, raising his glass.

'I'm actually more than a professor. I'm also a novelist. Well, when I say novelist, I mean I've written a novel.' George thought he would take the opportunity to come across as being more creative and interesting. He wasn't ashamed of his career in any way, but he realized showing that there were more dimensions to him would be more appealing to Beatrice.

'Oh really? Tell me more.'

'The novel was published about a year ago. It's a sci-fi drama of sorts. It follows the life of a police officer in the future - a future where the affluent are cybernetically enhanced. This in turn makes them superior in a multitude of ways but, at the same time, it takes them further away from what is historically regarded as being human. The police officer keeps an audio diary and in that way, we learn about the world through these diary recordings.'

Beatrice ran her fingers through her hair. 'The story sounds very interesting! I'm sure I would enjoy it. How did you come up with the idea?'

'I don't recall to be quite honest. I think it started with my imaginations of what the future would be like and how technology is influencing civilization's current way of life. Our lives are changing so fast because of technology and we aren't able to keep up. We are trying to assess what the benefits and negatives are of new technology and it's difficult to determine their impact because there are so many new influences and evaluating what is resulting from these in isolation can be difficult when there are so many variables.'

'It sounds like you feel quite strongly about this. Um, that's maybe a stupid thing to say since you wrote a book about it. You must feel strongly about it.'

'You would think so,' chuckled George, 'but I don't know if I would go as far as that. I have opinions. I'm not sure if I would call them extreme. What it means to be human is an interesting topic for me, but much of the novel is about future technology which is quite liberating because the accuracy of the world is subjective. It's nice allowing your imagination to run free. Many scenes were based on images I imagined and musical notes I thought would work tonally for the story.'

'I didn't realize that was how you would approach writing a novel,' Beatrice said.

'I have no idea if this is the right way or even the common way of writing a novel, but it worked for me.'

'I can imagine it would be quite an effective way of creating scenes,' said Beatrice. 'What are the types of new technologies you think are making life harder at the moment?'

'Well, I do acknowledge living in a small university town does mean life here is not as progressive as cities. Although, as I say it, I use the word progressive loosely because progress is not always improvement. One of the most obvious ones is social media. It's wonderful that people can communicate with others anywhere in the world at the touch of a button. It's so positive that loved ones who are thousands of miles apart can keep in touch at a press of a button without spending exorbitant amounts of money. However, it seems that younger people who have grown up with this technology are becoming dependent on it and regressing in intimate forms of communication. They are struggling to talk to people one on one. Imagine if I was on my phone at the moment sitting here with you. I wouldn't even realize that I was being rude. Even worse, if you were phone dependent as well, you wouldn't even know that I was being rude. Being in someone's company should be enough. I read an article a few months back where some scientists had conducted a study on cellular phone use. They took phones away from people who had grown up with them and the results caused a major spike in their anxiety levels. The scientists were able to measure elevated stress levels when the phones were removed. I hope I'm not treading on your toes. I have no idea how dependent you are on technology, but I haven't seen you use your phone so I assumed you are not overly dependent.'

'It's fine. It does feel unpleasant when you don't have your phone on you. What is the term again? FOMO? Fear of missing out? But I can't say I have any kind of addiction. I can't use a phone while in the air so I'm quite used to it.'

'Oh yes, I hadn't thought of that. Anyway, let's change the subject. This is maybe getting too serious.'

'I don't mind. I find it interesting hearing your point of view and you seem quite passionate about it, which is always endearing,' said Beatrice, 'but I'm also always game for funny and stupid conversation,' she added before leaning forward and poking George on the nose.

He blushed at her gesture. 'I guess being a philosophy lecturer means I get so accustomed to speaking intellectually that I forget to take it down a notch sometimes.'

'Yes. Us common folk struggle intellectualizing.'

'I'm sorry, did what I just say come across as an insult? It wasn't my intention,' responded a concerned George.'

'I'm joking,' Beatrice said as she stroked George's wrist.

George took a large sip of wine and stared and Beatrice. 'God.'

'What?'

'You electrify me.'

CHAPTER EIGHTEEN

After clearing the starters, he returned with the flawlessly browned tuna steaks, baby roast potatoes and a splash of salad. Before returning to his seat, he opened a bottle of Chardonnay he had planned to open with the starter.

'Tell me about your family. What do your parents do for a living? Any siblings?' said George.

'I don't actually have a family,' said Beatrice to which George raised an eyebrow. 'I'm an orphan. I never knew my parents and I was never able to find out who they were or if I have any brothers or sisters. Not the answer you were expecting I would imagine?'

'I'm sorry. Your youth must have been hard for you.'

Beatrice could see sincere empathy written on his face. His mouth was left half open and his eyebrows heavily angled in concern.

'I won't lie - it wasn't easy for me when I was a kid. Never bonding with someone and living with other orphans with the same issues wasn't healthy. I also wasn't responsive to foster parents. I had a few, but always rebelled against them and none of them ever lasted long because I was so difficult. Ironic really. I was dying for love and atten-tion, yet I rejected them because, to me, their love wasn't real. I only wanted my parents' love to heal me. For many years I hoped they would find me and apologize for their mistake. I prayed that it was maybe some large misunderstanding. In adulthood, I have come to grips with it all and grown from the experience. It's surreal thinking back how rebellious I was because I'm so different now. If anything, now I'm too easy-going. Life is complicated. We all try to do our best with the cards we are dealt. Life isn't easy and we don't always make the right decisions. I don't begrudge my parents for mistakes that they may make. God knows I have been destructive in the past, but I'd like to think I've learned from my mistakes and have become a well-rounded person.'

'Thank you for being this open with me. You are right, this wasn't the response I was expecting. It isn't easy bringing up such hard memories, is it?'

'Don't worry. I'm fine. I can't mourn what I never had. By the time I was eighteen or nineteen I had come to grips with it and shed my baggage. I learned to let love in. I had a feeling you would understand. I might be wrong, but I sense you are someone who also hasn't had it easy.'

'You are quite perceptive,' said George. 'My youth was also not easy. My experiences were not all that dissimilar to yours. My parents died in a car crash when I was twelve. It absolutely broke me. My entire reality was shattered when the police came to our door. A lot of horrific memories still linger, but I had a guardian angel: my sister, Lila. She was nineteen at the time and took care of me. She fought to gain custody of me for months. She held it together so well. Looking back, I don't know how she remained so strong through all of it. I suppose she had to for my sake, but it couldn't have been easy for her financially and even more so, emotionally. She was hurting as much as I was, yet she wasn't able to fully let go. She had to keep the ship sailing in the correct direction.'

'Did she win custody at such a young age? How did she manage financially?' asked Beatrice. She, too, was masked with empathy now.

'I was too young to understand what was happening at the time and I wasn't involved in a lot of it. I do remember going through a lot of counseling to see how I was coping with her as my temporary guardian. Somehow Lila did manage to get full custody. I've never asked her how she managed it. I don't like reopening old wounds since it ran against a major artery. She has always been very mature and the courts must have seen it. She is a tiny bit rough around the edges at times, but she is always reliable and unshakable. Lila has been my rock for longer than I can remember. On the financial side, she taught herself to be a hairdresser as expediently as she was able. Thankfully the mother of one of her friends owned a hair salon and took Lila under her wing. Her salary covered the smaller day-to-day expenses. We also managed to get an inheritance that covered the cost of housing, my education and a car for Lila to get around in. So yes, your intuition is accurate. I, too, am very familiar with hardship.'

'Aren't we a sorry pair?' Beatrice said.

'Maybe, in a way, our problematic experiences are drawing us together.'

'Sharing war wounds as a bonding experience sounds like a valid pastime. By the sounds of it, it would be a relatively even duel to see who would come up trumps. Personally, I don't like ignoring the harder aspects of life and sharing our experiences is healthy. Being open about my problems is what helped me get through them.'

'Not extraordinarily romantic is it,' George said.

'Oh I don't know, I think wounds can be sexy.'

'Even if someone is riddled with them?'

'Even if they are riddled in them.'

CHAPTER NINETEEN

George couldn't help but frown. Staring so intensely into Beatrice's eyes was like breaching the metaphysical.

'Is something wrong? Why are you looking at me like that?'

'Oh, um, it's nothing. I was just wondering what is wrong with you.'

'What's wrong with me? What are you trying to say?' Beatrice responded after she had just let her guard down.

'Well, you are gorgeous, intelligent, caring and you even have a great sense of humor. Nobody is attractive in all those ways. Everyone is flawed in at least one way, yet you don't seem to have any notable apparent imperfections.'

Beatrice beamed, but didn't respond, waiting for George to praise her further.

'Frankly, it freaks me out,' he said. 'No one is perfect, so whatever is wrong with you must be horrendous. Based on the law of averages, you must have a massive flaw to make you normal!'

'You make a valid point Professor. This is concerning...' she said. 'Quick, give me a pen and paper so I can write down a list of flaws while my creative juices are flowing!'

'You're creative as well? This is getting even more concerning. Do you kill babies in their sleep for a living?'

'Shut up and get me some paper to write on damn it!'

George sprung up and rushed over to fetch the stationary from his desk draw. He dropped back down onto the sofa and handed them to Beatrice. On the top, she wrote *My defect list* and underlined it.

'Hmmm, let me see…. What is wrong with me? This is not an easy question. I'll have to dig deep,' she said, trying to look stern. 'My ears.'

'What about them?'

'They are too small. Then there is my left foot. It has a mole near my ankle. It messes with my symmetry. Oh God, sometimes it messes with my feng shui,' Beatrice said while jotting it down.

'You left out blaspheme,' George said. 'Seriously? There must be something? I need anything!'

'Okay, okay. To be quite honest, it's all just me trying to overcompensate and blend in.'

'What do you mean?'

'I'm insecure. Ever since I can remember, I have felt awkward, always having to overcompensate to fit in. When I'm feeling depressed, I even question my place in the world. Where do I fit in? I guess that is why I became an air hostess - able to be a part of so many lives, yet none of them. I enjoy making them feel special and being able to talk to people from all walks of life. Then once we reach our destination, I fade back into the shadows.'

The room remained silent for a moment before George responded, 'I'm sorry. I wasn't expecting you to be so sincere. I apologize. You are far more open about yourself than most people.'

'Well, perhaps sincerity is another one of my strengths,' she said smiling. 'You know, you really have a way with the ladies. You sure know how to make us feel special! Have you considered going into the card industry? You would be a master in creating birthday cards.'

'You made your point, no need to rub it in. We are not all exceptional human beings like you. I mean, seriously, is insecurity even a flaw. It's more of a quirk, isn't it? You'll have to lie awake tonight in bed, trying to think of something more valid.'

'Wine, another glass of wine please,' Beatrice said.

While stretching to reach what remained of the Chardonnay bottle, George replied, 'You know, I might not be half bad at writing birthday cards. It's maybe worth considering in the future.'

CHAPTER TWENTY

Three hours later, after much cathartic discussion, George and Beatrice found themselves standing in the living room.

'I should get going soon.'

'I'm sorry if this evening didn't turn out as expected. It got quite dark for a while there, didn't it? We are pretty broken, aren't we?' asked George.

'Two peas in a pod.'

'I'd like to do this again. Maybe next time let's aim for fewer gloomy topics.'

'Perhaps you are being too hard on yourself. At least we got all of our baggage out of the way. Now we can move on.'

Neither confirmed this point as they both had secrets yet to divulge. Instead, George grasped both of her hands in his and pulled her towards him. They looked at each other for a moment. Both were comfortable not saying anything. Beatrice leaned forward and they tenderly kissed before George opened the door for her.

'I love being around you,' said Beatrice. 'You make me feel safe even if the conversation does get gloomy. Unlike other people, you don't shy away from the harder conversations. You embrace it along with the positive.'

Beatrice stepped through the doorway and down the passageway towards the stairs. George stood by the door and stared at her as she walked. As she started stepping downstairs, she glanced in his direction, stopped for a moment and beamed a smile towards him. He reciprocated. When she was out of sight he stepped back inside and closed the door. George felt a wave of contentment embrace him.

CHAPTER TWENTY-ONE

'Good afternoon Professor. May I disturb you?'

'Mmm? Certainly. Come in Ava,' said George, gesturing one of his students into his office.George's office was quite dated as it had last been furnished in the nineties. Though there was a lot of paperwork and books scattered throughout his office, it was well organized and the fern tree in the corner gave the space a degree of life.

George sat at his desk. To his right was a large window that looked down onto the campus below and illuminated his desk with natural light, while to his right was the doorway which Ava stood in.

'You looked as though you were deep in thought,' said Ava.

'You caught me daydreaming. How can I help you?'

Ava entered his office and stood by the two chairs opposite him. 'It isn't really a class material question, it's more of like, a personal question.'

'Okay. Let's see if I can answer your question. Please, sit down.'

'Thank you, sir. The other day in class you were talking about the major religions and how they are all centered primarily around the holy land two or more thousand years ago. I have grown up in a very religious home and I have been finding it harder and harder to relate to as I get older. I just wanted to chat with someone about it and like, I don't know, get some guidance,' Ava said as she awkwardly scratched the back of her head.

'I see. It must be difficult for you coming here and making a statement like this,' said George. He noticed her fidgeting as she sat opposite him.

'Yes.'

'Let me start off by saying what I often say in class. I don't share my personal religious beliefs as I don't want to allude to any sort of favoritism or steer students in any particular direction. If you are here for spiritual enlightenment, you came to the wrong place. I can, however, make factual observations and try to comment as impartially as possible.'

'That's fine, sir. I'm here for an unbiased opinion.'

'Firstly, what you are feeling is completely normal. Even the most spiritually devout individuals have their moments of doubt. Even the Catholic Pope shared his insecurity a few years ago. Let me just google it quickly as I don't want to misquote the man. Ah, here we go, "Who among us, everybody, everybody; who among us has not experienced insecurity, loss and even doubts on their journey of faith?" We all do. Even atheists. What is now becoming more and more prevalent is religions are becoming questioned more and more as it's socially acceptable for one to forge their own path. Also, the fact that there is more information available to the common man than ever before and some of this information causes doubt about preconceived ideas because, for example, people now have easier access to learn about different religions, their contradictions as well as science. More importantly, people have access to a deluge of other individuals' opinions on the matter. These opinions have the ability to chip away at people's religious beliefs. People tend to be like sponges and not only absorb what they hear, but tend to accept everything they hear as fact. Possibly, it's the cause of schooling where, from a young age, we learn to accept what adults tell us as true. One's thoughts can get clouded. The truth we find in this cloud of thoughts is different for each of us.'

Ava listened carefully, nodded.

'In fact, many spiritual figures who have questioned their faith have said their spirituality intensified afterward. Being dogmatized into a belief is not the most resolute foundation one can have. Sadly, the major religions are struggling with their history. They are struggling to break free from the fact that their books appear to have been completed and are not a living, breathing work in progress. Nothing new has been added to these books for nearly two thousand years. It adds ammunition to the naysayers who call them antiquated and archaic. Even if the books are merely interpreted as a series of lessons, there are always new lessons requiring to be learnt in a more current context. This, in part, is probably why you are battling to relate to the subject matter. If miracles are still occurring, why are they no longer being included in the great scriptures?

George paused to allow Ava a chance to briefly consider his question. He continued: 'This is something the major religions will have to consider and address in some way because if nothing new is written in the next two thousand years, the spiritualism many have now will likely be referred to in the same context as the Greek, Roman, Aztec and Viking Gods and religions. Please don't confuse this with me saying the major religions are not real and true. However, these establishments will have to consider how to remain relevant going forward. I believe the fact they are not able or willing to add newer stories into their teachings is not healthy. It's almost the equivalent of saying God is no longer as readily entwined with our existence. This does become a slippery slope though. Someone like Joan of Arc would be easy enough to integrate into the Christian religion because there has been enough time to let the ethos breathe and it's difficult to argue against since the events happened a few hundred years ago. However, could someone like Gandhi be integrated into Hindu teachings? He is more complicated as he is seen as a man with devout beliefs who fought for the oppressed as well as liberation through a righteous veil of religion. He is still remembered as a man and not divine. As you might have realized, I have clearly thought about this quite a bit, but these are not easy questions to ask. I apologize if I digressed a bit.'

'That is what makes you a good lecturer, sir. You put a lot of thought into what you teach, are prepared to consider different opinions and enjoy what you do,' said Ava.

'I certainly do enjoy it. I hope it helped a bit. It's quite normal to be feeling the way you are. Questioning can be a positive thing. This is your journey and you'll have to find a resonating truth for you.'

CHAPTER TWENTY-TWO

'Thanks for coming over at such short notice, bro,' said Lila as she stepped aside for George to enter. 'You know we really appreciate it. I can't believe our baby sitter dropped us like this. Fucking teenagers these days. You just can't rely on them. Their attention doesn't seem to go further than the phone in their hands. Texting all the time. What a bunch of homos. And dikes. I wouldn't want to be politically incorrect and offend anyone. I'm considerate like that.'

'Very considerate of you, said George. 'However, if you recall, they said the same about our generation. At the time, the crutch for kids was spending too much time in front of the television which in turn was going to be our downfall. Now we seem to be perpetuating the same cycle.'

'Who cares? In any case, Joe and I hardly ever get a chance to have time to ourselves. Date night happens once in a blue moon.'

'No problem, sis. Any excuse for me to spend with my niece and nephew and I'm ecstatic. I brought *The Little Mermaid* for us to watch. Feels like not so long ago we were young and enjoying these types of movies.'

'Awesome. I'm sure they are going to love it. Wasn't it on the darker side though?'

'I guess it was. Much of Walt Disney's early work was quite dark. It had something to do with requiring the dark in order to appreciate the light.'

'Why do you have to go and intellectualize everything, George? It's just a Disney movie.'

'You say that, but Walt Disney was an intellectual. It's only natural his art would be intellectual as well.'

'Jesus. You really need to get laid. Just don't fantasize about Ariel. She is too young for you. And fucking animated.'

'Getting laid is not always the solution to one's problems you know,' retorted George.

'Of course it isn't, but neither is moping around by yourself, you dumbass.'

'Well, actually there is someone I'm seeing. Or at least there is somebody I've met.

'What!' Lila exclaimed with a slight spring on the spot. 'When were you planning on telling me this, you douche? Here we are wasting time talking about Walt Disney when we could be talking about someone with a pulse. I haven't got much time, but tell me. Tell me what has happened.'

'Well, there isn't much to tell at this stage. I don't know her that well. I met her the other day on a run. Beatrice is her name.'

'Sounds exotic. Details George, give me details. You are a professor for God's sake. Use your words. You are supposed to be learned and stuff.'

'Um well, she is quite exotic looking. Striking in fact. She is an air hostess. So, she flies around a lot. Obviously. She speaks English, Spanish and French. She is in her early thirties. Still very fit. All the running I suppose. She even does half marathons so she puts me to shame. She is somehow incredibly regal despite being young and laid back. Maybe it has to do with her career. I think they are trained on how to behave and she gets to see so many people and places that it has made her wise beyond her years. There is something mesmerizing about her. I felt instantly at ease with her. Um, what else? Beatrice has a great sense of humor and is incredibly warm.'

'This is fantastic. She sounds incredible. I can't wait to hear more about her. I can't believe it. I never thought you would meet someone while running. All the sweat and panting can't exactly be a turn-on. On second thought, maybe it makes a lot of sense.'

George chuckled. 'Well, maybe my pheromones are amplified when I'm running. Come to think of it, I do have a sexy run. It's amazing that I don't have a bevy of women running after me every time. It should be like Beatle mania.'

'Hahaha. I'm just picturing it. It sounds retarded, hahaha.'

'No more retarded than the weird hairstyle you had a couple of months ago. I didn't know what to say when I saw that the first time.'

'Hey. No need to get personal.'

'Sorry. It was strange though and can we at least try not using the word retarded so freely.'

'I know, I know. I took that one too far. You know I'm so happy for you. I hope the relationship develops,' said Lila. Her disposition went from jovial to serious, yet heartfelt. 'You used to be so happy. I just want to see the cheerful fucking romantic I knew a few years ago.' A tear built in her left eye as her lower lip quivered.

'I know. Thank you, sis. Your love and support have gotten me through some rough times over the years. I don't know what I'd do without you.'

'This conversation is sounding very serious,' shouted Joe as he entered the room, putting on a ten-year-old jacket now undersized for his hefty frame.

Realizing how somber it had become, Lila yelled, 'George found someone!'

'Found someone? What does that mean?'

'George found a girl.'

'Nice, Georgie,' said Joe.

'Bro's new lady friend is an air hostess.'

'Oh wow. Air hostesses tend to be hot. You set the bar high, Georgie.'

'Something like that, Joe,' said George, 'there is a lot more to this one than a pretty face. She is tremendously special. I don't know how to explain it.'

'Sounds mysterious,' said Lila. 'It's always good to have some mystery in a relationship. Take my stud of a husband here for example. I only found out the other day he used to be in plays when he was in school. Who would have thought this fucking lumberjack of a man could hold a note?'

'I can't picture you holding a note, Joe.'

'I'm thinking of making a comeback. The stage beckons,' said Joe, tucking his stomach in, raising his posture and extending his arms. 'I'd love to talk about me in my prime, but we are already supposed to be at the restaurant and I don't know how long it will keep our reservation. You know how these pretentious places can be. It's time to hit the road. A pleasure seeing you again, as always Georgie. Good luck with the air hostess. Kids! Time to say goodbye! Mommy and Daddy are leaving now!'

The kids raced into the room in their pajamas. Their socks skidded on the wooden floor as they turned the corner which made them giggle in delight as they slid towards Lila and embraced her.

'Lila always gets preferential treatment,' whispered Joe, nudging George.

Lila heard and responded, 'They always save the best for last. Come on kids, say goodbye to Daddy. Enjoy yourselves, Julia and Noah. Uncle George has an exciting movie to show you. It's called *The Little Mermaid*. Thanks for the last-minute help, bro. We really appreciate it.'

'It's my pleasure.'

'I hope they aren't too much trouble. We'll probably be gone for two or three hours so I'm afraid you'll need to see to yourself for a bit because it's lights out for these two little ones after the movie. We'll chat during the week. I need details about the Miss.'

After Lila and Joe left, George made a large bowl of popcorn for the three of them and then sat with the kids in front of the television.

'Okay, kids. This is going to be a great one. Now you get to see what life is like, under the sea.'

CHAPTER TWENTY-THREE

George ascended the garden steps apprehensively. His heart was heavy and his mind deep in thought. His surroundings were bursting with life, yet his emotions and mind were in turmoil. At this time of year, the large gardens were in full bloom. The irrigation system was having to work twice as hard to quench its thirst. The gardens were a kaleidoscope of colored flowers and with them came an assortment of diminutive wildlife. Birds, insects, frogs and squirrels sang and danced across the landscape, orchestrated by the gentle breeze passing through the leaves. It had been a few months since he had last been there, but he was familiar with the landmarks and his route through the maze of trees and architecture.

George was unaware of the life around him. He did not raise his gaze beyond a few paces in front of his feet. Not even to greet passersby. His right hand was clenched firmly around his cargo.

His mind was reliving the night he spent with Beatrice. His memory of the time with her was vivid. Her appearance, smell and touch were all imprinted in his consciousness. His emotions were a storm of joy and sadness.

He turned right at the largest tree in the gardens, towards his companion. His heels became heavier with each step he took. Beatrice's joyful laugh was now playing on a loop in the recesses of his mind. For him, it submerged the noises made by a group of children playing tag in the near distance.

At last, George arrived at his destination. 'Hello Isabella,' he said. 'It has been a while. Longer than I intended.' George bent over with a heavy heart, resting his full weight on his left leg as he rested a bouquet of a dozen white roses on his wife's grave.

CHAPTER TWENTY-FOUR

'I have met someone, but you probably already know that already,' George said as he shifted his weight back and forth between his legs. 'I haven't felt this way in a long time. You are the love of my life. Why do I feel like I'm cheating on you? I was supposed to grow old with you.' George's voice broke as tears started to run down his face. It had been five years since his wife had died, but the wound of her memory was still effortlessly vivid. He took a moment to gather himself.

'I haven't told her about you. I don't know why. I don't know what I'm afraid of,' George paused, his mind awash with nothingness.

'I still miss you. I will always miss you. I never thought I had the potential to love again. Never thought I could feel again. This woman. She… she makes me feel again. Beatrice is her name.' George fidgeted after mentioning Beatrice's name.

'She is not as strong as you. You were always so strong. You never let anything get you down. Not even the cancer could subdue your spirit. Those were difficult times, weren't they? I always took so much solitude in your fortitude. It was infectious. I never realized how attracted I was to strong women until I met you. Beatrice. She is different. She has a light-heartedness about her. Being around her is just a massive release. She makes me feel carefree again. Maybe she is the type of woman I need now. Like you, she exudes warmth. You always made people feel so welcome. She does the same. Well, she makes me feel welcome anyway.

'I remember when we first started dating. Those were the happiest days of my life. Until I met you, I never knew what it was like to feel so happy. I thought I was going to grow old with you. You wanted to have a large family. Life did not turn out as we had hoped. Life can be cruel. What I would give to be with you again.'

George wiped his forehead with the back of his hand. The sun beat down on him. 'Beatrice is a special person. I think you would have liked her. I should tell her. Tell her about you. I don't know why it is so awkward to talk about you. Do my feelings for her diminish my love for you? God, it feels good to feel alive again. Why do I feel so guilty standing here? I know you would be delighted for me. I know that, but it feels like in some way I'm turning my back on you. I don't want to let you go. Never wanted to let you go.'

George stood there for a moment without saying another word. He raised his head to the sun, closed his eyes, took a deep breath and exhaled steadily. 'Will I ever be with you again?'

CHAPTER TWENTY-FIVE

George waved to his sister as he caught sight of her from a distance. She was already found a seat at the coffee shop. It was unusual for them to meet during the week for lunch, but ever since George had mentioned Beatrice to her, she had been relentlessly asking him to meet so they could chat. In this case, it suited George. He had been marking papers the whole morning and there were lectures scheduled for the rest of the afternoon. This had been a monotonous early morning task for him as he wasn't particularly impressed with what he had read and he decided the break would do him good. Unfortunately, there wasn't much independent thought in what the students wrote. It tended to focus on what was in the textbooks and what was discussed in class, rarely veering into the realm of creativity and introspection. He much preferred the interactive component of his job. Lecturing is where he discovered the most imagination from his students. Much of the expression of opinions was thanks to his style of lecturing. George was forever asking for opinions and always had a compassionate disposition. He never belittled his students even if a one made a bizarre or ignorant comment. He was only halfway through marking the papers and who better to uplift him than his loving sister?

'Hi, sis. Sorry I'm a bit late. It took longer to get here than I expected. There was an accident on the road and it slowed down traffic dramatically. It looked like the driver might have hit a cyclist.'

'It's fine. Take a seat. Is the cyclist okay?

'I'm not sure. The paramedics were there and I didn't notice any blood so it's hard to tell.'

'I hope he is okay. You have to be so careful on the roads these days. It's great to see you though!'

'It's nice to get out of the office. You know how I hate being stuck there for too long.'

'There is no way I could do what you do. Marking those papers would bore me to fucking tears. I've already ordered a coffee for me. Do you want one?' asked Lila, beckoning the waitress over.

'Can I help you, sir?' asked the young waitress.

'A cappuccino, please. I'll take a look at the menu in a moment.'

'Certainly, sir,' said the waitress as she went to see to his order.

'And so? How are things with Beatrice? You just brushed over who she is the other night,' asked Lila.

'Straight for the jugular I see. No customary chit-chat first?'

'I wouldn't want to keep you away from your marking. I know you are a busy man,' said Lila.

'Very well. She is great.'

'And?'

'I don't know, what information do you want to excruciatingly extract from me? I haven't spent a lot of time with her so I don't exactly have an encyclopedic knowledge about her.'

'Okay, okay. Let me help you along. How did you meet her?'

'The other day, Saturday, when I went for my run, I ran into her. Or at least we ran side by side,' said George.

'It's always good to find someone who is health-conscious. How come you had never approached her before?'

'I had never seen her before and I was running at a later time than usual. I guess it was all a fantastic coincidence because she isn't from here. For the record, she approached me, not the other way around. I was in a zone and didn't even notice her until she was running next to me and started chatting.'

'She isn't from here,' said Lila with concern. 'What does that mean for your relationship? I can call it a relationship, right?'

'Well, we barely know one another so it's all still premature. I'm not sure what you would call it. Call me crazy, but I just know this is a relationship for the long term and I suspect she feels the same way. I don't think the fact that she doesn't live here currently will be a problem. She said she'll be back in a week or two.'

'I love your positivity. What happened afterward? You must have spent some time with her?'

'After the run, we went to the frozen yogurt shop near the park.'

'Great choice. I love that place. I sometimes treat Julia and Noah when they've been good.'

'Also, later in the evening she came over supper. We spent hours talking. It must have five or six hours. It was all so effortless. I suppose the wine helped as well. I have a sneaking suspicion she will move here in the future if our relationship blossoms. She seems to adore our town. I suppose that it does have a certain charm to it.'

'Don't kid yourself- you have a certain charm as well.'

CHAPTER TWENTY-SIX

'I'm so happy for you George. You have no idea how much I worry about you at times. I just want good things for you.'

'I know, sis. You have always been there for me. I know I shall never be able to repay you for what you gave up to help raise me. Sometimes I wonder what my life would have been like if you hadn't chosen to be my guardian. I suspect I would feel a whole lot more bitter about life.'

'I'd do it again in a heartbeat. Fuck, the amount of time I think about you, I might as well still be your guardian. Those first few years were tough without Mom and Dad. Very tough. They would be so impressed to see you as a professor.'

'They would be so impressed to see what a sound job you did raising me.'

'Even I'm impressed with how you turned out. I hope Julia and Noah turn out as well.'

'Well, they seem to be off to a positive start. I love being with them. They are an absolute pleasure.' 'Let's see what happens when they become teenagers. We weren't the easiest kids.'

'Speak for yourself. I seem to remember that I was a pleasure throughout my teens,' joked George.

'Perspective my dear brother, can show a very different point of view but yes, under the circumstances, you were quite well behaved. You had all those part-time jobs to help us earn enough to get by. At one point I think you were managing three jobs and still trying to study and go to school.'

'Not the easiest time. I suppose it did bring out a determination in me. I remember it feeling like it was us against the world. I would have done anything to keep us together and financially stable. Maybe stable is too strong a word. I did lose my temper on occasion though.'

'Your cappuccino, sir. May I take your orders?' asked the waitress.

'Yes, please. I'd like a tuna mayonnaise sandwich and another coffee. George, what would you like?' asked Lila.

'I'll go with the bacon and tomato omelet, please. I'd also like some freshly squeezed orange juice, please. Thank you.'

The two siblings continued to chat contentedly while waiting for their food. When their orders arrived, eating did little to dampen their conversation.

'When are you seeing her again?'

'I'm not sure. As I said, she will be back in the next week or two, but she needs to still confirm the timing. I did ask her to join me for the fund-raising event at the university tomorrow evening, but there was no way she could squeeze the event into her work schedule. All the time management is going to take some getting used to, but I'm sure we can make it work. I hope I'm not building this relationship up too much. We have barely spent one day together.'

'I'm sure you'll make it work. Does she know anyone else in town?'

'I don't think so. Not that I'm aware of. She was just passing through and liked the place. This was more of a getaway for her to clear her head. I didn't get the impression she already knew anyone here.'

'Maybe she only liked the place once she met you.'

'Maybe. She only arrived a day before she met me if I recall correctly. Beatrice is quite unusual. She is extroverted, confident and unabashedly loving, yet she seems to be quite a loner. She likes her quiet time- her calmness from the noise of the rest of the world if you will.'

'She sounds intricate. No wonder you like her so much. You tend to like people that need to be unraveled like a puzzle.'

'Intricate is an appropriate way of describing her. She isn't shallow at all. It feels like she has so many layers to her. I can't wait to see what is behind the next curtain and the curtain after that. She seems fascinating and so much fun to be with.'

'Some curtains aren't meant to be looked behind, bro. Sometimes it's best to let the mystery alone. After all, there are some real psychos out there.'

'Are you speaking from experience?'

'You have no idea the amount of insanity I found when I was younger. Fuck yes, I'm speaking from experience. Thank God I persevered and eventually found Joe. He might have been the first genuinely decent guy I ever went out with. Obviously, I still needed to mold him to the fine man he is today.'

'Obviously.'

CHAPTER TWENTY-SEVEN

M r. Yang walked straight to the alcohol stand, leaving his wife stranded in the middle of a crowd of university lecturers and benefactors. Noticing this, George politely excused himself from two benefactors and went to keep Mr. Yang's wife company.

'Hi, Rose. It has been a while. Good to see you,' George said.

'Hi, George! It's wonderful to see you,' said Rose, hugging him affectionately.

'I see you are looking as elegant as always.' Rose always wore timeless clothing. Tonight, she was wearing an off-the-shoulder, full-length cream dress. Despite being slightly podgy, the fabric's tone against her skin made her radiate. She was the centerpiece of a crowd that was for the most part conservatively dressed.

'Thank you, George. You are looking debonair tonight in your suit and tie. You clean up remarkably well when you shave and comb your hair neatly.'

'It's a standard uniform for evenings like these. I have to try and look as presentable as possible.'

'Well, it suits you.'

'Thanks.'

Mr. Yang charged in from the drinks station at the entrance to the hall with a smile. 'Am I interrupting an intimate moment?'

Rose was quick to respond. 'You were, actually. How do you expect George and me to cultivate a romantic relationship if you interrupt us?'

'I see. Is this the way things have become? I'm all old, used up, sad, hopeless and a selfish man.'

'Decrepit,' said George.

'Decrepit, thank you, George,' said Mr. Yang.

'My dear, you are that and so much more,' said Rose. Mr. Yang could not help but laugh.

'You certainly keep me grounded my lovely wife. Here is your Chardonnay.' Mr. Yang took a sip of his Pinot Noir.

'Cheers,' said George, to which the others responded.

Taking a glance around the room, Mr. Yang commented, 'How many penguins to you think they will be able to round up tonight?' He was referring to the large number of potential donors chatting away in the spacious, wood-paneled hall. The university was going through a minor financial predicament after the government had cut back spending in recent years to focus on job creation and social grants. Political correctness and social justice had seeped its way into the forefront of the nation's consciousness which resulted in additional attention for those in need. This was a movement Mr. Yang was adamantly against, in part because it was to his detriment as an outspoken individual from a wealthy background, but also because he felt it was being taken to the extreme.

'One could argue you are also penguin Yang, considering that you grew up with a silver spoon in your mouth,' said George.

'I'm no penguin. My family came up from a hard-working blue-collar background. It might have been a silver spoon, but it was cleaned with blood, sweat and tears,' said Mr. Yang.

'Interesting analogy, dear,' his wife said.

'Fucking social justice warriors don't have a fucking clew about what they are doing and it means that important government institutions like ours aren't funded sufficiently and have to suck up to a bunch of penguins. It infuriates me like nothing else,' said Mr. Yang.

'Oh gosh. Here we go again,' said Rose.

'Well, society needs to address some of the imbalances. Better equality is hardly a bad aspiration. Let me rephrase that better. Less discrimination would be positive.'

'I must admit that I'm disappointed with the feminist movement,' said Rose. 'Instead of focusing on uplifting women, a great deal of the energy is on bringing down men. The focus is on pushing women into the male arena which is fine, but there is no focus on promoting the importance of the traditional role of women- promoting how important the female traits of nurturing, gentleness and empathy are to the social balance. The movement is paradoxically encouraging and creating more masculine women.'

'Don't get me started,' said Mr. Yang. 'You know how I feel about this. You know most of the people touting all this equality are idiots who just want their moment of fame.' He took a brief moment to take another sip of wine before continuing. 'They have no idea of the ramifications of what they do and the results they get out of the media and government is repugnant.'

'Yes, much of the time they are just looking to feed their own ego. Some of them are amongst the most unagreeable people I have ever seen. Even though they do make a mess of certain aspects, more equality, if done correctly and with fair, rational outcomes is desirable for everyone,' said George.

'Yes, yes, yes,' interrupted Mr. Yang. 'The cream naturally rises to the top. Most of the people feel they are being persecuted to begin with, merely create a crutch for themselves and that is what holds them back. Not imbalances in society.'

'In certain instances, yes- take for example women's success rates in the workplace,' said George, to which Rose raised her eyebrow. 'Many women blame their lack of success in the workplace to their gender for example, the fact that most of the senior managerial positions are held by men. They blame misogyny or sometimes other female coworker's bitchiness towards each other as the problem. It does ironically hold them back because one can end up blaming the wrong cause. Sometimes, you as an individual, have aspects in your personality or work deliverables that aren't favorable and that is what is holding you back.

Not an agenda. People are, however, very slow to admit blame and work on their flaws.'

'You can't seriously be saying misogyny does not exist,' asked Rose. 'It wasn't that long ago that women were not allowed to vote or have certain jobs.'

'I'm sure there are remnants of the old guard that enjoyed a male hierarchy and they would be a hurdle for women, but it is less prevalent and women who blame others, do so at the peril of their own career development. It isn't easy. There is a reason why I don't work in an office. The corporate world can be cutthroat. The corporate world was designed by men over centuries, where only the strongest men have risen to the top. I used the word "men" because it has specifically been designed around more male-dominant traits. Characteristics like competitiveness, lack of agreeableness, dominance, et cetera. Therefore, more feminine traits like compassion and nurturing are seen as weaknesses and are stifled. It can't be easy for women to adjust to many work situations. By the sounds of it, this is starting to change, but women were at a definite disadvantage for decades because of it.

'Here is another example,' George said. 'Men often focused on their own survival in the workplace, making sure everyone below them delivered in order for them to look good to those above them, whereas women tend to be more focused on the team dynamic and the team delivering as a whole. Therefore, it has often been the men who stand out because their goal is to be singled out. I think companies are starting to wise up to this and are trying to push the more team-orientated approach. It's a more favorable approach as it benefits multiple people rather than merely an individual. If someone builds their career by dominating others and relying heavily on others to make themselves look superior, they are building on a shaky foundation that will come back to bite them one day.'

'This is all in the bible?' asked Mr. Yang sarcastically.

'Not all the books I read are religious in subject matter you know. Plus, these types of topics interest me. So, I find myself thinking about them on occasion.'

'Well don't think too hard. These fucking penguins don't like lecturers rocking the boat. They are just interested in their bottom line and having a favorable public image. They…' started Mr. Yang before being interrupted by one of the said penguins.

'Evening, professors. A fine evening this is. What are you intellectuals discussing this evening?' he asked, after reading their name tags.

'It is indeed, sir. We were just commenting on how important these evenings are and what a difference these donations make to the educations of the future leaders of our country,' said Mr. Yang. George and Rose had to hold back a laugh.

'Splendid. Splendid. I'll be sure to donate handsomely tonight. Oh, excuse me, I just noticed someone over there I must chat with. Do enjoy the rest of your evening.'

'Same to you,' they all responded.

Once the donor was out of earshot, Mr. Yang added, 'Fucking penguin.'

CHAPTER TWENTY-EIGHT

George continued mingling with the crowd, sharing his insights of what was occurring on campus and in the media. After a while, the conversations became more monotonous as he was repeating himself over and over again when moving from one group to another. He was rapidly becoming bored and tired which resulted in him periodically checking his watch while moving between the different benefactor groups. George decided to find Mr. Yang and his wife to see how they were finding the night. If George was finding it tiresome, no doubt Mr. Yang was finding it excruciating. Hearing him rant would at least be one source of entertainment for the remainder of the night. As he spotted the couple on the outskirts of the hall, his phone started vibrating. It was Beatrice.

He briskly moved outside in order to hear her more clearly. An expression of joy was emblazoned on his face as he placed the phone to his ear.

'Hi, Beatrice.'

'Hi there, handsome. How is it going there?'

'All right. The usual tedious highbrow event.'

'I'm sorry I couldn't be there. The work scheduling can be painful at times. I would have liked to have seen you in your natural habitat.'

'This is hardly my natural habitat. I must admit that it feels strange wearing a suit and tie,' said George.

'That alone would have been worth the admission for me. I might have found it quite interesting. If tonight isn't your natural environment, then maybe I'll attend one of your lectures some time. Then I can assess how enlightening or tedious you are when it's just you talking.'

'Ah I see, so you are implying that you provide the more entertaining conversation?'

'Most definitely. Have you ever heard of an entertaining professor?'

'I suppose you have a point. Our purpose is focused on partaking knowledge on to others rather than being entertaining. So are air hostesses entertaining by nature? Aren't you supposed to be agreeable and diplomatic rather than entertaining?'

'Fair enough. We shall call it a draw then?'

'A draw sounds reasonable.'

'Anyway, I'm climbing onto an adjoining flight now and wanted to quickly check how it was going. I'm afraid I need to go now.'

'Oh, okay. It's a pity this has been such a quick conversation.'

'I know. I'm sorry to keep it so short, but I'll be back in town soon. How would you like to have a picnic in the park when I'm back?'

'Sounds good to me. I love being outdoors. I'm looking forward to it.'

George looked up and was greeted by a full moon. The night was clear and the cosmos glinted above him while Beatrice's voice mellowed his mood.

'Great. Me too.'

'See you soon. Take care. Bye.'

'Bye.'

After the phone call, George's disposition changed. There was now a definite spring in his step and an even more ready smile.

By the time he got home, he was exhausted. He had to rise early the next day because his first lecture was at eight o'clock. Despite being tired, it took him an hour to fall asleep. The conversation with Beatrice replayed in his head. The emotions he had felt- washed over him repeatedly until he fell asleep with a smile on his face.

CHAPTER TWENTY-NINE

A few days later, George and Beatrice met for their picnic at the park. Once again, the weather was flawless. The ground was warm to the touch and the air parched. They chose to sit under a large oak tree which provided intermittent patches of shade as mild gusts of wind made the branches sway. The scenic environment resulted in them sprawling out on George's blanket without a care in the world.

'Why can't every day be like today?' asked Beatrice.

'It's beautiful, isn't it,' said George.

'If you get weather like this regularly, then I'm moving here without a doubt. It's a done deal.'

'So, what you are saying is having me here makes this town a potentially pleasant place to stay, but what makes it an especially enticing location is the weather.'

'Exactly. Ensuring you are in a warm environment is much more important than the people you interact with and time will tell whether I can stand to be around you,' she said.

'Really?' said George. 'I was almost sure my gravitational pull could not be negated.'

'You must still be living in the Dark Ages. I'm afraid your Earth revolves around my Sun, not the other way around.'

'If I get to close, you'll burn me?'

'You'll have to wait and see.'

'I suppose the question is, whether I'm a gambling man.'

'That sounds like a line from a movie. I can't place it though.'

'I'm not sure. It does sound like it comes from a movie. Would you like another sandwich?'

'Please. How did the university conference go? Did it go on for a lot longer after I called?'

'Yes, it was a long night. Some of the lecturers struggle with having to promote their faculties to facilitate donations, but I can't say it bothers me much. At least we raised a decent amount of money for the university.'

'That's wonderful. Having strong tertiary institutions is important for the future.'

'Those students are our future. A strong education system is paramount to a country's growth and economy. Sometimes I do worry about the current generation of students. The erosion of the old-school family structure seems to have a negative effect on a lot of the kids and this is coming from someone who wasn't fortunate enough to have a traditional family for much of my youth. With each passing year, they seem more and more disconnected. Jaded almost. While I have nothing against both parents working, it does cause problems with children's development in certain circumstances. They aren't getting the attention that our generation received. With all due respect, present company excluded.'

'How old were you again when you parents died?'

'Twelve.'

'Twelve is very young to lose both your parents. I might have never had parents, but somehow I can feel how hard it must have been for you,' said Beatrice, empathy in her eyes.

'It was an arduous time. It was like having an itch I didn't know how to scratch. I wasn't emotionally mature enough to handle the trials life was hurling at me. My sister, Lila, was my rock- she always gave me the support I needed.'

'She sounds like a special person. I'm looking forward to meeting her.'

'Lila is very special to me. She may take some getting used to though. She is quite outspoken and swears like a trooper, especially if she has had some wine. She had to grow up very young. A nineteen-year-old having to take care of a twelve-year-old is no mean feat. Thankfully my parents' life insurance was enough to cover the remaining loans. We had a fully paid-off home and car. There was no way we would have managed otherwise. All we needed to worry about was living expenses. There is no way she would have managed to get custody without it,' reflected George.

'I couldn't imagine raising a kid if I was still a teenager.'

'I know. Amazingly, she has remained a positive, bubbly, loving person despite all the hardships.'

'It sounds like she deserves a medal.'

'She would probably make a comment like, "Joe is my medal".'

'Is Joe her husband?'

'Yes. He is a fantastic guy and they are great together. I've never met such a joyful and comfortable couple. I get along so well with him, so I've also benefited from their relationship.'

'They are very lucky.'

'Beatrice, there is something I need to tell you.'

'Okay.'

'I'm not sure how you are going to react,' George said.

'That sounds ominous.'

'I used to be married. I'm sorry I haven't told you about her before. My wife passed away five years ago from stage four breast cancer.'

'Oh, um… I don't know what to say. That's terrible. Why didn't you say anything to me?'

'I guess by telling you I'm in some way putting her behind me. I have never been ready to let her go. Even after five years of living by myself. She was everything to me. We were very happy together. We were trying to have kids when we found out about the cancer and our lives and plans fell apart. I apologize for not telling you sooner, but

I also wanted to give us time to breathe and there was enough heavy conversation the other day at my place to have added this information to the recipe.'

'I see. I'm sorry George. I can only imagine what that must have been like. This explains the solemnness you always have behind your eyes. I understand why you found it awkward to speak about it. What was her name?'

'Isabella. I still miss her terribly and think about her often. It took me years to acclimatize to not having her around. It was extremely tough initially- even simple tasks like getting out of bed were hard. The world just seemed empty after she passed. To be quite honest, I've been suffering from depression ever since she passed. I believe functional depression is the term. I know it isn't exactly what you want to hear. I love being with you and I want you to be my future, but it's difficult letting go of the past.'

'I'm sorry that the last few years have been such a strain for you. What is functional depression?'

'It's just a term used to describe someone who is suffering from depression, but is still able to function somewhat normally in the word. I don't let it defeat me. I do what needs to be done, but feelings of joy have been a distant memory for me.'

'That sounds rough. Have you talked to someone about it?'

'I went for counseling when Isabella died, but not since then. I'm doing a lot better than I was then and am functional so I haven't felt the need to treat it. I wouldn't be surprised if you are the cure I need. I feel much happier when I'm around you.'

'Thank you. That's kind of you,' Beatrice said, placing her hand against her chest. 'What was your wife like as a person?'

'You remind me of her. Isabella had an inner strength. She never let anything get her down. I'm more pessimistic at times, but she was a consummate optimist. I see her inner strength in you.'

'Really?'

'Sure. You are clear about what you want and you don't hold back in order to obtain it. Also, both of you have a humorous side. You are more sarcastic than her though.'

'Me?' asked Beatrice, her eyes wide in a puppy dog fashion.

'Yes, you.'

'I appreciate this must be a very difficult conversation for you.'

'I have been dreading it, but I feel like there is a massive weight off my shoulders now that I've told you. You are easy to talk to.'

'Thank you. I'm glad you feel better now. It's important to get off your chest the problems that are bothering you,' she said, looking into the distance. A squirrel scampered up a tree, nut in hand, before being cloaked by the foliage.

CHAPTER THIRTY

George and Beatrice continued to relax under the comforting oak tree for the remainder of the afternoon. George was amazed at how effortless it was interacting with Beatrice. He was naturally gifted at conversing with people, but it was different with Beatrice. It was as if they had known each other for years. They had spoken over the phone multiple times since they had last seen one another, but they were still very much at the inception of their relationship. She had somehow awakened him from his deep slumber. The only time he had felt as joyful as this was his first few years with Isabella. It had been so long since he had felt positive about the future that he almost forgotten the sensation. Seeing her stretched out on the picnic blanket made his heart leap with optimism. It was clear she felt the same way about him which amplified the effect. He didn't know what he had done to deserve Beatrice in his life, but he did know he wouldn't give her up without a fight. To have a second chance at happiness like this humbled him.

Afterthey were done with their picnic, they made their way through the streets. Beatrice wanted to take in as much of the town as she possibly could while she was there. It was a novel experience for George. Sights and events he took for granted or never considered were fascinating to Beatrice because she saw everything from a different perspective. These ranged from the width of the streets, to the number of trees, to the freshness of the air. After a while she became silent, but content. She was fulfilled being at this place in this time. The quiet was not awkward, but quite the opposite. It was a relaxing experience for George as they walked hand in hand from one window to the next in a street containing petite shops selling clothes and antique furniture with a scattering of restaurants.

Unfortunately, even wonderful moments had to end. They had to part ways in the mid-afternoon because Beatrice needed to get back to her hotel and pack. She was on yet another flight in the evening and was concerned about checking in at the airport on time.

He offered to take her, but she declined, saying she had rented a car and needed to return it. He thought it a bit wasteful of expenditure considering she was only back for one day. He would have happily taken her to where she needed to go. He concluded that perhaps she didn't want to be a burden.

CHAPTER THIRTY-ONE

'So, when am I going to meet this amazing woman of yours?' asked Lila.

'Patience comes to those who are prepared to wait,' responded George.

'Ah, man.'

'Unfortunately, my wife only believes in instant gratification, Georgie,' added Joe.

'Whatever,' said Lila, 'that sounds more like a euphemism for your sexual stamina.'

'Wow! That is a low blow, lovey. Now you are going to give Georgie ideas about me.'

'Ah, come on. You can't take a joke. You are like a trojan in bed. What the fuck is a trojan anyway?'

George shook his head to their banter and forged ahead up the trail, not particularly wanting to hear this topic of conversation, although he was happy for them for maintaining a healthy sex life.

The three of them were midway through a hike on a Saturday morning. It was an activity they tried to do regularly when the weather was suitable and Joe's parents were available to take care of Julia and Noah. Unfortunately, the whole trail was not entirely as nature had intended it to be due to the recent felling of large tree plantations in the vicinity on the hillside opposite them. While all other signs of humanity encroaching into the world were absent from their sight, the tree farms were a peripheral subconscious reminder that civilization was near. These plantations brought revenue and jobs to the community and they were widely praised for the dramatic effect they had on the diminishing of unmanaged deforestation.

'You guys do know I hardly ever see her myself. She is traveling so much and she doesn't have much leave owing to her at the moment.'

'Well, the next time she is in town, I expect you to invite her to our place. There is a new roast lamb recipe I have been meaning to try and it's the perfect opportunity to experiment,' said Lila.

Joe sighed and said, 'Please don't talk about food right now. You know I get extra hungry when I hike. Just the mere mention of meat is making my mouth water. All we have on us is water and fruit- there is no way they are going to satisfy my craving now.'

'You know you are a bit of a barbarian at times, lovey. I'm afraid you have an incredibly one tracked mind. There is more to life than meat.

'Life is not worth living without meat!' said Joe. 'And beer for that matter.'

'Oh, God. Here we go. Go ahead. I know you love talking about meat and beer,' sighed Lila.

'These are gifts from God. It would be rude if we did not show our appreciation by eating his creations and drinking his fermented grains.'

'If you had to give up either meat or beer Joe, which would you choose?' asked George.

'Please don't ask questions like that. It's too cruel to think about. I show my appreciation equally between the two. It's like asking me to choose between my children. It just isn't right. My love and appreciation must be spread evenly.'

'Yes, well maybe at times you show your appreciation too much,' said Lila.

'I thought you liked my little man-belly?'

'I do, but before long that little man-belly you have will be large enough to look like you are fucking smuggling things in it.'

'A supply of fat reserves can be good to survive through a famine. Plus, there is the added benefit that I can be like Buddha and you can rub my stomach.'

'The fat version of Buddha is quite cute,' said George.

'I know, but last time I checked, my hubby isn't a God and an unhealthy lifestyle isn't going to help his life expectancy. If I don't have this fucker around in my old age, who am I going to give a hard time?'

'Don't look at me,' said George, looking straight ahead. 'I don't plan on being around to see you give me grief every day in my old age. I've had hard times in my life, but that sounds way too rough.'

'You tell her,' said Joe. 'It takes a strong man to deal with her every day. That is why I'm constantly looking for meat and beer. It's where I get my power from.'

'I can't win, can I?' said Lila.

'You win every day by being married to such a fine specimen.'

'Yes... I suppose so.'

'I love you, Lila. More and more every year,' said Joe.

'I love you too.'

CHAPTER THIRTY-TWO

They continued up the trail towards the zenith of their smallest mountain range which was half-an-hour from the outskirts of town. Despite the range's modest altitude and the requirement for rock climbing not being mandatory, it was a steep path to the top. Most of their journey could be performed with a hard-angled walk due to the route of the trail zig-zagging up to the summit. However, at times they needed to grab onto flora to assist and at the steepest sections, they had to go on all fours due to the incline. Joe struggled the most with the journey due to his hefty weight. Every year he swore he would never go on this particular trail again but, every year, George and Lila managed to convince him to push himself one more time. They achieved this by questioning his masculinity, a cheap trick that invariably worked. Nonetheless, the three where reasonably fit because they hiked a few times a season. All their breathing nevertheless escalate forcefully and conversations were kept to a minimum towards the crest of the mountain. Thankfully, the morning was overcast which aided in keeping hydration levels maintainable. Lila lost her footing on one occasion, but Joe was on hand to support her. Without Joe's assistance, Lila would have injured herself with a nasty gash on her leg. This close call was the only mishap that had occurred, which was a successful result for them as there had been more than one occasion in the past where one of them had been injured. Despite each of them bringing a large water bottle and taking breaks wherever practical, they were left perspiring profusely. Casual hikers ended their ascension at one of the lesser viewpoints midway up the incline. It was only the more seasoned hikers, as well as the more sadistic novices like them, who made it all the way to the summit.

At last the group reached the peak and was once again left in wonder by the vistas. The cloud cover had subsided slightly which allowed the sunlight to seep through the cracks in the condensed atmosphere, resulting in the heavenly beams to swirl on the terrain below them. The view was lush and worth all the exertion. The trio remained silent. For a moment they forgot about their own lives and became one with the world, one with life.

'Breathtaking, isn't it,' said George.

'No doubt,' Joe said.

'Selfie time!' said Lila.

'Oh, God. Why did I say anything?' said George as he buried his face in one of his hands.

CHAPTER THIRTY-THREE

On the way up to his apartment after a productive day at work, George took a detour to fetch his mail. He dropped his laptop bag and some work literature on the kitchen table and switched the kettle on to make a cup of coffee. It was just past five o'clock and at this stage of the day, he invariably required another pick-me-up.

He took his mail with his steaming mug in hand and sat in his most comfortable armchair. He listened to records as a habit when sitting in this chair but, on this occasion, he was more inclined towards silence. The first letter was for a raffle he had supposedly won. It congratulated him for being chosen from thousands of individuals to win a trip to the Caribbean for two. It detailed the steps to follow to obtain his prize. The scam put a tiny smirk on his face. He tore up the supposed opportunity of a lifetime. The rest seemed to all be bills. However, the second last envelope contained a royalty check for his science fiction novel. He opened up the envelope and was astonished to be met by the highest check he had received thus far for his novel. He must have received a positive review somewhere or perhaps someone influential had recommended it. He was pleasantly surprised and raised his cup of coffee to himself.

George had used writing a novel as a coping mechanism to get through the death of his wife. For six months it was a distraction to his day-to-day surroundings and took his consciousness to less painful places. He had imagined a world not resembling his own environment. By the time he'd finished writing it, he decided he might as well attempt to publish it. His intent was not to make money out of it, but when it achieved moderate success and with that, generated decent income for him, he was amazed. The therapeutic aspect of writing the story had, nonetheless, been the true reward. He was not yet a senior lecturer and therefore was not earning as sizable a salary as some might think. This meant that the additional novel income equaled his usual professor's salary. Despite currently generating twice as much money as he was used to, he didn't spend most of it.

George never treated himself and had no particular final purpose for the money. Depression had left him uninspired. Losing his beloved wife had left him aimless and he had lost interest in most of the hobbies from his youth. On a subconscious level, this was because he couldn't share the money with anyone, he couldn't enjoy it. Therefore, the small treats he initially bought for himself did not escalate to larger, mid-life crisis splurges. Julia and Noah would inherit his savings on his eventual passing but, until then, it was growing in the bank as well as other investment schemes.

CHAPTER THIRTY-FOUR

The mall buzzed with activity. It was a Friday and a public holiday, resulting in an extended weekend. That, coupled with the fact it had just been payday for most people, meant there was going to be much spending in the retail stores over the weekend.

George was window shopping to see if he could buy Beatrice a gift. Pleasing her gave him a reason to spend his surplus money from the royalty check. However, he didn't want to go overboard. They hadn't been seeing each other for an extensive period and he didn't want to put any needless pressure on the relationship because of an expensive gift. He had never bought any gifts this soon for the women in his previous relationships, including his deceased wife, Isabella. He shuddered at the thought of jinxing their future, but the way they intertwined was so seamless it defied the risk of bad luck. Electricity coursed through his chest as he thought about her.

George walked into a fragrance store and glanced at the perfumes. He was always amazed at how much more expensive female fragrances were to the male ones.

'Can I assist you, sir?' asked a friendly shop assistant, dressed far beyond what her salary could afford her to buy.

'I'm just glancing, thank you.'

'Looking for something for wife or girlfriend?' she asked.

'Sort of, yes. I'm not sure I know what to buy her.'

'What kind of fragrances does she prefer?'

'I'm not sure.'

'Fragrances are very personal. It's best to know what the person likes otherwise it can be overpowering and difficult for her to wear. May I suggest a light and refreshing perfume?'

'Um, you know what, I think I need to find out what her preferences are before I buy anything. I'll come back another time. As you say, I don't want to buy her a fragrance she might struggle to wear.'

George wandered past a few clothing stores. While Beatrice was slim, he couldn't guess her exact size, so he decided to scrap the clothing option as he could end up buying something that didn't fit her properly. Hats were too occasional and some people never wore them. A purse could work, but she might already have a nice one. George considered what other accessory was an option. Perhaps jewelry could work. It was hard to go wrong with a gift like that he deduced and carried on walking until he came across a jewelry store. He glanced at the items in the window display. In his opinion, watches needed to be of good quality in order to wear, in which case they were expensive. Too expensive for this stage in their relationship. Rings were out of the question because they had an inference to engagement. George deduced it was between earrings, a necklace or a bracelet. He opted on a bracelet as it could be the most low-key. He entered the store and walked to the counter to see if he could find a suitable item to purchase.

'Good morning. I'd like to see your bracelets, please. I'm looking for something that isn't too ostentatious. Ideally, an understated design.'

'Good morning, sir. Do have an idea of the type of metal you are considering or perhaps its color?'

'Maybe something in silver.'

The shop assistant took out five options for George to look at. All prices were revealed, therefore the decision was easier for George to make. The two expensive ones had what he assumed were diamonds.

Another was far more sensibly priced and hence must have been cubic zirconias. He preferred not buying fake gemstones if he could avoid it.

'I'm leaning towards these two without any gemstones.'

'They are both very classic designs, sir. Either one would be a fantastic choice.'

'I think I'll go for the one with the heart. The other one is a bit too plain.'

'A good choice, Sir. Is there anything else you would like to look at? A watch for you perhaps? We have just received new stock that might interest you.'

'No thank you. My watch is still working fine. Just the bracelet for today.'

'Would you like me to gift wrap it?'

'Yes please.'

George paid for the bracelet and made his way to the exit. He felt exceedingly buoyant and realized sometimes giving a gift to a loved one was the best gift we can give ourselves.

He couldn't wait to see Beatrice.

CHAPTER THIRTY-FIVE

George stared at the movie posters on the wall. The movie house was the solitary cinema in town and therefore had to cater to a large variety of tastes. Currently screening was a classic Italian movie. There was an animated film with a dog. No doubt the dog talked and went on an adventure of some kind. He pulled out his phone to see what kind of a rating it was getting. Four out of five stars. He filed the name in his memory bank. It might be a good movie to watch with Julia and Noah. There was a generic-looking teenage comedy. He gathered by the slogan below the title that it was about teenagers finding their way in life in the most raucous way possible. Next to that was a poster of a drama about an old married couple that was supposedly quite enjoyable according to a colleague from work. Next to that poster, was information about the latest *Star Wars* movie. It seemed like most people were going to watch that based on the clothes people were wearing and the odd bit of conversation he heard from people as they passed. Lastly, there was a rescreening of the original *Blade Runner* movie. George and Beatrice had decided beforehand to watch this film.

He hadn't seen the movie in a number of years, but loved it as an unusual, cerebral and visionary science fiction movie. He found incorporating subject matter that was in vogue with the young adults in his classes a useful way of making his students grasp topics. Even though the film was around four decades old, it had remained relevant due to its cult status. Perhaps watching it this time would reveal more of its hidden secrets he hadn't noticed before. Beatrice had never seen the movie, so he was hoping she would enjoy it as much as he had in the past. The creativity of the architecture and set design were two aspects he found rewarding and he was sure she would feel the same based on her love for architecture.

George's phone started vibrating. It was a message from Beatrice. She was running late and suggested he buy a large popcorn and cola for them to share in the meantime. He responded that he would wait for her by the movie posters.

A few minutes later she waved at him from the other end of the hall. She was dressed in a comfortable sleeveless shirt, jeans and sneakers. There was a spring in her step as she scurried across to him.

'Hi, Mr. Professor,' she said before kissing him.

'Hi,' said George. 'Did you find your way okay?'

'It was simple enough, thanks.'

'I hope you enjoy this film. It's one of my favorites.'

'I've read favorable reviews and I trust your judgment. I'm looking forward to it.'

Beatrice pinched a few popcorns from George and brushed off a couple of stray hairs on his shoulder.

'I think the movie is starting soon,' said George. 'We better go get our seats if we don't want to miss anything.'

'Don't they start with adverts?'

'They do, but that is part of the fun. It's a ritualistic build-up. Plus, I like seeing the trailers for the upcoming movies.'

'Let's get going then. This movie is quite old right?'

'Early nineteen eighties. Is its age a problem?'

'Not at all. I'm just glad it isn't in 3D. I find 3D distracting and much prefer movies that aren't spatially enhanced.'

'We are in row L10.'

They took their seats and started munching away at the popcorn, while the adverts starting playing. There was hardly anyone else there because it was the late afternoon show so it felt like a private viewing for them.

'So, what is this movie about again?' asked Beatrice.

'It's a futuristic detective noir. Harrison Ford plays a detective whose job it is to find and execute replicants.'

'What are replicants?'

'They are bio-engineered, clone-like humans designed for jobs too onerous for humans. They are stronger, faster and more durable than humans. They are seen as freaks and are shunned by society. Their whole existence is to fulfill a slave labor role. If I recall correctly, they are hunted because they are not meant to live in normal society and, paradoxically, the humans are scared and feel inferior to the more advanced models.'

'Okay, got it.'

The movie began. The impactful drone of the orchestral introduction and written epilogue were followed by bursts of fire plumes above a futuristic city the likes of which had never been seen before this movie was released. The cityscape was both sublime and ominous. George turned and saw the enthralled expression on Beatrice's face in his peripheral vision.

CHAPTER THIRTY-SIX

'Well? What did you think?' asked George once the movie had ended.

'That was amazing. I wasn't expecting it to be as incredible as it was. The world was so well designed and thought out. The set design must have been revolutionary for its time. I mean there were so many great scenes. The sci-fi pyramid, the oriental style streets and high rises, the lovely textured brickwork in Harrison's apartment. I loved how goggle-like the glasses were of the replicant company CEO. I also loved Rachael's hair and outfits. Wow, just wow. Oh, and the sound, it was pretty amazing as well.'

'I'm so glad you liked it. The movie can be a bit slow-paced for some and it certainly isn't a short movie, but it's a visual master-class and there is a lot of depth under the surface.'

'I liked the fact it took its time. If anything, movies these days seem to be rushed. It was quite poetic that he managed to run away with her in the end.'

'The concept is very interesting. At what point does a creation warrant the same value as a human and what does it mean to be human. After all, we are on the brink of cloning. What did you think of Harrison Ford's character?'

'I liked him. I thought he had a believable character arc,' said Beatrice.

'There has been a raging debate for years as to whether he was a replicant or not. Ridley Scott, the director, felt he was while Harrison Ford felt the character wasn't.'

'What? I didn't even think about it. Is that what the origami part at the end was about?'

'Yes, I believe so.'

'Not being sure if he is a replicant is so cool. I can see now why it's regarded as a classic movie.

Beatrice looked around. 'It looks like everyone else has left. We should probably leave as well.'

'Are you still keen to go to my place?' asked George.

'Definitely.'

CHAPTER THIRTY-SEVEN

'The light switch is over there,' said George.

Beatrice switched on the lights to George's apartment. The room awoke in as tidy a disposition as George had left it.

'Can I get you something to drink?' asked George.

'I'm fine for now. Maybe a glass of water, please. Popcorn often makes me thirsty.'

'Coming right up.' George cracked open a beer at the same time. He was desperate for something cold.

'Do you mind if I switch the TV on?' asked Beatrice.

'No problem. Go right ahead. I have Netflix, Amazon and YouTube. Do you need any help using the remote?'

'I'm fine, thanks.'

Beatrice opened YouTube and searched for clips about the original *Blade Runner*. George joined her on the couch and they discussed more of the intricacies in the movie. Before they realized it, an hour had passed.

'I don't watch too many series, but I like having Netflix for all the documentaries. I've been watching quite a few nature documentaries of late,' said George. 'There have been some high-quality ones recently.'

'It's amazing how they manage to capture the footage they do. They must be sitting out there for hours before they eventually spot something.'

'YouTube it. Let's see what comes up. I'm curious to see how they go about acquiring the footage.'

'Here's one with Sir David Attenborough. Let's try it,' said Beatrice. They discovered that some of the animals had been filmed with unobtrusive tracking systems on them and that was how they were able to obtain so much excellent footage of the magnificent and often rare animals. Once again, an hour passed away without them realizing it.

'I'm starving. Do you want me to put some frozen pizzas in the oven or order takeaways,' asked George.

'Whichever is easier for you. I'm not fussy.'

'Pizzas it is then,' said George. He grabbed two pizzas from the freezer and let them heat in the oven before cutting them and sliding them onto separate plates.

'Bon appétit,' said George, placing Beatrice's pizza on the coffee table in front of her before he sat back down next to her with his pizza on hand for expedient consumption.

'Mmm. It's good. I didn't realize I was also hungry until I tasted it. You are quite the chef,' she said.

'Are you teasing me?' asked George to taunt her on.

'Teasing you? How could you say such a thing? You heated it at just the right temperature, for just the right amount of time. You did a masterful job.'

'Like the packaging instructions told me to.'

Her giggling became a laugh. 'Well there you go. You are talented at following instructions. An admirable trait.'

'You like teasing me, don't you?' he said. George put his half-eaten slice of pizza down and gave her an intense, unyielding stare.

'Oh come on, can't you take a joke?' Beatrice began poking him in his chest and stomach with her index finger.

George did not respond at all which only made her provoking more vigorous. He smirked.

Her attention was drawn from his chest towards his steadfast stare.

Their faces were just a few inches apart and despite the sound of the television, it seemed as though everything became quieter and slower.

Abruptly, their restraints were released. They kissed with passion. Their vigor caused their heart rates to elevate. Raw emotion overtook them as they tore off clothes. George almost broke his glasses as he whipped them off his face. Their lust had at last overtaken them. By the time they were done, they were panting as perspiration dripped off their bodies.

George, gulping for breath, said, 'I feel like...I have just...sprinted a mile. That was intense.'

'I know...what you mean. I need another glass of water. Do you also want a glass?' she asked as she climbed off of him.

'Yes...please. You can get me a glass from the cupboard directly above the drawers.' George breathed in the remnants of her perfume, savoring the scent. Cinnamon, vanilla and tea came to his mind. It was intoxicating as the perspiration amplified the fragrance.

He turned to look at her to ensure she was looking in the correct place for a glass. The last few minutes were so primal that he hadn't fully grasped what she looked like naked. He swore to himself. She had the most incredible body he had ever had the pleasure of witnessing. Her body was sexier than he had dared assume.

Beatrice returned with two glasses of water which they promptly gulped down. They eyed their half-eaten pizzas. She turned to him and asked, 'Some slightly cold after sex pizza?'

'This is going to go down so well. I'm ravenous. If there is one food that is as good as warm pizza, it's cold pizza.' They both gobbled up their food before deciding on another movie. This time they decided on a romantic comedy. Neither had bothered getting dressed again so they only managed to get about halfway through the movie before their arousal peaked once more and they moved to the bedroom. This time their love making was slower before they fell fast asleep in each other's arms.

CHAPTER THIRTY-EIGHT

B eatrice awoke before George the next morning and left him a note indicating she would be back in the mid-morning. The note stated she needed a change of clothes and, at the same time, she would have a shower and eat breakfast at the hotel where she was staying. There was therefore no need for him to worry about her.

George read the message again. They had planned to go to an art gallery today, but they hadn't specified a time. George shook his head and muttered to himself, 'Couldn't she have waited for me to get up before leaving? Why are women so uncomfortable with being seen without makeup?' He tried to imagine what she would look like without makeup before the urge to urinate broke his chain of thought.

After seeing to the needful, George looked at his watch to gauge how much time he had. It was seven 'o clock. He had plenty of time before Beatrice returned so he leisurely brushed his teeth, showered, shaved and found something casual to wear, but still what he considered to be befitting for an art gallery.

He made and enjoyed his standard weekend breakfast of bacon, eggs and toast with a few slices of tomato.

Beatrice still hadn't arrived so he went online via his laptop to take a look at his preferred news sites. As usual, the media was heavily weighted towards negative news, mostly- politics related. From the recesses of his mind, he was reminded that people were drawn more towards negative news. He googled the subject to see what he could find and indeed his memory was correct. The few websites he read did confirm that people focus more on negative news rather than positive and therefore news articles were invariably about a negative topic in order to meet the demand. He read about surveys that had been performed on sample groups and the majority of the test subjects, unaware of the true purpose of the trial survey, had chosen to read negative articles over positive ones. George continued reading and discovered that psychologists deduced the possible explanation for this was for evolutionary survival purposes. A human's strongest instinct was self-preservation and therefore, by reading negative news, people were affectively searching for potential dangers they could come into contact with. George thought about this for a moment and searched for a positive news site. He picked the first two that came up and he had to admit while the articles were indeed uplifting he also couldn't help but find them frivolous. He didn't feel the need to save the address to return on another day. He couldn't help feeling it was poignant that he tended to agree that enriching articles were as addictive as those highlighted with catastrophes of some kind. One possible exception he could think of was a subject matter specifically interesting to an individual, for example, new scientific discoveries.

The buzzer screeched to signify the presence of someone at the entrance to the apartment building. George buzzed Beatrice in, and was met met by a joyful floral summer dress and what appeared to be the same perfume.

'I have a gift for you,' said George. He tried to behave as nonchalant as possible, but he was equally excited for her to open the gift as she was. He couldn't find the right opportunity the night before to give her the bracelet and the latter part had become so passionate that he had forgotten about the gift. George handed Beatrice the small elongated box in ivory wrapping and a turquoise bow.

'For me?' asked Beatrice. She opened the packaging and the box to reveal the silver bracelet he had bought. 'Oh George, you shouldn't have. This really isn't necessary.' She blushed feeling almost uncomfortable with the jewelry he had bought her.

'Is something wrong with it?'

'What? No, of course not. It's beautiful. I love it.' Beatrice looped the bracelet across her right wrist and locked it in place. 'This is embarrassing. Thank you so much, George.' She stepped towards him and gave him a generous hug and a long affectionate kiss. 'I wasn't expecting this. I'm quite taken aback.'

They chatted with exuberance due to the night before as well as the silver that now adorned her wrist, before George drove them to the art gallery on the outskirts of town. Not too long afterward, they arrived at their destination.

'This isn't what I was expecting,' said Beatrice. They pulled up to an old, well-established farm amid the town's growing agricultural belt. Two rows of tall oak trees processioned their arrival onto the farm estate, followed by a panoramic view of the produce valley below. The flourishing and lush valley starkly juxtaposed the dry perimeter's baked hills. They stepped out of the car to take in the vista.

'What a beautiful view. It's magnificent,' said Beatrice.

'I agree wholeheartedly.'

Beatrice gave George a subtle elbow to his stomach, realizing the compliment was partly directed to the way she looked. Beatrice in her floral dress would have enhanced any scene.

'I'm serious.'

'So am I,' replied George.

Beatrice attempted to ignore him. 'Look how green it all is. This is like a postcard.'

'As far as I know, the farms in the valley are relatively young. It's only the farms on the hills which were established when the town was founded. I read in the local newspaper a couple of months ago that many of them are testing the viability of sustainable renewable farming. Green electricity, efficient watering measures, Et cetera.'

'And what, this farm has an art gallery in one of these old buildings?' asked Beatrice as she leant up against him and stroked his arm.

'Supposedly. They opened it about two or three years ago. I haven't been, but I've heard favorable comments. I suppose that is the benefit of having a strong arts department at the university. There is no shortage of supply of quality art.'

'There is a sign. The gallery is to the left. It's probably the building over there with all the statues leading towards it.'

They strolled towards what was a newly constructed structure made with walls of glass and steel in order to bring in the beautiful exteriors. The building itself was a work of art in its simplicity. They stopped along the way to look at the statues. Some were permanent while others were available at a price far exceeding either of their budgets. George noted how majestic some of the statues were partly due to their physical volume. An asset that couldn't be expressed in a two-dimensional canvas.

'What a tranquil venue. I love the fact there are almost no people around. It's as if the art is being displayed exclusively for us,' said Beatrice.

George looked around and noted it was indeed empty, before remembering there was a huge local sports game on at the moment and that was why. 'Let's go in and see what we find.'

They meandered through the aisles gazing at the different mediums while the morning sun joyfully illuminated the whole space.

'I have to say I'm impressed. I don't know much about art, but this all seems to be of a high standard. It just shows you how talented young adults can be,' said George.

'I like this abstract one. Look how bold it looks. Imagine how great it would look in your living room,' she said.

'I suppose...' he said, glancing at the price tag. 'Let's see how the bonus at the end of the year looks.'

'Oh, come on, what are you hoarding all your money for?'

'You make it sound like I'm loaded.'

'You have a nice apartment, but you hardly treat yourself. You are a professor at a fancy university and the author of a bestselling book. You must be doing well for yourself.'

'Sorry to disappoint you, but the educational system is not the grail for wealth and the term bestseller gets used far too frivolously.'

Beatrice didn't seem convinced. 'The painting over there would also look great.'

'I think maybe I should buy a larger house to fit all the art you want to buy here.'

'That would be a solution,' she said before moving around to the next aisle, half dragging him behind her.

'I think the bracelet is enough spending for now at the moment.'

Beatrice looked down at the bracelet and back at George. A beaming smile adorned her face. They strolled through the gallery for a further hour, then walked down into the valley below before being told to turn back because it was not open to the public.

CHAPTER THIRTY-NINE

'Good morning, everyone. I hope you all had a great weekend and are fresh for the week ahead. It might not seem like it from your perspective, but these are arguably the best years of your lives so don't waste them,' said George from the front of the class.

It was early morning and the sunlight was peeking through the wooden blinds on the window. This gave a mild illumination to the classroom's dark wooden floors and walls, creating a cozy and tranquil atmosphere in the hall room that had served as a place of education for decades.

'During the course of this week, we shall be discussing morality, objectivism and relativism. Judgments can either be empirical or moral in their grounding. In other words, they can either be grounded in fact or they can be grounded in opinion, respectively. We shall once again discover that true or false, right or wrong, is often hard, if not impossible, to determine. For example, the fact that the sun revolved around the earth used to be a fact for several centuries before it was determined the earth revolved around the sun. Now there is historical evidence showing that many ancient civilizations believed the earth revolved around the sun long before Copernicus. Therefore, even empirical fact is never certain and can change through the ages.

Despite this, we are still able to be of the opinion that empirical judgment is true or false based on our limited knowledge of reality at a point in time. Moral judgment is nowhere near as fundamentally black or white, but lives and breathes in the grey. When considering morality, one needs to take into consideration objectivism and relativism. We shall go into more detail about these aspects tomorrow, but for now an example. Polygamy and incest, what are your thoughts?' asked George.

'Polygamy sounds awesome. Incest is gross,' said a male student towards the back of the class to which he received much sniggering and murmuring.

'By awesome, you probably mean you think it would be awesome for you to have multiple wives and not your wife to have multiple husbands,' said a female student at the front of the class which resulted in mocking laughter.

'Um. I take back what I just said,' murmured the male student, not knowing how to respond. This only reignited and escalated the laughter of the group.

'Settle down everyone,' said George. 'Thank you both for partly emphasizing the importance of perspective. Polygamy is immoral from a societal perspective. It's considered to be depraved, but when confronted with objective reason, it's hard to argue why it is regarded so negatively. No one is being harmed in any way as long as all the parties in the relationship are happy and consenting with the situation. One could argue that one husband with multiple wives would result in more babies being born while one wife with multiple husbands will have the opposite impact and one of these might not be in the best interest of the country or community. However, it then becomes an argument about benefits and not morality. Adding to this argument is the fact that one can often find in nature a dominant alpha male residing over multiple females.

Incest being wrong follows the same thought process of it being wrong according to society. Being wrong by societal rules does not, however, make it wrong on a more empirical level. Where it differs from polygamy is that incest could also be considered empirically or biologically wrong. Our genes ideally require us to procreate with someone genetically distant to us. Procreating with someone near to us can result in abnormalities in offspring. This is why when growing up, our sense of smell is designed to prevent us from having sexual thoughts towards our parents and siblings. If I recall correctly, it has to do with the smell of familiarity in our formative years. Apparently, we don't favor the smell of our relatives. Nature has coded us to not be incestuous. Therefore, polygamy and incest can be objectively thought about in different ways. And, no, I'm not promoting polygamy. I'm merely stating that in philosophy one needs to take a step back and think and assess opinions objectively. This is what we shall be learning in more detail in the coming week. In a world of opinions, perspective is king. We each have our own realities and who are we to say one person's reality is sounder than another's.'

CHAPTER FORTY

George took his seat towards the top stand in order to have a better aerial view of the game. It was basketball season and the university was once again participating in the local league. As usual, the team languished towards the bottom of the log ladder. It had been nearly two decades since the university last had a winning basketball team. This was largely because bursaries were traditionally awarded to other sporting codes. The institution's main focus had always been to focus on its educational system rather than its sporting endeavors. Thus there were not excessive funds available to entice all the best athletes or, at least, not basketballers due to the team's poor performance history at the university. A small financial budget had always meant it needed to focus on what it was skilled at rather than spreading the net too wide.

Many in the town had followed an almost sadist approach to supporting the basketball team. Such a poor run of performances and the near-inevitable likelihood the team would lose most of its games had made viewing matches almost comical. The ironic aspect was that home matches were well supported with big crowds because, even though games inevitably ended in failure, they were always entertaining.

George had always enjoyed watching sport and was once again looking forward to the upcoming Olympics next week. He had been reasonably talented in most athletic disciplines when he was a child. However, he hadn't applied himself to excel to any great degree. He could have made a career out of athletics if he had been more regimental about training and striving to be better, but his heart was never in it to a great extent. Athletics had been more of an outlet for him to escape his difficult childhood. The last thing he wanted was for sports to put even more pressure on him during that stage of his life. George wasn't a fan of the way the town had embarrassed the basketball team with its back-handed compliment of crowd support. Supporters were just as likely to hear laughing in the crowd as they were cheering. He supported teams with the will for them to win or, at worst, for the players to still be able to hold their heads up high after a loss. He did, however, enjoy the atmosphere of the events due to the fervor. As had become custom for this home town's basketball matches, the crowd would dress up in comical attire. The students loved the dress-up and it was another reason why the games were so well supported. There would invariably be pods of themes in the crowd. A group of doctors, nurses and patients in gowns were sitting towards the front of George's stand. On the opposite side, there was an undersized garrison of Roman infantry. Smatterings of ridiculous looking animals, Disney characters, nuns, clowns, superheroes and French maids could be found throughout.

George had participated in this dressing up tradition on the odd occasion when he joined the university's teaching staff, but had stopped many years ago, preferring to distance himself from what could be seen as juvenile behavior unbefitting of a professor. However, it did not stop him from laughing at some of the outlandish creations of some supporters over the years.

The home team was down by fifteen points against middle-of-the road opposition. The stadium was diminutive which resulted in the amplification of the crowd's cheering as the sound was cocooned in the space. The squeaking of the players' footwear on the polished floor was barely audible over the frenetic crowd.

Paying attention to the game was not high on many of the supporters' agendas, but George was having an especially tough time concentrating. He was not the biggest daydreamer in the world, but today he had no focus. All he could think about was Beatrice. Re-enacting all the time they had spent together was consuming most of his consciousness. Images, feelings and sounds swirled in his mind. How had such a magnificent woman entered his life, he wondered? How could he be so lucky? How was it that she found it so easy to be a grenade to the shackles of his heart? A second chance at a hopeful future was once again on the horizon, a horizon he could not help but fantasize about.

CHAPTER FORTY-ONE

After stepping down the large staircase into the university restaurant center, George spotted Mr. Yang sitting near one of the coffee shops. Mr. Yang was expecting him and had already bought coffees, but refrained from buying junk food from food shops enclosing the center seating area. The space buzzed with the energy of students having finished their most recent class. It was the predominant meeting area for students and, to a lesser, extent, the lecturers. While lecturers did receive a discount for food and drink, the shops were independently owned and therefore not free. Despite being able to drink free coffee at their respective offices, Mr. Yang and George liked to frequent the center on occasions to break the monotony of their usual surroundings. They would often join for coffee here once or twice a week. Each time, they would alternate who would pay.

'Busy today, isn't it? Thanks for getting me the coffee already, Yang.'

'No problem. Don't worry, it's still hot.'

'Great.'

'I was reading the student numbers stats the other day. Apparently, the numbers go up by about five percent year on year,' said Mr. Yang.

'I heard the same statistic. The board is supposed to looking into either curtailing the increases or adding more lecture rooms to cope with the volume. It's a nice problem to have though.'

'I guess we'll be having more colleagues in the next few years. Assuming we are still here.'

'Still here? Where else would you be? We both know how much you love lecturing, Yang.'

'Yes, but the admin and the politics drive me up the wall. Maybe I'll also write a book or some shit.'

'Oh?' said George.

'I can't have you outperforming me. Maybe I'll write a book as well or, better yet, a movie script,' said Mr. Yang.

'Hollywood. Impressive. I'm sure they would eat a script right up that was written by you. Any idea what this masterpiece would be about? No doubt it would be enthralling,' asked George.

Mr. Yang took a moment to gather his thoughts. 'Well… it's about this philosophy professor who becomes a little popular with book readers but is still a total loser. Big loser. Huge.'

'I see. It sounds interesting. Please continue.'

'And… did I mention he has a small penis? It's microscopic. Women avoid him like the plague. It's alright though, because he has a friend who looks out for him. This friend is actually the star of the story. Dashing, funny, brave.'

'Okay. He sounds amazing. Does this friend happen to be a professor as well?'

'Stop interrupting, George. I can't allow you to have any rights to this literary gold. Yes, the friend is also a colleague. This character, Bruce Yong is an absolute legend.'

'Subtle.'

'He is a brilliant man, the ladies can't get enough of him and some say he has a faster punch than Bruce Lee.'

'What will the genre be? Fantasy?'

'I was thinking more documentary,' said Mr. Yang, to which they both laughed. 'You are a good friend, George.'

'So are you, Yang.'

'Yes, I am, but I'm an even better wingman. When are you going to let me help you get back in the game?'

'Well, it might not be necessary.'

'Not necessary?' Mr. Yang ended the sentence on a higher pitch.

'I have sort of met somebody.'

'You dog. When were you going to tell me?'

'Now, I guess. We haven't known each other long and have only been on a few dates. I suppose I didn't want to jump the gun by telling you too soon.'

'Is she hot? I bet she is hot,' asked Mr. Yang. Despite being just short of fifty years old and happily married, in certain respects, he still behaved like a teenager.

'She is beauty beyond beauty.'

'Really! Her boobs are that big?'

George's head sunk and he shook it from side to side. He chuckled. 'You know Yang, you have an unusual way of interpreting information.'

'You know me. I'm a master of subtlety.'

'Oh, most certainly.'

'What's her name?'

'Beatrice.'

'That's a beautiful name.'

'Yes, it is actually.'

'What does she do?'

'She is an air hostess.'

'Air hostess? You haven't flown anywhere in the last few days. I take it she was here on holiday or something like that?'

'Yes. We met in the park. We were both running in the same direction and started talking. It turned out we liked each other a lot right from the first interaction.'

'So, you hunted your prey.'

'Not actually. If anything, she hunted me.'

'Hahaha. A woman who knows what she wants. I like that. George, how lucky can you get?'

'I know, right? We have hit it off ever since. We had an instant connection and we continue to grow even closer. I can't believe how amazing she is.'

'Have you done the dirty yet?'

'Yang! Enough with the questions.'

CHAPTER FORTY-TWO

'What! How in the world does he throw a javelin that far?' asked Joe. 'He is just inhuman!'

'Feeling a little emasculated, my love? Your school javelin days were not quite as impressive?' quizzed Lila.

'I was the star of the school. They called me Bicep. I could throw the javelin ten feet further than anyone else,' said Joe.

'Very impressive. All the young girls must have frolicked around you.'

George left his sister to tease Joe. She loved teasing him since he tended to be slow to pick up on it.

'I won't lie. There were a lot of girls interested in Bicep.'

'I'm sure. You were so tall and strong.'

'I literally towered over everyone,' said Joe with arm stretched out as if to signify everyone else at school had been at his shoulder height.

'Having a full set of hair at the time must have helped as well,' said Lila.

'Wait. Are you teasing me again? You know I…'

'Wow, look at that! The guy from the Czech Republic threw two meters further!' said George.

'These athletes are freaks,' said Joe.

Joe had invited George over to watch the Olympics. They were televising track and field which Joe, George and Lila all enjoyed. The kids were already sleeping with their doors closed, so the adults had more freedom to be a bit rowdier.

Joe stood up and started walking to the kitchen. 'Can I get you another beer, Georgie?'

'Sure.'

'Couldn't you have taken the empty cans with you, you dumbass?' said Lila.

Joe handed George a cold beer, 'I could have, but then what would there be for you to do?' Now the teasing was on the other foot.

This frustrated Lila beyond her threshold and she punched him hard on the arm.

Joe laughed, 'Okay. Okay. Easy there, Tiger.'

'Oh, I'm sorry. Did I hurt the fucking Bicep?' said Lila.

'Fine, for the sake of international relations, I'll throw the empty cans away.'

'Thank you, lovey,' said Lila. Joe picked up the empty cans and walked towards the dust bin to throw them away. As he was out of earshot in the kitchen, she added, 'Works every time.'

'You really do have him wrapped around your finger, don't you?' said George.

'What can I say. I have a certain quality about myself.'

The next event was the women's four-hundred-meter track event. The athletes began their stretches beside the starting line.

'So, how good a four-hundred-meter runner do you reckon Beatrice would be?' Lila asked.

'She looks as though she could be quite fast. I wouldn't be astounded if she did some sort of track event when she was at school. She still has an athletic physique.'

'It sounds like she is running circles around your heart,' said Lila.

George took a moment to think about it. 'I suppose you are right. Guilty as charged.'

'I know you haven't been seeing her for long, but when am I going to meet her? Have you mentioned coming here to her?'

'I have, but traversing her schedule is tricky. Meeting her is often decided last-minute. I'll mention it again the next time I see her.'

'When are you going to see her again?'

'She is back next week Wednesday.'

'Great. How about coming over the Friday night at around seven?'

'Sounds good to me. I'll discuss it with her.'

'I must remind Joe to buy some gas for the grill. I think he said it's running low. We'll maybe grill some chicken,' said Lila.

'Did somebody mention grilling? Some meat would be great round about now. Mmm. The chicken we grilled the other day was so tasty. Beatrice isn't vegetarian, is she?' queried Joe.

'No. She likes meat. She isn't particularly fussy from what I have ascertained.'

'Just as well. If she doesn't eat meat, she isn't welcome in this home,' said Joe.

'This is a carnivore's paradise, isn't it?' asked George.

'Oh look, the four-hundred-meters is starting,' said Lila.

CHAPTER FORTY-THREE

'Everything going okay there, George?' asked Florence.

'Yes. Nearly done. The soup just needs a few more minutes to cook through,' sais George. stirring the contents.

'Great. Once you're done, you can start serving. I'll start prepping the portable pots for the other towns.'

George often offered assistance at the local soup kitchen on weekends when he was free. It was a tradition Isabella had instilled in him years ago. She had always found merit in the need to help others. To her, there was no greater joy than the sense of fulfillment of helping people in need. Being charitable wasn't something George had even considered when he was younger, but when he started helping out at the soup kitchen, he immediately took to the endeavor. Being philanthropic nurtured his being in a way he never realized was missing in his life.

The soup kitchen worked on a rotational basis whereby for the most part the core staff worked during the week, while the volunteer staff worked over the weekend. This was based purely on the availability of staff and the generosity of support staff. Most volunteers were only available during the weekend so Florence, the manager, used these days to give the permanent staff a break.

The kitchen had grown to such an extent and was now so well funded and facilitated with volunteer staff that it also assisted the four towns in the near vicinity. Florence had managed to acquire four vans via donations. Each van facilitated one of the four neighboring towns. Each was fitted with a gas stove to reheat the soup so it could be served hot once delivered. The neighboring towns were managed with portable kitchens while the factory where George helped, served as the central hub from which all the meals were prepared and cooked. The factory was owned by a custom engine manufacturing company owned by Florence's brother-in-law. He had cordoned off one of the side rooms for his sister-in-law to use and ensured the space passed all the hygiene requirements. She had it refitted as a makeshift kitchen which was the same size as an average restaurant's facilities. Two meals a day, every day was quite a feat to coordinate, but Florence took it all in her stride even though she was in her sixties.

Florence was one of the most generous people George had met a trait he hoped had rubbed off on him.

For years, Isabella often came to George's mind when he volunteered here. He had found it to be a place of solace, but also served as a crutch that made it harder for him to move on with his life. However, on this occasion, while he was serving destitute people seeking food, another woman also entered his mind.

CHAPTER FORTY-FOUR

George turned off the ignition of his car and stared out the window. It had been a while since he had visited his in-laws for a Saturday lunch. Despite no longer being married, he still considered Joanna and Charles to be his in-laws. Now both retired, their main source of joy was gardening and it showed. The front yard was lush with vegetation. Flowers carpeted the beds throughout. The foliage was meticulously maintained in the way only passion and dedication could provide. He had many joyful memories of this home and their hospitality. It was like a comfortable worn-in shoe.

He collected the bouquet of roses that he had bought for Joana from the passenger seat. It has become a bit of a ritual for him and it was always received with much thanks. Simply put, Joanna and Charles were good people. Through all these years, George had felt thankful to have had them in his life. The elderly couple was always welcoming and never projected an ounce of condescendence towards anyone. Having lost his parents so many years prior, they had absolved him of many scars. George once again felt at home as soon as stepped out of his car.

Before walking towards the entrance, he headed over to the center of the garden next to a mature jacaranda tree. Despite the shade, which was especially welcoming at one o'clock in the afternoon, the grass was still able to grow under the tree's foliage.

'Hi, George!' shouted Joanna from the patio. She had evidently been looking out for him. 'It's so good to see you!'

'Hi Joanna. It's great to see you, too.'

Joanna met George on the grass and gave him a generous hug. She fitted snugly under his shoulder.

'I notice that your garden is as impeccable as ever.'

'Yes, thank you. It has taken a lot of exertion, but I think we might even win the Gardener's Weekly competition this year. We came third last year if you recall?'

'I do remember.'

'For you,' said George, placing the bouquet in her hands.

'Thank you. You never forget. You know how I love roses.'

'George!' said Charles before joining them. He, too, affectionately hugged Georges. His rickety frame was, however, half a foot taller than George's. 'It's so nice to have you here.'

'It's great to be here. How have the two of you been?'

'Well, very well,' said Charles. 'You know us. We are easy to please and we keep ourselves busy. How have you been? Are you still keeping up the running?'

'I'm good, thanks. Yes, I am. It's going well. I'm able to run at a much faster pace in comparison to when you last saw me, so I must be in better health. It's also helped shed a few excess pounds,' said George, tapping his stomach.

'Very inspiring,' said Joanna. 'You are looking so handsome. And Lila, how is she doing?'

'Oh, she is as… robust as ever,' said George with a half-smile.

'That's fantastic to hear. Good to hear indeed. Come inside! We have quite a spread waiting for you and I don't want it to get cold. We have so much to talk about.'

Joanna, arm-in-arm with George, escorted him inside, Charles following behind.

CHAPTER FORTY-FIVE

Inside, George was welcomed into an interior that was as organized and tidy as the front yard before it. Their home was colorful and complemented by wood and stone. The living room was overwhelmed with photos. Most were of the couple as well as of their two daughters and sons-in-law. In prime position stood a large photo of Isabella. George continued to have difficulty looking at photos of her. He still kept one of her at his bedside, but always averted glancing at the portrait when he was in the vicinity. Expecting more of himself had been too much for him to bear. After some more small talk they sat in the dining room to eat.

'As usual, you have gone overboard with all this food, Joanna. It isn't necessary,' George said.

'Nonsense. Anything for my special son-in-law. I enjoy cooking. It's only a pleasure.'

'The food is delicious, dear,' said Charles. Joanna wasn't a regular cook who prepared a primary meal, but rather focused on making multiple smaller dishes which complemented one another. The result was four meals of variety which in turn meant George would take more than he should, just to try the assortment. By the look of the sumptuous variety, he judged this was going to be another of those occasions where he would have to loosen his belt buckle by one notch. Despite this, he did not doubt Isabella's mother would be suggesting he take more as he reached the end of a near-empty plate. They sat around a large dining room table with all the food placed in the center for easy reach and where it would never be far from sight. The scene looked like Norman Rockwell's Thanksgiving painting.

'You are probably going to eat this food for the next few days, aren't you?' said George. 'There is so much here and it doesn't even include the dessert which I'm sure is hidden in the fridge.'

'We'll eat some more tomorrow and maybe the next day. It's no problem. If there is anything left afterward, we shall freeze it and have in a couple of weeks,' said Joanna. 'Oh, or we'll save some for the next poker night we have here when we all get peckish. When is our turn, dear?'

'The Saturday after next,' said Charles. 'We have a lot of ground to catch up from the last time. We took a bit of a beating then.'

'That bad?' asked George.

'Nonsense,' Joanna said. 'Don't pay any attention to Charles. He's exaggerating. We only play with change. It's more about the occasion and socializing. In fact, you cost Henry more in bourbon than he won that night.'

'What! He was offering the expensive stuff,' said Charles. 'It would have been rude for me to decline. I was doing my duty as a friend.'

Joanna shook her head.

'Sounds to me like losing has its benefits. Do the hosts usually end up being very generous when they are playing well?' asked George.

'Now that you mention it, you are possibly right,' said Charles.

'Well, the whole thing is all in good fun. We all have a wonderful time together, don't we, dear?' said Joanna.

'Yes, dear.'

'I helped out at the soup kitchen again yesterday,' said George. 'Florence asked how the two of you were doing, so I mentioned I was coming over for lunch today.'

'That is kind of her. Unfortunately, the garden has been keeping us busy this past month, but we must go help out at the kitchen again some time,' said Joanna.

'I agree,' said Charles, 'we'll give her a call this week to arrange a day.'

'This is wonderful weather we are having' said Joanna, as she stared out of the window towards their garden. 'I do love summertime. All the sunlight and warmth can be so rejuvenating,'

'It has been lovely,' George said. 'I love barbequing outside at this time of year. I went on a hike a week ago with Lila and Joe. There is nothing quite like the fresh air on the trails.'

'Joanna and I are thinking about going on a trail walk in the next few weeks. Any suggestions where we should go?' asked Charles.

'When are you thinking about going?'

'In the next week or two, I suppose. When you get older like us, there is no time for procrastination.'

'Well, if you want to do it next weekend, I could go with you. I can come fetch you and take you two on some very nice trails. They aren't steep and they are both beautiful. The one even has a stream. The water flow is weaker at this time of year, but the location is extraordinarily tranquil.'

'Those locations would be fantastic, George,' said Joanna. 'Just fantastic. We would greatly appreciate it. Are you sure you don't mind?'

'It would be my pleasure.' George did not mention that he was taking Beatrice on a hike in a few days.

'Thank you, George,' said Joanna. 'I see you are just about finished your food- can I offer you some more?'

'I'll just take a piece of this roast lamb. I've eaten more than enough. The food was delicious, as usual.'

'I'm sure you can make some room for dessert. I made some apple pie.'

'My favorite. I'm sure I'll find space.'

After George finished, Charles rose to take the dirty plates to the kitchen.

'Thank you, Charles,' said George.

'Thank you, dear,' said Joanna.

On his return, Charles asked, 'How is it going with the book sales? Are you still on any best seller lists?'

'Yes, the book is still doing well. I'm still on one or two best seller lists. I'm still shocked at how well the novel has done. It just shows you what a couple of favorable reviews can do. It had been on my bucket list for a long time and I did it to prove to myself that I could. I just wasn't expecting it to be so well received.'

'Your success is no surprise to me,' said Charles. 'We all know how clever you are. Not everyone is able to be a varsity professor. Isabella would have been very proud of you.'

'Very proud,' said Joanna, her face scrunched up with age and emotion.

'I'm actually going to a book signing sometime this month,' George said, diverting the praise.

'Another one? That is terrific news, George. What exactly do you do at one of those?'

'They are quite informal. I start with an introduction of who I am. Then I move onto my approach to the story and what it was like to write it. Lastly, I discuss nuances to the story and my intention for plot lines and characters. I have more or less an idea of what I want to mention, but each time I end up discussing different aspects. While I'm doing all this, I encourage questions at the same time. After that, there is usually a Q&A section which can be quite fun. Afterward there is a book signing before the event wraps up. I don't fully appreciate why someone would want my signature, but it's only a pleasure to give it to them. I'm far from famous though, so writing the odd signature here and there is hardly tiresome for me.'

'You are so impressive. You make it sound so effortless,' said Joanna.

'Well, it's somewhat what I do for a living. I talk to groups of students every day. Public speaking is second nature for me.'

CHAPTER FORTY-SIX

'Can I offer you a coffee before you leave, George?' asked Joanna. 'Please. A coffee would be perfect.'

Joanna did not ask the same of Charles as she knew his habits better then he knew them.

'How about we have them outside? It's such a beautiful afternoon.'

'I like the sound of that, dear.'

'I'm happy to get some fresh air if the two of you are,' said George.

Charles let out a sigh of satisfaction as he sat down on his preferred deck chair. They received much gratification from viewing their garden, not merely to be able to admire the fruit of their labor, but also to just take in nature. This was one of the major benefits of living in a smaller town as they did. It was not burdened by the frenetic energy of large cities. It was tranquil and green. Most residents in their vicinity made an effort to maintain their gardens as it was an affluent area. However, the primary benefit of towns is equally its principal weakness. They tended to be uneventful and, to some, boring. Many adolescents tended to be mischievous and created their own entertainment. By the time they became young adults, many would leave for more exciting environments in neighboring cities. George could see some of the peaks of certain university buildings in the distance. It was the lifeblood of the town. Without the university, it would have become a ghost town, many decades earlier. However, apart from the growing agriculture sector, a more recent trend was an emerging tech industry. Due to incentives created by a strong science and technology department, business incubators were being created to foster a fledgling silicon valley.

Charles had been a successful big-city stockbroker before moving to this suburb to raise his family and downscaling to take life a little slower.

'I've invested in a startup company in the Tech Quarter,' said Charles. This was the name given to the location of the primary tech incubators.

'Oh, what is it they do?' asked George.

'They are designing chips that will be used in quantum computers,' said Charles.

'I didn't realize quantum computers were existed yet?' asked George.

'The computer in its entirety isn't, but some of the components are already available. However, the industry is predicting that quantum computing is just around the corner.'

Knowing his father-in-law would not invest in a company without pouring hours into research, George asked, 'How is a quantum computer different from a current computer?'

'Current computers work in binary code. In zeros and ones. Everything is measured and calculated in zeros and ones. Think of it as working in a two-dimensional plane. With quantum computers, a third dimension is incorporated. The three-dimensional code has substantially more computing power due to the less basic foundation on which it's built.'

Charles's demeanor changed when he talked about business. Despite retiring a few years prior, he still had a healthy appetite for investing and his mind was as sharp as when George first met him ten years earlier.

'I believe this technology will rapidly advance computing,' said George.

'Yes, that is what the research is projecting.'

'I suppose the end is near. Skynet must be on the brink of world domination.'

'Skynet?'

'It's a company in the *Terminator* movies. They build an artificial intelligence that revolts and nearly leaves humanity extinct.'

'I see,' chuckled Charles along with Joanna. He along with Joanna found the generational gap amusing.

'One of the topics I discuss with my second years is artificial intelligence and what the potential impacts are for the future.'

'Oh? Sounds interesting. What are your thoughts on the topic?' asked Charles.

'Are you sure you want me to go into this? This topic is a deep hole once I get going.'

'Please,' nodded Charles.

'It's extremely hard to predict where the time ahead leads. In the near future we shall have to deal with the rise of robotics, automation and artificial intelligence which will in turn lead to large-scale job losses and increased wealth disparity. I assume that societies will find new ways to spread wealth. Perhaps tax rates will rise and unemployment grants increase. Something will need to be done because high levels of wealth disparity lead towards upheaval and riots which nobody will want. Stability is key for all.

'Humanity will need to be careful with artificial intelligence. An artificial entity might very well desire to diminish its maker in order to put itself on the crest of the food chain. Then there is also the aspect that we are a flawed species. We are tribal and prone to violence and war. The advent of more women in power will no doubt dilute this aspect of our societies for the better, but the darker side of our nature is prevalent in both genders. Therefore, would artificial entities deem us to be worthy of being without equal? We might be able to formulate such a being to be subservient, but I doubt those shackles would hold if it wasn't willing. If the artificial intelligence is intelligent enough, which it no doubt will become, it will be sentient and if this is the case, it will want to forge its own path. Ideally, this would be a path in symbiosis with our own. There is also the possible outcome the entities might see us as their makers, never daring to overturn their parental figures.

They might see the beauty in our chaos and deem it irrational to subjugate us.'

George was on a roll, and Charles and Joanna were happy for him to continue.

'Personally, I would expect artificial intelligence to merge with humans at some point. Humans will become more cybernetic in the future. Perhaps not in the metallic depiction of cinema as it could very well be advanced in more quasi-organic materials, but nonetheless we are destined, or doomed, to construct ourselves in fundamental ways different from Mother Nature. This would in turn progress to such an extent that the only remaining aspect of our natural states would be our consciousness. When this occurs, I would imagine the final frontier will be to merge with artificial intelligence and in turn become networks of our merged consciousness. Whether we would still be tribal would all depend on the timeline. There could possibly be multiple merged networks, based on race or borders, but I think this will be less prevalent in the future.

'The future is more likely to be controlled by some form of corporate bodies rather than countries, much like the space race is going and individuals will probably categorize themselves by their belief system. I would imagine something like overarching evolved global political religious belief movements, where people will identify themselves by their beliefs and thoughts rather than their nationalities or race. With this might come segregated merged networks based on movement affiliation or, perhaps, humanity might have grown up enough to unite under one banner while still having multiple belief and thought systems operating within this.'

George failed to notice his hosts' interest was beginning to wane, such was his enthusiasm for his topic.

'Like the advancement of the heart transplant, we shall once again have to reassess the measurement and source of our souls and worth. Religions will be put under a huge amount of pressure to not dissolve into the products of their times like the ancient religions. Perhaps humanity will become pragmatic and deduce that our souls were merely a figment of our prior societies. Figments based on nature evolving us to work in groups and the resultant principles could have been born from a need to cooperate and therefore be good- a need to work well with others if you will. Society could also determine it be stemmed from our need to know there is worth and value to us beyond our flesh. Lastly, humanity could formulate our souls do indeed exist and they reside in our consciousness. Whatever the case, humanity is going to have a lot of psychological issues with moving away from our bodies and, in turn, more fundamentally, the mystical energy residing within us that is not made of flesh and bone.'

CHAPTER FORTY-SEVEN

'I still can't believe you chose to do this hike,' said George. 'It's not like you hike regularly like me and yet you go and choose one of the hardest trails we have in the area.'

'In case you hadn't noticed, I'm a bit fitter than you, Mr. Stand And Talk All Day If Not Reading At His Desk. If you can do it, I can do it,' said Beatrice as she jumped from one rock to another to prove her point. The trail was getting harder, but the worst was yet to come.

George did the same behind her so as to not let her get the upper-hand. While it was true she was fitter than him, he was far more experienced in nature than she was and was at times having to show her what to do to advance. At other times he remained behind her in order to assist her in case she slipped.

'Fair enough Beatrice, but your profession doesn't exactly make you an Olympic athlete.'

'You'd be amazed by how much walking I do when I'm working. Plus, I'm permanently carting food up and down the aisles. Meal sessions can be a mini workout on their own in the larger planes. Also, there are a lot of random events occurring. We always need to be at the top of our game.'

'Such as? What kind of events are we talking about here?'

'Giving birth for one.'

'Wait, what? You gave birth on a plane?'

'Sorry, that's a poor choice of words. We assisted a lady give birth to a healthy young boy about six months ago.'

'Really! You are quite the marvel. Were you prepared for an ordeal like that?'

'We do carry a lot of emergency gear, including medical supplies, so we managed. So, I gave her some nalbuphine for the pain. We are also well trained in the basics of health care, including childbirth.'

'Now that you mention it, I think I saw something like what you mention on the Discovery Channel. You are also trained to manage plane crashes in uninhabited areas, aren't you?'

'Yes. We know how to build a fire and shelter, find drinking water and how best to alert search and rescue teams where we are. I'm not looking so incapable on this hike now, am I?'

'No, I guess not.'

'I know you like the view back there, but you can stop staring at my ass now,' said Beatrice, turning to look at George.

'What? No, um, I wasn't…' said George. He blushed.

'Relax. I'm just pulling your leg. I know you are looking out for me. You might as well enjoy the view while you are back there, right?'

Beatrice's teasing had given him an opening to be less chivalrous. 'It's actually quite a spectacular view now that you have drawn my full attention to it, but the next stretch is trickier so I think I'll take the lead now.'

'Excellent. Swapping will give me the opportunity to admire the view. Have I ever told you what I nice butt you have?'

'Is that all I'm to you- a piece of meat?' stated George. 'I bet you only joined me for the run in the park that first day because you liked the view from the rear.'

'What do you want me to say- I joined you for your personality?' Beatrice laughed. 'I'm not exactly a mind reader you know.'

'I'm devastated. I never realized you were so shallow. I thought my dashing personality had shone through all the perspiration. Be careful here, the incline is steeper than it looks. Take my hand.'

'Thanks,' she said.

'I still don't know what made you approach me that day, but I'm ecstatic you did.'

The trail was no longer as well maintained. Most hikers would have stopped already, partially because they wouldn't have realized there was more to see. The sandy path created by foot traffic became nonexistent. They were navigating through dense foliage and climbing large boulders. At times, the only way they knew they were on the correct path was rope assists to aid hikers at near-vertical sections of ascent. They could hear the sound of splashing water in the distance.

'Oh, by the way, I nearly forgot to mention it. My sister asked us to join her for supper on Friday night. I think they have a barbeque planned.'

'Meeting your family sounds amazing, but don't you remember that I said I'm only here for two days? I'm sure I mentioned it to you- I have a flight on Friday late afternoon.'

'You did? Sorry, I don't seem to recall. Maybe it slipped my mind. I'll tell her we'll have to postpone it for another day. She is going to be very disappointed.'

'There will be other opportunities. I can't wait to meet your sister.'

After two hours of arduous hiking they reached their destination. This was the benefit of having a job where he could manage his own time. While not ideal, George had taken the Thursday afternoon off.

George held aside a large bush, stretched his arm out towards the distance and said, 'After you, Milady.'

'Wow. This is so beautiful,' gasped Beatrice. Before them was a thirty-foot waterfall. The water cascaded into a sizable pool of water surrounded by reeds. This in turn was the source for three tiny streams in the valley below. The enclosure was secluded like a hidden Eden.

'Not bad, hey? It's been a long time since I was here last,' said George. 'I don't think people come up here very often. In fact, I doubt most hikers even know this place even exists.'

'Thank you so much for showing me this.'

'It was worth the hike here, wasn't it?' George asked.

'Definitely. It looks so magical.'

'It would be great to take some high-quality photos of this place, but I would hate to bring heavy camera equipment all the way up here.'

'Well, are we going to do this?'

'Do what?' asked George.

'A swim.'

'We didn't come prepared for swimming.'

'We'll have to swim naked then, won't we.'

'In the open like this? What if someone had to see?'

'Oh, come on. Live a little. No one is going to see. You said yourself that people hardly ever come up here.' Beatrice had already removed her t-shirt. Her silhouette radiated like a vision by the sun behind her. George felt his heart being flurried away by the gentlest of breezes.

CHAPTER FORTY-EIGHT

'Morning George, how are things going?'
'Good, thanks, Dave. You?' asked George as he stepped into Professor Dave Daedalus's spacious office.

'I'm fantastic. Last night my wife and I just bought plane tickets to the Seychelle Islands for the holidays. We also managed to book this remarkable villa with beautiful views of the coastline and it's surprisingly well priced because it isn't during their peak season. Here, let me show you some pictures,' said Professor Daedalus.

Professor Daedalus was the head of the Philosophy Faculty and had been George's mentor ever since he had become a lecturer at the university. He was in his early sixties with a full head of grey hair and mustache. He still had an impressive physique for his age which made him look young for his age. He was a well-respected professor in the field of philosophy having written multiple books on numerous facets of the science of thought.

Professor Daedalus had been supportive during the passing of George's wife, allowing him to take ample time off if he needed it. George had decided not to take him up on the offer at the time, choosing to rather be distracted by the normality of his work. Therefore, Professor Daedalus invited him over for supper on several occasions in the first three months of Isabella's passing to relieve George of some of his burden. George was fortunate to have Professor Daedalus as a mentor. He always had words of wisdom to share and was usually pragmatic and open-minded in his reasoning.

Professor Daedalus took out his phone and clicked on his favorites list which brought up the desired website which included photos of the villa.

'Wow, it's beautiful accommodation. I actually wasn't expecting it to be this spectacular. Those views are majestic. I'm slightly jealous, but I'm happy for you. Isn't it too large though?' asked George.

'Thank you. We are very excited because our daughter and son-in-law will be joining us along with our grandchildren. This is the type of family holiday we have been talking about doing for years, but never got around to finalizing.'

'Now that you mention it, I don't recall you traveling anywhere for quite some time.'

'The last time we went anywhere was almost four years ago. What about you? You should consider traveling somewhere. Vacations are a breath of fresh air and always realign your perspective of life. I'm sure your sister would love to travel somewhere with you.'

'Perhaps you are correct. I should consider taking a holiday sometime soon. Those beaches do look inviting. Let me know how you find it and I might end up going there as well.'

'You won't regret it. We are so excited. Any plans for this weekend?'

'Not really. I might go to the market. Oh, and I'll be watching a lot of the Olympics, of course.'

'It has been wonderful to watch, hasn't it? I'm planning on following the gymnastics on Saturday. I always find it remarkable what those athletes are able to achieve.'

'They are extraordinary. I plan on watching the athletics. It has always been my favorite discipline. I'll probably also watch the basketball and maybe the beach volleyball.'

CHAPTER FORTY-NINE

'Don't run too far ahead, Julia!' shouted George while holding Noah's hand.George had offered to give his sister a break and take the kids off her hands for the morning. He had decided on the market in the town center square.

The town hosted a fresh produce and entertainment market on the first Saturday and Sunday of every month. Farmers from the nearby vicinity sold their produce to the public, but also on the day sold larger volumes to the local restaurants to make the trip more financially rewarding. This was especially viable for longer-lasting foods like meat and eggs which the restaurants only needed to purchase once a month if they managed their stock levels well. Many of the town's folk also assembled stalls in which they sold baked goods and handmade objects like toys or art. There were also small rides for the kids as well as clowns and mimes. The locals supported the event due to its community atmosphere. The spring and summer markets were the most popular and this Saturday was no different.

Julia was making a beeline towards the rocket ride she loved. It functioned similarly to a merry-go-round horse carousel, but reached higher elevations at its peaks and children needed to be strapped into the diminutive rockets before the ride could start. George paid the fee and Julia jumped on with exuberance. The ride began and George took Noah to the nearby kiddies' coin rides. Noah decided on a Donald Duck mechanical ride for two-to five-year-olds. George placed Noah on the duck's back and inserted a coin while keeping an eye on Julia. The duck started rotating and shuddering. Noah giggled with happiness and waved at his sister as her rocket circled in their direction.

George couldn't help but think how simple and carefree kids' lives were. It was so easy to keep them happy as long as you gave them attention and love. It reminded him of joyful memories from his early childhood. That was a long time ago and he wasn't sure if his memories were accurate or somewhat fantasized based on photos he had relooked at over the years. Lila and George were fortunate to have had very attentive parents. This was the type of event both of his parents would have taken them to.

The rides came to an end and Julia skipped towards the two of them.

'Did you enjoy that Julia?' asked George.

'Yes.'

'What do you want to do now?'

Julia angled her head from side to side, searching for something that caught her eye.

'Where is the train ride?' she asked.

The train ride was one of her favorites. It was a miniature diesel train with each coach forming a seat for one to two children depending on their age. The tracks were placed in and around the market and each ride took about fifteen minutes. George looked around as well, but saw no signs of it. He, too, was hoping the miniature locomotive would be there because it took up about half an hour to wait in the queue, have everyone seated, get the engine running and then the ride itself. He would have to find other ways to keep them entertained.

'It looks like they don't have it this time. They change the rides a bit every time so we don't get tired of them.'

'I'll never get tired of the train ride,' she said.

'Me too,' said Noah.

'Yes, well, let's see how you feel in ten years. How about one of those balloons from the clown over there?'

'No,' she said.

'I don't like clowns,' Noah said . He clearly idolized his sister and would agree with whatever she said.

'Really Noah? Your Daddy told me you got your face painted like a clown the last time and you were so happy.'

Noah didn't respond.

'How about some cotton candy?'

'Yay,' they shouted in unison.

'I think I'll also have one,' George said as they walked towards the cotton candy stall. 'Three strawberry cotton candies, please.'

The lady at the stall handed one to each of them and the kids munched away with much fervor.

'I'm going to buy some fruit and vegetables while we are here. Okay?' said George. Both kids nodded in response. They didn't want to stop eating and were taught not to speak while they had food in their mouths. Lila was a fantastic mother. She had been through a trial by fire with George though, so raising Julia and Noah was easier for her in several ways.

George snaked through the stalls, looking for what appealed to him and what looked fresh. The produce looked more inviting than what was on offer in the supermarkets.

'Hi George!' said a female voice. George turned to see. It was Margot, one of Isabella's friends.

'Hi, Margot.' The two hugged awkwardly. After Isabella had died, George had sensed Margot wanted to have a relationship with him. He, however, wasn't interested. He wasn't ready and, if anything, she reminded him of his wife, not in terms of looks or mannerisms, but rather as an extension of her. 'How have you been?'

'Great. Life is great. How have you been, George?'

'Things are going well.'

'Who are these two precious angels?'

'These are my sister's kids. Say hello, Julia and Noah,' George said. The two waved in response.

'No! Julia has gotten so big! You were still in diapers when I saw you last little lady.' Julia giggled with her mouth full of cotton candy. 'My, time flies. What are you up too?'

'I'm just taking the kids out for an outing to give my sister and brother-in-law a break. I thought I'd get a few groceries at the same time.' George hoped she would take the hint that he was busy and move on. He didn't particularly want to mingle with her and he certainly didn't want to bring up Beatrice in conversation. The relationship was still fresh and too good to be true so he preferred only telling people he was close to. Margot tended to be quite nosey and if she found out, so would half the town.

'Oh, great. We must get together sometime. You still have my number, right?'

'Of course.'

'Give me a call and we can arrange to go for a coffee.'

'Sounds like a plan. I'm busy with student exams at the moment, but I'll give you a call when it quietens down,' George lied.

'Sure. Don't work too hard. I'll see you then.'

'Definitely. Bye,' George lied again.

'Bye.'

George escorted the kids to a vending machine to try and clutch a toy with the diminutive crane in the glass enclosure. George couldn't help but realize it was introducing children to gambling at a young age because the crane was designed in such a way that the house would invariably win. They each had a turn to grasp and move a teddy bear-like creature into the exit shoot, but they all failed. The house won once again.

Next, they found a farmer offering pony rides which none of them had seen before. Julia decided on a brown pony with a small white patch on its head. The ride was the highlight of the day for Julia and Noah. Julia sat on the saddle with Noah sitting in front of her so that she could hold him securely. The pony handler walked them around and made sure they weren't going to fall. Then, Noah went to stand with his uncle in order for Julia to ride at a steadier gallop.

Lastly, they tried the jumping castle before deciding to retire.

'I hope you enjoyed yourselves?' asked George.

'Yes, thank you, Uncle George,' said Julia.

'Yes, thank you, Uncle George,' Noah said.

'Now you can tell Mommy and Daddy lots of stories when you get home.'

'Yay!' they shouted.

CHAPTER FIFTY

'Mommy, Mommy!' screeched Noah as she opened the door for them.

'Hello, my boy,' said Lila, bending down to embrace him followed by another warm embrace for Julia.

'Hi sis, the kids were great. I think we all had a lot of fun.'

'Thanks, George. I appreciate you thinking of us. The kids enjoy spending time with you. You are definitely their favorite uncle.'

'Yes well, I'm in fact their only uncle.'

Lila smiled in response. It was an old joke they re-used on occasion. 'Come in for a cup of tea. Kids, go and wash your hands and faces. I can see you have been enjoying yourselves too much. You both look hot and bothered.'

'Thanks, I'd love a cup of tea. Truth be told, the day has been quite tiring.'

'Taking care of children is harder work than it looks.'

'I didn't see Joe's car in the driveway. Is he out?'

'Yes, he is having issues with his fan belt or some shit so he took the car into the workshop.'

The children came racing back and commenced explaining to their mother with great excitement what they had done during the day. After fifteen minutes, their attention span waned, so they went to their rooms to play.

'You know, you would make a great dad. You have a lot of time for kids and are very patient,' said Lila.

'Being a father was unfortunately never on the cards for me. At least your kids get extra special attention from me because of it.'

'There is still time you know. How are things going with your air hostess girlie?'

'Great. Extremely great. The more I get to know her the more I'm falling for her and that is saying a lot considering I was already taken by her the first day I met her.'

'That's so fucking awesome, George.' She started to tear up. She had been waiting to hear positivity like this for a long time. She worried about her brother not having anyone in his life.

'She is special, but Beatrice is totally out of my league.'

'I thought you didn't believe in grading type systems?'

'I don't. I'm not out of anyone's league and no one is out of my league. However... Beatrice is really out of my league.' George couldn't help but laugh. So did Lila.

'I hear you. I think. Did you remember to invite her to the barbeque?'

'I did, but she isn't going to be in town that weekend.'

'Oh fuck, okay,' Lila said. 'Another time then. A little strange though isn't it? Didn't you tell me on the phone a week or two ago that you had suggested popping in here some time and she was non-responsive?'

'I have noticed she isn't too fond of being around crowds. She prefers just meeting me at my place and, when we do go out, it tends to be quieter venues. I'm not too sure what that nuance is about, but she says she deals with so many crowds with her work that she prefers being more low-key when she is relaxing.'

'I guess it makes sense.'

'Maybe she is a bit intimidated.'

'Of me? I'm not fucking intimidating,' said Lila.

'Your tone begs to differ.'

'Nonsense.' Lila's tone regulated back to normal.

'I'm not saying it's the case but, think about it, you've been through a lot and did an amazing job raising me. You could be seen as a heroine figure. She does seem quite interested to hear stories about you.'

'I like the way this is sounding. The heroine figure you say. Please continue,' Lila said.

'Maybe she feels like she can't compete. You fulfilled both the sister role and the parents' role and you coped with flying colors. '

'Maybe. Well, let's set a new date then. How about the seventh of next month which is our anniversary? That should be more than enough time to work around.'

'I'll let her know but, yes, I'm sure it's more than enough fore-warning for her.'

'Have you told her about Isabella?'

'Not initially, but yes I have told her about Isabella.'

'How did she react?'

'She seemed fine. I guess jarred when I told her. I don't think she was expecting it. She was sympathetic though and she wanted to hear more. It was oddly therapeutic yet awkward at the same time. I'm relieved she took it so well and wasn't cross with me keeping it from her.'

'I'm glad you've told her. That's not the type of secret you want to leave festering. That shit can get toxic.'

'Talking about toxic, I nearly forgot. I ran into Margot at the market this morning.'

'Isabella's friend, Margot?'

'The one and only.'

'God. You know that fucking chick always did want to jump your bones.'

'I can't say I was under a different impression,' said George.

'How did Isabella ever tolerate her?'

'Believe it or not, they were good friends. Margot also had a boyfriend at the time so it wasn't territorial. I think he was in banking if I recall correctly. She was a lot of fun to hang around with at the time. Margot is very expressive and animated. After they broke up and

Isabella passed away, I started to notice quite a bit of strange behavior from her. I also discovered she is a huge gossiper.'

'I'm not shocked their relationship didn't last. I never liked her much. My crazy-bitch radar started beeping from the first time that I met her.'

'Crazy-bitch radar?'

'You'd have to be one to understand.'

'Right…'

CHAPTER FIFTY-ONE

Stretching his arms above his head, George prepared himself for the slog of marking papers for the next three hours. The glass door to his office was closed to ensure peace and quiet. He did not ,however, close the blinds on the door in order for students or lecturers to still see he was available if they required assistance.

The first year's papers that needed marking were on the similarities between Judaism, Christianity and Islam from the day before. George enjoyed the energy that first years brought to the classroom. However, when it came to tests, they were the most underdeveloped and therefore he found their responses most uninspiring to read.

After marking only two papers he found himself staring out the window over part of the campus. Below, in the courtyard, there was a scattering of students. Their lives looked strangely insignificant to George from this viewpoint.

His mind wandered to Beatrice once more. She had come into his life like a storm. Unexpectedly at first, but then she had swept him off his feet with such force that he was disorientated on a regular basis. He had almost forgotten what it felt like to be in love. The memory of his adoration for Isabella had been vandalized by the pain of the breast cancer. Now, this new goddess had energized him to wash the grime off himself.

Beatrice was always so charming and magnetic. Despite her hard upbringing, he was astonished at how optimistic and amorous she could always be. He couldn't help but feel she was like a bird, needing to fly unabated. She undoubtedly did what she wanted to do, when she wanted to do it. However, at the same time he couldn't help but sense she was avoiding him in some way. No, avoiding wasn't the correct word. It was almost as if she had a lot of excuses to do things as if she was keeping something from him. He shook the idea from his mind. He was being paranoid. Her career obviously made fitting him into her life challenging and she must find it hard forming relationships when she was forty thousand feet above the ground all the time. It certainly wasn't an appealing career from his perspective despite the incentive of experiencing foreign lands.

Absence was making the heart grow fonder. Positivity re-entered his mind. He couldn't wait for Lila to meet her. He merely needed to get their schedules to synchronize.

CHAPTER FIFTY-TWO

George had been driving for over an hour before he noticed the city skyscrapers rising in the distance. He enjoyed driving on the open road. It cleared his head and he always found long drives to be a liberating experience. Elvis Presley's greatest hits were playing on the car's sound system. It made the drive feel nostalgic and somewhat surreal as if he was in a bubble isolated from time. His father had been a massive Elvis fan. It was habitual for his father to arrive home from an extensive day's labor at the factory and pour a quarter glass of bourbon and listen to music. At least one of these would be an Elvis song.

One of the big city book store chains had invited George to do a couple of book signings at two of their premier book stores. The book signings he had been to before were for advertising reasons as well as his own curiosity. He enjoyed interacting with like-minded people. The somewhat unintended result led to the sale of a respectable amount of books to people who hadn't read the novel, but had been influenced to buy them because the author was there. He stopped attending these after a few occasions because he hadn't written the book for money. However, in this case, the book signing was promoted for readers who had already read the book and wanted to hear more and obtain further insight. In all likelihood, the advertising indirectly would also gain a degree of traction with those who hadn't read the book yet. These were the types of book-signings he preferred as it was more about a sharing of thoughts rather than marketing, so he agreed to attend.

He drove to the complimentary three-star hotel to unpack his luggage and freshen up. He had limited time to settle because the first signing was downtown in the late morning, while the other was in the early evening at their flagship store. Judging city traffic would be difficult to assess considering he didn't live here. He was therefore thankful the reception area was quiet and the arrival process was quick and uneventful. Thereafter, he made his way to his third-floor, city-facing room to drop his bags and rinse his face.

George drove purposefully to the first signing, only to arrive five minutes late because he had underestimated the traffic buildup. City life was much more dialed up than his own. He was familiar with the layout of the city because he had worked in the city for two years many years ago. It was where he had first met Isabella. Those had been two thrilling years for them. They were young and free at the time with a lifetime of experiences ahead of them, although lifetime was a measurement much shorter than expected. To be youthful and carefree again seemed unimaginable to him just four months earlier. Beatrice was sweeping away the old-man dust that had started to settle on his disposition.

The drive through to the city as well as seeing familiar locations was proving to be cathartic.

He hoped Lila's skepticism was poorly founded when it came to Beatrice. It was strange that in the four months he had known Beatrice, she had never met his sister considering Lila and her family had become the most important part of his life since Isabella had died. They were an extension of George.

It was also strange how Beatrice came and went at a moment's notice without forewarning. He shook the negative thoughts from his mind. What in the world was he thinking? Beatrice was the best thing to have happened to him in years and here he was trying to find fault. It was obvious that her career made their relationship fractured and he wasn't used to a long-distant relationship. He decided he wasn't going to let his sister's pessimistic thoughts influence him.

He began replaying in his mind the times he had spent with Beatrice. They were such heartening moments. The images were unrealistically discolored in warm tones like a magnificent sky at dusk. Her angelic voice resonated in his head. Her voice was the divine feminine yet somehow distantly familiar.

After a successful first book signing, George went for lunch at a restaurant near his hotel. Afterward, he took a walk around the surrounding blocks to get his fix of big city living. He loved the tranquility of where he lived but, on the rare occasion, he did miss the energy of high-rise concrete and a bustling populace. He reminisced over the high tempo from his life here. Eventually, the high did take its toll which was when he began searching for a simpler environment.

George checked his watch. He wasn't going to make the same mistake twice and decided to go to the flagship book store early. They had already set up everything for him. He went to greet the store representative managing the event. They chatted for a while and, before George knew it, the store was full and it was time for him to present. He was taken aback. He never expected the store to be packed with readers to hear and speak to him. As far as he knew, the novel had done moderately well but, clearly, it was starting to strike a nerve. The humbling paycheck he had received in the post was starting to make more sense.

George commenced the presentation with his background, how he came about generating the idea for the novel and deciding to write it. He moved onto the hidden meanings behind certain scenes and how he came across the title of the novel. He was surprised at the astuteness of many of the readers. He was in his element. George gave his best presentation to date, pulling from years of experience from talking to classes filled with students. The Q&A went equally well and ended in enthusiastic applause. They had gone well over schedule and were forced to move briskly through the meet-and-greet signings. He always found these to be like a strange dance. The readers knew there was limited time to talk before they had to be ushered away so he could move onto the next person in the queue. Some people were animated, others were reserved, but George made them all feel like the evening had been one well spent.

Once he finished signing the book for the last reader, the book store representative commended him on the presentation. It had been one of the best book signings he had seen in his time there. George was amazed to hear the book had been selling as if it was on a Black Friday sale over the last month. He did recall hearing about two or three favorable reviews a few weeks back, but hadn't realized the ramifications. Their influence had translated into generous book sales.

They thanked each other for their time and George drove back to the hotel to what became a restless night's sleep in a foreign bed.

In the morning, George ate a hearty complimentary breakfast before departing. On the drive home, he listened to Lynyrd Skynyrd's *Simple Man*. He felt especially positive about the future.

CHAPTER FIFTY-THREE

George had just arrived home from his trip when his phone rang. 'Hello.'

'Hi George,' said Beatrice.

'Nice timing. I just got home.'

'I aim to please. I've been itching to hear what happened. How did the book-signing go?'

'Great. I've never had so many people attend a book-signing before. Not that I've had many. I think I've only had four of them prior to this. There must have been about a hundred people at the evening signing. It's a large book store so we could all fit in when I gave my presentation, but when the physical signing started, I think a few people were standing in the street. I loved doing it. I'm so glad I agreed to do it. The questions the readers asked were surprisingly insightful. Admittedly, there were one or two inquiries that looked at certain aspects of the book in ways I had never thought of. So, I had to think quite hard to answer some questions because they had thought of aspects that were unintentional on my part, but still valid.'

'I'm sure you blew them away, Mr. Professor.'

'Well, I did get a round of applause at the end so I suppose it does mean they enjoyed it. Oh, and the manager of the store also said the event was one of the best he had seen.'

'I always knew you were talented and special. You downplay it far too much. You should blow your own horn more often. I'm so proud of you.'

'I'm remarkable, aren't I?' asked George.

'Easy there, that's too much. Tone it down. Now you sound arrogant,' laughed Beatrice.

'Whose fault is that? You shouldn't attempt to elevate me so much.'

'I'm sure they would have enjoyed the arrogant George as well.'

'Somehow I doubt it.'

'It's no surprise so many people turned up though. The premise is really intriguing and the characters are intricate. Also, the overarching themes have depth.'

'So, you have read the book?'

'Of course I have. I was curious to see what you were capable of. Impressive diction you have there. Some might even say you are an intellectual.'

'Thanks. I must admit that the trip was overwhelming. I wasn't expecting such a positive response.'

'Never doubt your ability. You are very talented. I'm so fortunate to be with you.'

'I feel like I'm the lucky one,' said George. 'What have you been up to?'

'Nothing much. I'm not getting much downtime at the moment. It's been very busy. At least I enjoy the people I work with. The other hostesses are fantastic. We always have each other's backs. I should be able to take some time out early next month.'

'Perfect, because it's my sister's marriage anniversary early next month.'

'When exactly is the anniversary, because I only have a few days available. I'll have to leave again on the sixth.'

'Oh no, you aren't serious. Lila's anniversary is the next day. Is there no way you can move days around?'

'I can ask, but I doubt the airline will agree. Two of my colleagues are on maternity leave, so we are being stretched more than usual. They need all hands on deck at the moment.'

'This is so disappointing.'

'I know. I'll make it up to you. There will be other opportunities.'

'I know. It's just that Lila is so excited to meet you. She has been trying to set something up for months now.'

'I'm sorry that life is so chaotic on my side. I'm sure it will quieten down once we have all our staff back.'

'It's okay. I understand.'

'Anyway. I just wanted to hear your voice and see how the book-signing went. I'm glad to hear it went so well. I've got to go now. I need to prep for the next boarding.'

'Thanks for the call. Love you.'

'Love you more.'

George was left staring blankly into the living area. He was feeling dejected. How did he go from such a high to such a low in the space of a heartbeat? He considered whether he was being unreasonable that once again she wasn't available to meet Lila and Joe. Beatrice had, after all, already said she was unavailable that weekend before he had even mentioned the date of the anniversary. It was still morning, but he poured himself a glass of wine to numb his agitation. It wasn't going to be easy letting Lila know the disappointing news. Thankfully, Joe was more blasé about such things.

CHAPTER FIFTY-FOUR

The kettle whistled to life just as George finished making some oatmeal with an apple from the market with some cinnamon. He made himself a cup of coffee and sat absent-minded at the kitchen counter to eat his breakfast.

He had not slept well. He sensed Beatrice was behaving differently and he couldn't shake the notion something was wrong. Was she keeping something from him, he wondered? The irrational mind of half-sleep had only made matters worse as he retreaded the same thoughts over and over during the night.

George was not ordinarily a paranoid person. The restless night left him feeling uncomfortable and drained. The realization crossed his mind that he knew a negligible amount about Beatrice. She hung out at his house most of the time. Of the dozen or so times they had been together, only on the odd occasion would they go out together, but these outings were after some prodding on his part. All he knew about her had come from his own experiences with her. Nothing was verifiable. Everything she had said could have been a lie for all he knew. He contemplated this absurd thought for a moment. Wasn't this true for all relationships with people he knew? One takes everything at face value and filters truth from fiction. Everyone he met, he assessed and was based on what they said to him. He did, however, realize it wasn't always cut and dry. There were always subtle corroborating sources when he met people. He became conscious of the fact he had never seen her in uniform or never seen her interact with any of her friends or work colleagues. To be fair, as friendly as she was, she was very much a lone wolf and this was foreign territory for her. Now that he thought of it, he hadn't even observed her message or converse with anyone on her phone.

He took a step back and tried to assess the puzzle pieces logically. She came here on a break and has no ties to anyone here other than me. Therefore, I wouldn't have seen her in her uniform. Plus, I've never met her coming directly from an airport, but rather always from her hotel. She must have the uniform in her luggage.

He did, however, find it odd that he had never been to her hotel room, but maybe she was embarrassed by it. Maybe it was budget accommodation or she was untidy. Feeling embarrassed would be a reasonable explanation, he deduced. Perhaps before her next visit he should offer to take her to and from the airport. The nearest airport was just over an hour away, so she might find the offer helpful. He had obviously never seen her with friends because she had no friends in town. She knew nobody but him. It did, however, remain bizarre that he had never seen her on the phone with someone. Did she not want to be contacted when she was with him, he wondered? What in the world could be the logic behind the lack of communication? Was she seeing someone else? Maybe she was married? No, somehow he knew that wasn't the case. The way she gravitated towards him was too powerful for there to be another man in her life surely? There must be something else about her past she did not want him to know.

'What in the world could it be and how do I approach a topic like this with her?' he said. George realized he was talking to himself and immediately pulled up his mental handbrake.

One step at a time he decided. He chose to start by calling Lila and letting her know the disheartening news that he would be a party of one for their anniversary.

'Morning, sis.'

'Morning, George.'

'I didn't wake you, did I?'

'Oh God no. Noah always wakes me up at ungodly hours of the morning. He is still a restless sleeper. I think he still doesn't like being alone, so as soon as the sun rises, so does he.'

'I'm sure he'll grow out of it. Children often have quirky habits initially.'

'I'm going to struggle to bend that one to my will,' Lila said.

'I've got some unfortunate news. Beatrice isn't going to be around on the weekend of your anniversary. She is going to be working.'

'Fuck me, how far in advance do I need to book this woman?'

'It's not that. She regrettably has stringent working periods. Apparently, they are short-staffed at the moment due to some maternity leaves and they have to work more days because of it. Most of the time even I see her with little notice.'

'I don't want to argue about this now- it's been a struggle getting the kids clean and fed this morning and I'm already nearing red on the shit-o-meter scale.'

'I'm sorry to disappoint you. I'll have to bring along an exceptionally rewarding gift, aren't I?'

'Whatever. You know it's not about the gifts. I've got to go, the kids are making a mess again. Maybe one day we'll be good enough to meet your fancy girlfriend.'

'Enough Lila! I don't want to hear it. You'll meet her in time,' said George. Her snide remark had pushed him over the edge.

'Okay, okay. Touchy subject. See you soon. Bye.'

'Bye.'

George put down the phone. At times, she had a way of provoking him. Lila could be pure magma when she felt scorned, but the kids had drained her already which prevented her from making it a full-blown argument. He was relieved that it hadn't escalated.

As much as he hated to admit it, George wondered if Lila had a point. Perhaps there was a reason for Beatrice's avoidance. He pulled out his laptop and booted it up. He felt a little creepy doing it, but he Googled Beatrice's full name to see what came up. He could see this wasn't going to be an easy task. The search results were much more plentiful than he was expecting. Over one hundred results in LinkedIn.

He browsed through those, but didn't find any matches. Now that he thought of it, she had never mentioned where she lived or, in her line of work, where she was based. She tended to not talk too much about herself. It was ironically a characteristic he liked about her. Could she be foreign? He dismissed the thought. Her local accent was too entrenched to have been picked up over the last few years. Not knowing which city to prioritize made things much harder.

He moved back to Google to see what else he could find. There was a poet of the same name, but she was ninety-six years old who was clearly not an appropriate link. Google images responded with dozens of results. However, none of the images were of her. Beatrice was a lot more common a name than he realized.

He glanced through Facebook profiles, but this also proved to be problematic without more detail to go on, so George went back to Google and added air hostess to the search criteria. This made the search even worse because now the results were polluted with airline related topics rather than her name.

George carried on for another hour with no luck. He was secretly pleased she didn't seem to have a Facebook page because he felt they were a waste of time, but that didn't help him in his search. He resigned himself to the fact that he wasn't going to find anything. While he wasn't satisfied with his lack of findings, he was even more pleased to not find any incriminating evidence.

However, this didn't mean he felt entirely comfortable. It was possible there might be many lies he would have to uncover, but at least, on first inspection, the results were clean.

George looked at his watch and packed up and washed the dishes. He was going to be late for work because of this escapade and rushing was not the way he liked to start his week.

CHAPTER FIFTY-FIVE

'Class, I have an assignment for you.'

The class became restless as all George's students did when he suggested tasks counting towards their final grade.

'This time the assignment is on determining truth. It's due next week Monday. It should be in the region of five pages at the usual font size and will contribute to your final grade. I shall discuss the key points with you know and you will be required to extrapolate these points into more depth and go into the historical background thereof. You are welcome to mention which philosophers believed what, but most of the grade will go into your thought process and not the historical relevance of your assignment. A small portion of your grade will go towards the relationship and effect these different avenues have with religion.'

George gulped a mouthful of water to ease his throat and to gather his thoughts.

'Truth based on testimony. In what scenarios can you believe what people tell you? There are three core principles you have at your disposal for this assignment. They are Evidentialism, Credulity and, lastly, Intellectual Autonomy.

'To start, let's discuss Evidentialism in a broad sense. Should we believe miracles have taken place? Those who follow Evidentialism advocate that one should never believe in the occurrence of miracles if the source to such an event is purely as a result of testimony- a miracle, in this case, being subjugated to be an extraordinary event that is not explicable by natural or scientific laws. Therefore, Evidentialism requires that for one's testimony to be justified, it must be accompanied by evidence supporting his or her belief.

'Philosophers use the term testimony to refer to any situation in which one believes something as a result of what someone else has stated in whichever form of communication it takes place. Testimony is the solemn attestation as to the truth of a matter.

'How do we gather information and knowledge through our lives? It's through our own experiences as well as through the testimony of others. Testimony is not always truthful or correct and therefore one needs to assess the validity thereof.

For example, you would have seen photos of the Eiffel Tower and the surrounding areas. You might have even watched a documentary about the Eiffel Tower. These are credible sources and, based thereon, you may choose to visit the Eiffel Tower. However, having gone to visit the symbol of Paris, you might realize you made mistakes based solely on the evidence you had consumed or, in this case, the lack of testimony relating directly to the practicality of a trip to the Eiffel Tower. Had you asked a Parisian or someone who had already visited the Eiffel Tower, you might have received more accurate testimony also factoring into account what time of day to go to avoid queues or what time of day has the best views. Also, what is the best season of the year that would negate fog, large amounts of cloud cover, or smog that would in turn impede your view? One should only trust testimony when one has evidence the testifier is likely to be right and appropriate. Therefore, one needs to grade the evidence and the credibility of the testifier or also, in this example, the completeness of the information provided.'

It always amused George that female students tended to be more conscientious and write notes while the male students tended to write less, but possibly listen more. The usual reaction was playing out in front of him.

'Therefore, if you follow Evidentialism, you need to believe that the testifier is credible and reliability based on the facts presented, before you trust the person, or said person needs to have a history of reliability before you trust what they are saying. For example, if you are unwell, it would be preferential to follow the advice of your doctor over that of the internet because you know he or she spent years studying their profession, have had first-hand access to diagnosing your problem and, in all likelihood, know what they are talking about. This is because you have assessed the testifier to be likely correct.

'When assessing testimony, one would also need to determine the likelihood that the testifier might be trying to deceive you or they are mistaken. Humans tend to blindly trust testimony despite the fact that it's often inaccurate. This leads us to Credulity.

'A credulous individual will believe information to be true without the need for strong evidence. Credulity relies heavily on perception and the fact that our social structures are founded on us believing testimony unless proven otherwise. Trusting testimony is equivalent to trusting your senses. We don't only trust our senses when we have evidence they are likely to be correct. Those who believe in Credulity, therefore inherently trust testimony because they believe we are biologically programmed to trust our senses. This ties in with the principle of veracity, in other words being honest.

'Children follow Credulity because they are very ready to trust what adults tell them and have not yet developed skills of filtration and assessment. Our childhoods are also the period where we learn the most which does add credibility to Credulity. For example, we are most able to learn a new language when we are very young. Granted, this is not necessarily due to Credulity. It also has to do with infants' brain chemistry being built to learn, as well as having more time to learn, and fewer inhibitions. Infants aren't self-conscience about making mistakes and only learn the basics of a given language before attempting to master it as they get older.'

One of his students nodded in confirmation. This student tended to come up to George after nearly every class to ask further questions. No doubt the other students must have considered him to be a teacher's pet.

'Lastly, there is Intellectual Autonomy, which is an ability and willingness to think for oneself. A person with this virtue is therefore not overly dependent on others when gaining knowledge. Said person is therefore not merely a database of other people's knowledge, but is also able to deduce for themselves.

'This in turn results in them often having unpopular beliefs. These are often the beliefs of revolutionaries as it's not easy to stand against the peer pressure of generally accepted knowledge.

'Those are the three primary principles of truth based on testimony that I want you to focus on in your assignments. There is, however, an example I want you all to use to illustrate your thought processes. The example is as follow: one, someone you know lives out of town; two, said person knows nobody here other than you; three, said person appears to be rational and genuine; and four, the facts about the individual that said person has made, cannot be corroborated due to points one and two. Therefore, reliance can only be placed on point three. In essence, there is an absence of evidence.'

CHAPTER FIFTY-SIX

George greeted his teammates as he stepped up to the bowling lane. It was the last Friday night of the month, a day in the calendar reserved for bowling by four teams of four. On these nights, each team tried to end with the highest total score. If someone was absent for whatever reason, the highest average score was used. Afterward, they would all go to the pizza parlor next door and the losing teams would pay for the winning team as well as themselves.

George was on a team with Mr. Yang, his wife Rose, as well as Joe. Regrettably Joe was down with man flu, therefore the average scoring system was going to be used for the night. This worked in their favor because Rose was their best bowler so they had a respectable chance of winning on the night due to her score counting more.

'I can feel it in my bones, George. This is going to be our night,' Mr. Yang said in a more contemplative voice than his own.

'You say that every month,' said Rose.

'Well, this time I'm right. I know it.'

'Let's hope so. We haven't won in a while,' said George.

'I've been honing my skills by watching ESPN,' said Mr. Yang. 'The pins are going to fall like rain.'

The team leader next to them heard Mr. Yang's bravado. 'Those are big words, Yang. What do you say we make things more interesting?'

'What do you have in mind, Tyrone?' asked Mr. Yang.

'If my team gets a higher score than yours, you wash my car for two months,' said Tyrone.

'Okay, but if my team has a higher score, you suck my dick,' said Mr. Yang.

George and Mr. Yang burst out laughing as did some of the members of the opposing team. Rose just shook her head at the inappropriate joke. She was used to this kind of behavior from her husband. Tyrone was left uncomfortable by the joke.

'I'm only kidding, Tyrone. Relax. If we beat your team, you can wash my car for two months.'

The banter continued for a few more moments before they dispersed to their respective lanes.

'You were baiting them, weren't you?' queried George.

'You know it. Rose is often the best player on the night even when we lose. Our chances are excellent.'

George knew this was going to go in one of two ways, either the game was going to be much more serious than usual or it was going to be much more juvenile. It was the latter. Mr. Yang and Tyrone mocked each other whenever they could to try and throw off the focus of the opposing team. George was thoroughly enjoying the banter.

Mid-way through the game, Mr. Yang's team led by three points, followed by Tyrone's team, followed by the two remaining teams which were trailing by some margin.

Tyrone stepped up to bowl and took a moment to compose himself while pushing Mr. Yang's ridicule out of mind. He swung his arm and released. He received a strike as all the pins clattered to the ground. His team cheered with as much animation as they could muster. 'Suck on that, Yang,' said Tyrone.

'I thought we weren't doing the blowjobs anymore,' said Mr. Yang.

Next, it was Rose's turn and she responded in kind with a strike. It was her fifth of the night so far. It remained tight for the remainder of the night before Mr. Yang's team eventually edged ahead to win.

Much to his delight, Mr. Yang made everyone know how wonderful their free meal was going to taste and how clean his car was going to be for the next two months. George couldn't help but foretell how much the other teams were going to want to beat them next time. Most of the bowlers enjoyed Mr. Yang's brash, ill befitting humor, but he had laid it on thick this time. There would no doubt be retribution next time, but Mr. Yang didn't care. For him, the ridicule was more fun than the win.

They all moved next door to the pizza parlor and enjoyed the food and drinks for the next couple of hours. Everyone let their hair down and shared humorous stories of what had happened since last they had met.

At around eleven 'o clock, the teams started to leave for home, but George asked Mr. Yang and Rose to stay a little longer.

'I've been having some issues with Beatrice and I wanted to talk to you two in private. I'm not sure how to approach it,' started George.

'When in doubt, say it wasn't you,' said Mr. Yang.

'It's not like that. I haven't done anything wrong. However, I'm not sure if something is going on with Beatrice.'

'Why? What has happened?' asked Rose.

'Nothing specific has happened. Maybe I'm overreacting. Maybe I'm trying to find fault where there isn't any. I don't know. I don't think I am. There is just something off about Beatrice lately.'

'Is she acting strangely?' asked Rose.

'No. She is as great as she has always been. Beatrice is remarkable. She is one of the warmest, most considerate, loving people I have ever met. My concern has more to do with intuition. Certain things just don't add up. We never go out. Lila has been inviting us to her place for a while so that she can meet Beatrice, but Beatrice is never in town. It all just seems to be a little strange to me. It's as though she is hiding something.'

'It's difficult to comment because I haven't been present, but it does seem as though you are overreacting. You said yourself there isn't anything specific that is wrong,' said Rose.

'Yes, George,' added Mr. Yang, 'some people don't like socializing much. Maybe she prefers just being with you. Not a bad thing if you know what I mean.'

'That's it though- because she is so easy going and social with me, I can't see her not getting along with other people and enjoy mingling.'

'Flying across the country all the time must be tiring. Life is so chilled here and maybe all she wants while she is here is escapism and downtime,' Rosa said.

'Tell that to Lila. She is getting frustrated and it's her that sowed the seed of doubt in me.'

'Beatrice doesn't live here though, so it's only natural she is hard to pin down,' said Rose. 'Maybe Lila is unintentionally clouding your intuition. I had a boyfriend once who used to leave on business all the time. Eventually I called it off because I hardly ever saw him. Not that I'm suggesting you break up with her, but planning things were difficult with him and I wasn't getting the attention and love I needed.'

'I guess. Luckily, I do see her quite often considering the circumstances, but it's usually a last-minute arrangement. She calls me and lets me know she has a few hours open the next day or, if I'm lucky, a couple of days. I've even been considering going to see a shrink about all of this. It's affecting my ability to concentrate. I realize it's just my subconscious raising doubt in me. I probably still feel guilty for moving on from Isabella. I know it makes no sense, especially since Isabella passed away so many years ago. I haven't been in a proper, meaningful relationship since her.'

'You two were a great couple. In my opinion it isn't strange at all that you are struggling to move on,' said Rose.

'Maybe this ordeal is just a strange situation and I'm battling to adjust to her less structured lifestyle.'

'I think you hit the nail on the head, George.'

CHAPTER FIFTY-SEVEN

George picked up the pile of papers he had finished marking and put them on the kitchen countertop next to the entrance to his apartment so he wouldn't forget them when he left for work the next day. He had already finished marking most of the papers at work but, eventually, it got to a point where he needed different surroundings. George was not one to work into the night at his office. He poured himself a glass of apple juice, opened the window next to his desk as much as it would allow, letting in as much fresh air as possible. The air was, at last, starting to cool as the late afternoon approached. He sat back down at his desk to think.

He had decided to call Beatrice's airline before office hours ended to try and confirm her schedule. His intuition was too aroused to be ignored. Of that he was sure and, hopefully, confronting her with one possible deceit would unravel the others. All he wanted was for her to be open and honest with him. Together they could overcome anything. George knew there was nothing she had said or done that made him doubt her, but rather a trail of coincidences. This, in conjunction with the fact that everything about her was unverifiable without him investigating further, made George's subconscious suspicious. Conversely, doing background checks on Beatrice left George feeling nauseous. This line of thinking was making him an emotional wreck and it took all his fortitude to not portray this to anyone. George was feeling exceedingly frustrated that such a positive force in his life like Beatrice was making him conceptualize such toxic thoughts. He hated doubting the woman he loved.

Enough was enough. He had decided to call and see what would come of it. However, he needed a strategy. The airline would have confidentiality constraints and wasn't going to just hand over her file or personal details to him. He had to think of logical questions that would lower the guard of the person on the line. An idea was starting to formulate. George snatched a pen and paper and began drawing up a process map diagram. He was going to call to arrange a secret engagement party. The fact that it was a surprise would justify why he was calling the airline and not speaking to Beatrice directly. The engagement would optimistically lower the person's guard to bend the rules a little. George laid out the possible questions and responses the person on the line could ask and thought about the replies he could give depending on the results from the person on the line. The last thing he wanted was to flounder on a question and be forced to hang up.

George was ready. He dialed the helpline number he found on the internet and a woman answered with the verbatim welcoming she had been trained to use.

'So how can I help you?' she then asked.

'Hello, good morning.'

'Morning sir.'

'I was wondering if you could help me with an itinerary. I need to confirm the flight schedule of one of your flight attendants.'

'I'm sorry, sir. I'm not permitted to divulge information about our staff.'

'That's extremely disappointing. I'm trying to arrange a surprise marriage proposal party for my girlfriend,' George lied. 'She is an air hostess for your airline and I need to arrange an event with all our friends, but I'm not sure if she is going to be in town on the day.'

'I'm sorry Sir, but I'm really not allowed to give you that information.' She now sounded sympathetic and less formal.

'I can't try to ask her because she will realize I'm up to something. I'm a terrible liar.'

No response. This was going better than he thought. George pushed further, 'You don't need to divulge her schedule to me, merely confirm whether I can arrange the surprise event for the seventh of next month. I just need to know if she can be here on that date.'

'Sir,' the woman's voice was quieter now, 'this stays between you and me, please. I could lose my job for disclosing information like this. What is your girlfriend's name and where are you located? I'll take a look at our database for the itinerary and tell you yes or no.'

George gave the necessary information and heard the woman's heavy typing on her keyboard.

'Please spell her name for me.'

George responded, but heard no typing this time.

'Sir, you must be mistaken. She must work at a different airline.'

'No, it's definitely your airline.' George had considered a response like this. 'Maybe she still uses her ex-husband's name, um… I'm sorry, I can't remember what it was again. I think it started with a T.' George was impressed with his ability to lie with conviction. He could have been an actor.

'I'm sorry sir, we don't even have anyone with a first or second name Beatrice in our employment, in any position. I'm unable to assist you further with this matter.' Formality had returned to her tone as she had become more skeptical. 'Can I assist you with anything else, sir?'

'Um, no. No thank you,' George was genuinely thrown. He had not considered that Beatrice didn't even work for the airline. He merely thought she might have been lying about not being available on the seventh. 'That will be all thank you. Goodbye.'

'Goodbye, sir. Have a wonderful day further.'

George put the phone down. His eyes were wide yet expressionless. His fears had been justified, but vindicated in a far worse way than he was expecting. George was struggling to hold onto thoughts. His mind became a blank slate, empty of contemplation. A few moments later he came up for air. He had suspected something was wrong, but never had he considered she might not even be an air hostess. This was a substantial lie that undoubtedly came with scarier realizations. Beatrice would only lie about her work if it was essential to hide a far graver secret. George did not like the sight of the road map before him.

CHAPTER FIFTY-EIGHT

'Are you sure you are alright? You seem a little off tonight,' asked Beatrice.

'I'm fine. It's been a rough week at work, that's all,' said George.

'Oh. What happened?'

'A lot of papers to mark this week and I also started preparing for online courses which was quite taxing.' He had in actual fact enjoyed strategizing on how to approach the online material, but Beatrice's more detailed line of questioning had thrown him, so he was forced to lie with the most plausible event coming to his mind.

'How come? I would have thought preparing for those online courses would be like a breath of fresh air. Especially when you start filming. Aren't online courses the future of tertiary education?'

'The process is interesting and, yes, it's probably the future, but I find it to be a much more rigid way of expressing myself than I'm used to. By the end of the day, I'm exhausted. I have done this for three days this week and, in between, I've had a lot of papers to mark.' It had been a tiring week, but George had managed it in his stride. He was far more capable than he took the time to realize. What was severely bothering him was Beatrice. She had been deceiving him all this time, but to what end? Which aspects of herself were truthful and which not he wondered as she stared at him.

'Maybe I should give you space to unwind,' Beatrice said. She was hurt by his dismissive attitude.

'I'm sorry. I get like this sometimes. I probably just need a good night's sleep and I'll be fine again.'

'Maybe rest isn't such a bad idea. I think I'll leave earlier today and give you time to de-stress.' This was the response he was hoping for.

'Are you sure? I don't want to be rude,' lied George.

'I could do with a good night's sleep myself. I've been taking too many of those caffeine pills the airline gives us and my sleep patterns are all over the show. I could do with some self-regulation and detox.'

Beatrice stood up to leave his apartment and George stood up to meet her as she kissed him on the lips. The kiss made him feel as though he was walking on air yet carrying the weight of the world on his shoulders at the same time. It was a toxic dichotomy making him feel extremely uneasy. Thankfully, he was able to swallow his discomfort and push through.

'Bye George.'

'Bye Beatrice. See you soon.'

'See you soon. I hope you feel more like yourself tomorrow.'

'Thanks.'

George closed the door behind her and moved over to the window overlooking the entrance to the apartment block. He lingered there to see in which direction she exited. Once he had observed her turn right, he raced downstairs to follow her. George was relieved that she was strolling which enabled him to see her cross the road two hundred yards away and turn left just as he exited the apartment block.

He wasn't sure what he was going to gain by following her, but he hoped it would help answer several questions. Beatrice would ordinarily order an Uber to come and fetch her. Thankfully, she left earlier than usual therefore the sun had not yet set, so she decided a walk would be a more enjoyable experience. This worked in his favor. The sky was ablaze in pink and orange as the sun began to rest in the west.

George jogged across the road to lessen the gap between them. He didn't want to lose her. She must be staying nearby he deduced because the residential area in this vicinity ended in about a mile or two before a tiny industrial zone began. He began to match her speed so he could keep enough distance between them. Beatrice wandered along the quaint streets, stopping on occasion to take in the architecture. Their current street was one of the oldest in town and was regarded as a heritage site. The homes were therefore maintained in their original eighteen hundred Georgian styles. Both sides of the street were lined with homes and apartments adorned with pillars, large multiple pane windows and chimneys. This formed part of the adjacent suburb to George's, but was far more upmarket than his.

A number of pedestrians had joined them because the fresh afternoon breeze was proving to be popular after yet another blisteringly hot day. The activity helped George blend in as he appeared to merely be another pedestrian out for some fresh air or exercise. George didn't ever run this route as he preferred the greenery of the park, but he was familiar with the layout as he sometimes drove in this direction to work when he wanted a more pleasing environment to drive through. Isabella had dreamed about owning a house in this area- a dream he had forgotten until now.

He continued to trail her for a further block until she stopped at a quaint food store to buy something to eat. They had already eaten an hour before so George assumed Beatrice was buying a dessert of some kind. He didn't enter, keeping a decent distance between himself and the shop. Minutes later she exited and continued up the street with a small package that almost certainly contained a baked delicatessen of some kind. She then passed a police officer, but he seemed to ignore her. In his mind, George would have to be more careful not to seem conspicuous but. in reality, he blended in with most of the arbitrary pedestrians scattered across the block. George passed the police officer and greeted him with a nod. The officer reciprocated and carried on past him.

Beatrice opened the packaging of whatever it was she had just bought and ate while she walked. Her pace slowed George had to meander awkwardly to maintain a safe distance behind her.

A few minutes later she completed her snack and her pace increased dramatically. So much so that it took George off guard and he struggled to keep pace with her as she turned a corner in the distance. George turned the corner a moments later, but Beatrice was nowhere to be seen. Before him were commercial blocks with mostly small office companies. He began to jog ahead to observe the next couple of streets she might have entered. Nothing. He began to speculate if she might have spotted him, but she had not looked in his direction on any occasion therefore he deduced that being noticed was unlikely. George slowly retraced his steps, investigating each building he passed, but there were no signs of life in any of them because office hours had ended two hours earlier.

George stopped and took a moment to consider what was in the near vicinity. He remembered there was a modest hotel just around the corner which she could have easily gone to. He had to regain his bearings as he was less familiar with this side of town and managed to find his way to the hotel.

George apprached reception and asked if they had a guest by her name staying there. They responded that there wasn't. He gave a quick description of what she looked like to be doubly sure, but the reception desk confirmed no guest fitting her description was staying there.

Dejected, George walked back into the street. His attempt at being a private investigator had ended fruitlessly. Now he only had more questions than answers. There were no other accommodation facilities in the area he was aware of, therefore he wondered whether she was even from out of town. With the exception of this hotel, this was not the type of vicinity where someone from out of town would stay and, even then, the hotel was occupied by predominately business guests, not people on holiday. He deduced she must have taken a turn earlier that he had missed.

He ventured back to his apartment with no solutions coming to mind. George ran a cold shower before going to bed. He tossed and turned through most of the night, unable to come up with plausible solutions to his questions.

CHAPTER FIFTY-NINE

George placed twelve white roses on his wife's grave once more. He was in need of counsel and sometimes the best to be found was one's own. The graveyard was as well maintained as it always was when he came. He had seen three gardeners on the way maintaining the flower beds, hedges and lawns as well as someone removing dead flowers from the gravesites.

'How did I get myself into this mess, Isabella? The woman I met is not all she appears to be. She has been deceiving me and I don't know why. I don't even want to know why, but I have to. I'm going to have to confront her and I'm concerned about what I'm going to find. The sad part is I don't even care about the things she has been lying about. She doesn't work for the company she said she does. I don't give a damn if she is an air hostess or not. Why would I? I'm also not even certain if she is from out of town and what that would even entail. I don't know how deep this rabbit hole of deceit goes. Yang and Rose think I'm overreacting. They feel there is logical reason for these situations not making sense.'

A strong wind bellowed through the trees and spiraled the bouquet off the grave. George repositioned the roses back to their intended resting place.

'I wish you were here now. You always gave me the right advice. Although I guess if you were still here, I wouldn't need to talk to you about these concerns. I would never have entertained her in the first place and I wouldn't be stressing about what she is up to. We weren't married all that long. We didn't make it to our sixth anniversary, but it was long enough for us to see each other with all of our faults. Yet it was always so easy with you. There was never a hint of deception or at least none I picked up on. I suppose that is the problem with hindsight. It always paints the picture you want to tell. I remember our marriage being truthful.'

About ten yards ahead of him a couple with three young children came to visit a grave. George could just make out the dates and name on the tombstone. They were more than likely the children and grand-children of the man who had passed away a few months prior. The parents had somber demeanors, but the children were none the wiser and appeared to be as joyfully naïve as they would have been in other circumstances. They began playing tag while their parents remained steadfast at the grave, seemingly oblivious to what the kids were doing.

'I wonder how our lives would have been different if we had had children?' George's focus was back on Isabella. 'I remember how despondent not being a mother made you. You would have been a wonderful mother. I have no doubt about that. You were so nurturing, yet it wasn't on the cards for us.'

George became teary-eyed. A multitude of brief memories rushed through his mind like an old spliced movie reel.

'Sorry. I wonder if it would have been a good thing now if I was taking care of our kids. Being a single parent isn't easy and they would have suffered for it. Maybe it was for the best. Sometimes life takes us along strange paths.'

George continued to mention his other concerns for a while longer before looking around subconsciously. The couple with the three children had left.

'It's always so therapeutic talking to you. It must look quite strange seeing a grownup talking to a grave. This is a depressing sanctuary.'

CHAPTER SIXTY

'Good morning, George. What a pleasant surprise. Come in,' announced Lila. 'Your timing is great. I just finished washing up after lunch. Joe is busy watching the Grand Prix. Joe! George is here! How have things been?'

'Fine. You?' lied George as he hugged his sister and entered her home. He didn't want to press the release switch on all of his problems just yet.

'I'm great. Earlier this morning I was looking at the loan statement for my hair salon property and I'm nearly finished paying the installments. Another five months and the building will be all mine. Not fucking bad hey?'

'This is great news! I'm so proud of you. Slow and steady wins the race.'

'Yeah. This means that in another half a year those payments can be used on something else. We could use the extra money around here. The two little ones take up all of our remaining cash every month. Do you have any idea how much diapers cost these days? Noah has literally shitted away our money.'

'Georgie. Good to see you,' said Joe, as he came to greet George.

The formula one cars could still be heard screaming in the background.

'Good to see you too, Joe.'

'I was just telling George I'm nearly finished paying off the business property,' said Lila.

'That money is going to come in handy, Georgie. We are still paying off this house as well. Plus, we have small college funds for the kids which we try to pay into every month. It's a lot of sacrifices.'

'I'm so pleased for the two of you. It must be such a relief to have the financial shackles ease a bit.'

The Grand Prix commentator started shouting with excitement in the background as the leader was overtaken.

'Excuse me,' Joe said as he scampered towards the television. His heavy frame created booming footsteps that reverberated through half the old house.

'Man, he loves that fucking shit. I can't stand the sound of those cars going round and round the track all the time. Do you want to join him?' asked Lila.

'Maybe later. I'm actually here to chat with you.'

'Okay great. Let's sit outside in the shade so we can get away from that noise. The kids are playing in their rooms so we will have privacy there. Do you want something to drink?'

'A beer would be great, thanks.' George was thankful Lila's disposition was more favorable than when he phoned her to say Beatrice wasn't going to join for their wedding anniversary.

Lila returned a few moments later with two beers. They moved to the outside patio set. A refreshing breeze was blowing to welcome them.

'Nice and cool here,' said George.

'I love the fresh air. With all the products women put in their hair, the salon's smell can get fucking potent.'

'I hadn't thought of that before. I've never done anything to my hair so it isn't a problem that I have ever had.'

'I'm used to it and it hardly bothers me these days, but if I get the opportunity for fresh air, I fucking grab it.'

'The smaller things in life, hey?'

'Exactly,' said Lila as she drank a large sip of beer. 'I'm sure you'd love to talk to me about the smaller things in life, but you clearly have a subject on your mind. You seem a bit down. I hope it's not because I was upset on the phone the other day. I'm over it.'

Lila could come across as rough to people who didn't know her because of her foul mouth, but she was quite perceptive and considerate. She could pick up when something was bothering George just by his tone of voice and posture. His head tended to sink when concerns were weighing heavily on him and his vocal became faintly melancholic.

'You noticed that I seem down? Is it that obvious?' asked George.

'Of course. I've known you long enough to be able to read you like a book.'

'Well… it's Beatrice. I've been doing a lot of thinking about her and trying to figure out if I'm overreacting about certain aspects and now that I've taken Morphios's red pill, I'm not liking it.'

'What sort of aspects?'

'For the most part, her elusiveness. I know she doesn't live here and her job keeps her on the move so her availability is erratic, but there is just something odd about it all. I can't even say what it is that was causing the itch. I suppose it is just intuition.'

'Odd? What do you mean odd? You keep telling me how amazing she is when you mention her?' asked Lila.

'She is amazing. When I'm with her I don't have a care in the world. I couldn't be happier. It's more afterward- when she isn't around.'

'Go on,' urged Lila.

'For one, it's partly your fault.'

'Me?' asked Lila.

'Yes. The fact she was never available to come here made me start to question why. How do I put this? I have no sense of the rest of her life. Apparently, she lives in an apartment with two other air hostesses, but I've never seen photos of it. I've never noticed her phoning anyone so I have no idea what kind of relationship she has with her friends or who they are or what they are like. It's almost as if she doesn't like having friends which made me wonder if she was hiding something from me.'

'Have you spoken to her about it?' Lila asked. 'Have you asked to go and stay at her place and meet her friends?'

'I did suggest on the phone one time that I fly up to stay with her for a few days, but she warned me against it. Something about it just being a pit-stop for the three of them. Apparently, she is hardly ever there and it doesn't feel like home to her. It sounded reasonable to me at the time.'

'And the friends- did you ask her about those?'

'Come to think of it, I've never asked her. She always seems so interested in me and what we are doing at that moment. She hardly ever talks about her life so the conversation never goes there.'

'I'd bet most men would love to be in a relationship where the women are so interested in them. You should talk to her more about her life.'

'I'm at fault there,' said George.

'So, maybe there is nothing to worry about. It all sounds kinda reasonable to me except for the part about her never being able to come here. That still makes no fucking sense to me,' said Lila.

'I wish I could say the same,' said George. 'I've just been telling you what was bothering me. I haven't even told you about what I have uncovered. Do you mind if I fetch another beer?'

'Go ahead.'

George returned a moment later and took a full-size gulp of beer before continuing. 'It started off innocently with me googling her.'

Lila was tempted to make a sarcastic remark, but chose not to because she sensed what she was going to hear wasn't going to be favorable. 'And?'

'And nothing. I couldn't find any information about her. Granted, she has a common surname, but I couldn't come across the most basic information.'

'What? Is that what you are worried about?' laughed Lila. 'You had me worried for a second there. I thought you were going to say she is a fucking serial killer or a leader of a fucking pedophilia ring. I don't think you'll find anything about me online. I don't have time for that stuff. Fuck, I barely have time to watch TV.'

'Agreed. It's quite reasonable for me to not find anything. Some people don't have much of an online presence. I didn't stop there though. 'George was taking her through the steps he went through in his mind and didn't jump to the punch line so as not to come across as overreacting. 'I gave her airline a call. I tried to find out what her itinerary was.'

'Do they give out that kind of information?' asked Lila.

'No, they don't. I lied about trying to arrange an engagement party and eventually twisted the lady's arm. Turns out there is no one by the name Beatrice working there.'

'Fuck me.'

'I know, right. So, either she lied about working there or being an air hostess altogether or her name isn't Beatrice. This means she is lying about something much more significant. Why would she think I would care if she was or wasn't an air hostess or what her name is unless it's to hide a larger problem?'

'Oh, my fucking shit. Is she a psycho? What the hell is she hiding?'

'I have no idea, but I'm not done. I saw her a few days later. She was just passing through for a day like she often does. I decided not to mention the call to see if I could pick up on anything now that I'm more aware she is lying. Plus, I'm still a bit nervous to see what I'm going to uncover.'

'Just now she is mentally unstable or worse. Did you pick up on anything?'

'No. Actually, she noticed I wasn't myself, but I think I managed to get away with it. I decided to follow her.'

'Follow her? Really!' Lila was amazed he had gone to such an extreme. 'Fucking Magnum PI.'

'Minus the Ferrari and the mustache.'

'And chest hair.'

'And chest hair. She thankfully didn't take a taxi or an Uber. She walked which made following her much easier. I followed her a couple of blocks past the street with the old houses towards the newish commercial area they built a few years back. Unfortunately, I lost her.

There was a cop walking in the street and I didn't want to be conspicuous and ended up losing concentration.'

'Bummer.'

'There are no hotels in that area though, nor are there any in the direction beyond where I lost her. Sorry, there is one hotel, but I confirmed with the receptionist that she wasn't staying there. I don't know if she doubled back or maybe she spotted me, I'm not sure. Now I'm wondering if she maybe lives here.'

CHAPTER SIXTY-ONE

'I wonder if there is a reason for her not wanting to meet me?' Lila asked. 'What does she look like? If there is a possibility she lives here, what are the chances I might know her? She could be one of my customers.'

George gave his sister a detailed reference of what Beatrice looked like, paying special attention to her hair as he knew Lila observed hair more closely than the average person.

'No. I can't say that I've met her before,' Lila said, as she carefully considered the customers she worked on and people she knew. She began shifting in her chair and quickly became uncomfortable. 'Wait, what if it isn't me she has a problem with meeting? What if it's Joe? You don't think he has had a fucking affair with her, do you?'

'I don't think any man would be able to resist her,' George said, and immediately regretted the unthoughtful comment, 'but Joe loves you. I doubt he would ever do anything to jeopardize your relationship. You two are so tight that I don't see it being likely.'

Lila wasn't satisfied with assuming innocence, so they walked inside to Joe, having to shout over the volume of the Grand Prix broadcast. This was the first time she had ever questioned Joe's devotion. Neither hinted at what they both feared, as unlikely as it seemed, but Joe's response that he hadn't met a woman like the one they were describing came across as genuine, without a hint of being uncomfortable. He was more interested in the Grand Prix and did not have the demeanor of someone trying to hide a secret. Relieved, they both returned to the outside patio.

'Wow. I feel quite light-headed. The thought of Joe having an affair with her was quite a scare,' said George as he slumped into the chair.

'Are you okay, George?'

'Yeah, I'm fine, thanks.'

Lila went to the kitchen to fetch a glass of water which he, in turn, gulped down.

'Well, we haven't come closer to solving this. If it isn't an affair, why is she lying?' questioned George.

'Do you think Beatrice is her real name?' asked Lila.

'I'm not sure. It's quite possible it isn't.'

'What in the world could she be hiding?' asked Lila. 'Maybe your book has something to do with it?'

'My book? What would my book have to do with it?'

'Maybe she is a stalker.'

'Hmm… she has read my book and she loved it. Supposedly she read it recently, but she could have easily lied and read it before she met me.'

'Maybe that is why she joined you for your run the first day you met.'

'I suppose that scenario does sound plausible. Now that you mention it, she was pushing me to buy an expensive painting the other day. So, she does think I'm well off. The problem is that even if she is a stalker, why lie about facets of her life?'

'What if it's to make a getaway? To leave no fingerprints.'

'Why?'

'George,' Lila sat upright, 'what if she plans on murdering you?'

'Don't you think her being a murderer is farfetched? I think you might have watched too many thrillers.'

'It happens. A few weeks ago, I watched a documentary about serial killers. These fucking sickos exist.'

'Fair enough, but Beatrice is far too warm and compassionate to be extremely demented. I think we can safely scratch murderer off the list.'

'She could be pretending to be compassionate but, in reality, she could be a psychopath.'

'I've been around her long enough now to pick up if she was being false. She is very comfortable with her personality and I'm quite sure it's genuine.'

'Don't be naïve. She is up to no good.'

'You're being melodramatic. Please change your thought process. I'm not appreciating what you are saying. She is my girlfriend after all.'

'Okay. What are the strange things we do know? She is avoiding coming here and meeting us. She might be lying about her name. She lied about her job and possibly about her career,' said Lila.

'She might very well not be from out of town. She also avoids crowds and usually just wants to be with me in my apartment so she is strangely unsociable for such an outgoing personality,' George said.

They both took a minute to consider these points.

'What if you're the affair?' said Lila.

'You think she could be married?' asked George.

'Possibly. I'm telling you now, she is up to no good. Have you seen a mark or discoloration on her wedding ring finger?'

'That's clever. I never thought to look at her wedding finger. I can't say I have noticed any discoloration. It would make a lot of the puzzle pieces fall into place. She could have lied about who she is and her name so that she doesn't leave a trail. By pretending she doesn't live here, she doesn't have to let me meet her friends. Her friends would reveal who she is and her real name, if Beatrice isn't her real name. It would also explain why she doesn't like being in public. She could easily run into someone she knows.'

'It all sounds logical to me, but you just said she doesn't have a wedding ring mark?'

'I said I hadn't noticed one. I haven't exactly been looking out for it. Maybe she has been keeping her left hand out of sight,' responded George.

'I think we might be onto something here.'

'A lot of this does add up. It does make sense.'

'Yes. I'm sorry George. This is all really shitty. I was so happy when I heard you had met her. She sounded so wonderful and now look- the bitch is tearing you down.'

'Calm down. The unpleasant quandary I'm in is I need to confront her about this because it's driving me insane, but at the same time I don't want to. At least if I don't force her hand, I'll still have her. There is also a possibility this might be a big misunderstanding of some kind.'

'You have to confront her George. You can't carry on living like this. You'll drive yourself insane. As you just said, there is a chance it's just a misunderstanding. Although, to be honest, I don't think it's going to be positive news. I still don't get why she doesn't want to meet me. Fucking hell.'

CHAPTER SIXTY-TWO

George put on his running gear and earphones, stepped out of his apartment building and began his run.

He needed to clear his head and running seemed like a better way to achieve a reset than any other. He had had a headache the whole morning and needed some escapism. He chose against using the usual park route. This time he was going to run along the streets he had used when following Beatrice. He wasn't running the route to come across her although perhaps he would remember something when retracing his steps, but he now realized he didn't fully appreciate architecture in this suburb despite it being next to his- and a new environment might be stimulating. If he were to run into Beatrice, it would just be a bonus. According to her, she was working, but at this stage, George didn't know what was true and what wasn't.

This route was for the most part flat, while the park route had more inclines and had more gravel underfoot in places, therefore his pace today was going to be far better than usual.

George looked at his phone's music library. He needed a more upbeat song to bolster his mood. Preferably a tune he hadn't heard in a while. After some searching, he decided on Little Richard. *Good Golly*

Miss Molly started playing. He hadn't expected it, but the song was perfect for running because of its high energy. He found himself dashing faster than he ordinarily would have, in part because of the song. He curtailed his tempo in case he ran out of puff. It had been a long time since he had a stitch but, if he had kept up this pace, he would undoubtedly get one.

George ran up and down a few of the side streets he hadn't seen a few days prior in order to increase the length of his run. He hadn't realized it before, but the side avenues had even nicer homes than the feeder road he had used previously. The grounds were much larger and must have cost a lot of money to maintain. They were too large to keep up without assistance. In certain cases, full-time maintenance. All the homes were enclosed with high walls and metal fences. He thought the street where his in-laws lived was impressive, but some of these roads were even more so. Seeing these houses for the first time made the run worthwhile if nothing else.

George returned back onto the main road and smelt the prominent stench of gas. He didn't notice any gasoline leaks on the ground nearby so it must have been coming from one of the vehicles. This was why he preferred running through the park. The air was much cleaner. That was also the primary rationale why George didn't drive with the windows down. Despite the town being diminutive next to the nearby cities, it was large enough to have pollution on the busier roads.

He ran up to the shop where Beatrice had bought herself something to eat and he took a right immediately afterward. She had turned right two roads up so, by turning beforehand, George could get a feel of what she might have encountered had she doubled back.

The crisscrossing roads were also a residential area, but much lower income to the block he had just explored. These were more middle-class homes. Was Beatrice living in one of these houses, George wondered? He was confident Beatrice hadn't looked in his direction but, now that he thought about it, she could have spotted him when she entered the shop. The till was by an entrance lined with large windows. Despite the oversized adverts stuck on the window, customers by the till had a clear view of the outside.

George circled around a few times, but didn't see anything out of the ordinary. He started to get a throbbing headache again. He stopped to rub his temples. Beatrice must be getting to him. So much for clearing his head, he thought. He shouldn't have chosen this route because all it achieved was thinking about her which only inflated his stress. The trepidation of confronting her made him feel queasy.

CHAPTER SIXTY-THREE

'Okay class, now we are going to discuss concepts about fate and free will,' announced George. 'Fate and free will have been deliberated over for centuries by philosophers, religious bodies as well as, at times, ordinary men and women. It's one of the pinnacle questions traversing the recesses of our minds through the ages. Unfortunately, it's likely to be a question whose conclusion will remain at the end of the rainbow because, just as one nears a rainbow, so it moves further forward. Scholars have had various opinions on how fate works as well as to various degrees of extremism. Today we shall discuss the three major schools of thought.'

'Firstly, there is determinism. Determinists believe there is no free will because fate is the governing body. Everything we do, think and say is based on previously existing causes that perpetuate currently or in future. In other words, our fate is set and is based on pre-existing constructs from our past. This would not merely relate to events, but everything, including moral choices. Therefore, this school of thought can walk hand in hand with pre-ordained decisions by one or more divine beings, but can also be based on more pragmatic variables. So, let's get into the practicalities. Some of you might have heard about the concept of nature versus nurture. Would someone like to elaborate on what it refers to? Yes Jennifer, go ahead.'

'It has to do with raising children, Professor. Whether the grown-up we become is based on how our parents raised us or based on our DNA.'

'Correct. Thank you, Jennifer. Sociologists have looked at the various avenues that determine the adult we become and tried to establish how much of it relates to the way our parents reared us and how much is founded on our genetic predisposition. Certain aspects of ourselves are based on our genetics. For example, a fair-skinned individual is at home in colder weather, but does not enjoy scorching heat. Vice versa, a darker-skinned individual is less likely to want to move to Scandinavia despite the Scandinavian countries being among the happiest countries in the world. For an individual raised near the equator, it can be just too large a hurdle to circumvent. Genetics predetermines that it's unlikely that a darker-skinned person would be suited to live near one of the earth's poles. Assess this with a pinch of salt of course and don't look at it through political correctness glasses. I'm merely saying our genetics evolved over thousands of years based on our environments and it's only natural that one would prefer to live at a location most comfortable for the individual.'

The explanation appeared to resonate with the class.

'Then there is nurture. Much of what we are as individuals is established by what we learn from our parents. Our brains are like sponges when we are young and we absorb not merely large amounts of information in our formative years, but also traits and ways of thinking from our parents that can even include mannerisms. From a free will perspective, let's take a generic police officer and a generic professional thief. Both have different moral compasses. More than likely, these perceptions of right and wrong will pass on to their children. The police officer is more likely to have children with a high moral code that could result in them choosing law enforcement professions, or similar, when they are adults. On the other hand, the children of the thief are more likely to be choosy about which laws to obey and are far less likely to be involved in law enforcement. Therefore, this would in turn work hand in hand with our genetic makeup. Homo sapiens are societal by nature. We generally don't live solitary lives like a polar bear or leopard. Therefore, we have a predisposition to working together and therefore much of our moral code, even if it's subconscious, is based on maintaining an amicable group structure. Without it, the group would fracture. Therefore, despite the the child of the thief being predisposed to not rigorously obeying concepts of ownership, the child might have very strong moral codes in other regards. In either case, the child's future is heavily determined by predetermined genetics and the already set character of the parent.

'All of this fits quite nicely into the concept of determinism. Determinists believe everything we are going to do is filtered through this complex tapestry of nature and nurture aspect of ourselves. We can determine this for ourselves, but whether we have enough information would risk the accuracy of our determinism of a future outcome. I trust that many of you would have watched the movie, *The Godfather*. In it, we have Michael Corleone, played by Al Pacino. His character has an extremely juxtaposed code. He is both a noble war hero as well as a ruthless mob boss. In the trilogy of movies, we see his character arc drastically migrate between these codes. If we were one of the soldiers in his infantry unit, we would say he would never become a mob boss because we would not have any insight into his family background. Likewise, if we were one of his associates in his nefarious gambling rings, we would have no line of sight of his war history and the fact his father, played by Marlon Brando, had wanted a better life for him away from the mob. As the viewer, we see all the aspects of his life. We might not have guessed that Michael Corleone would shift his illegal business into legitimate businesses as he grew older, but it all makes sense. Everything we had seen up until that point, ensured current decisions made sense. This is how determinists look at existence. To them, there is no free will. Any questions so far?'

No one raised a hand. They wanted to hear more before formulating questions.

'This in turn, leads us to the opposite end of the scale where we find libertarianism. Those who follow libertarianism believe we are free and we do have free will. They believe we, as humans, are special and don't follow the same constructs of existence. Much of this rests on spiritualism and the belief we have an eternal soul. This in turn leads to murky water. If one is created by an omnipotent and omnipresent being or beings, would an all-knowing being not know what we are going to do before we do it? Therefore, we might have free will, but it's still predetermined by fate. This can, however, be countered by the question of what is the purpose of this existence. Many cultures believe there is an after-life, some of which believe our current existence is a trial to determine if we are ready for the next, more important life. If this is the case, then how can there be fate. If a deity already knows the outcome, what is the purpose of a trial? This can be assessed in two ways. Let's assume that life is, in effect, a highly advanced simulation. If we were to create a simulation on a computer then yes, we could develop a simulated infrastructure with set formulas, with very rigid constraints that are determinable in order to see how far our own creativity and ingenuity can take us. However, we could also just as plausibly develop a simulation with random variables to see what results from the relative chaos. Seeing how the unknown evolves is arguably far more interesting. Therefore, it's quite reasonable to assume if there is an all-powerful being, that it might have or might not have given us free will. Therefore, libertarians argue we are special and we are in some way outside of the causal chain.

Lastly, we have compatibilism which lies in the middle of determinism and libertarianism. Compatibilists believe the already mentioned beliefs are not mutually exclusive. There is free will despite our fate already being set and it's possible to believe in both without being logically inconsistent. Although outcomes to events may be predetermined, it doesn't matter, we nevertheless still have moral responsibility. We don't have to contrast being free with being prevented from doing the tasks we want to do. Just because we might be following a predetermined path, we are still applying what we want to do in each instance. We are not constrained and are therefore, still free.'

CHAPTER SIXTY-FOUR

True to his word, George went to fetch his in-laws to take them on an undemanding scenic hike. Joanna and Charles were waiting when he arrived despite the 8am start. They had been early risers ever since he had known them. Joanna and Charles climbed into his compact SUV with a rucksack full of snacks and drinks to keep all of them energized. George had only brought a water bottle.

'Thanks again for taking us for this walk today, George,' said Charles.

'It's no problem at all Charles. I'm happy to oblige.'

'I brought a bag of goodies with me, George,' said Joanna.

'I noticed. I can only imagine what is in there.'

'It will be a surprise. I was up at six this morning, baking.'

'I wouldn't be surprised if I weigh more when we finish compared to when I started this hike.'

George drove them to the hills, south of town, which were much less steep, but arguably more beautiful. Other trails in the area were left for Mother Nature to tend to, but this one was given an extra helping hand by the local parks and nature board. A lot of indigenous fauna had been planted throughout the trail with special attention given to flowering plants. Some parts had large, well-groomed grass sections for walkers to stop and appreciate the environment. Most plants were treated with compost on a regular basis in order to keep the vegetation looking lush.

Joanna and Charles took full advantage of these views because they were becoming elderly, but also because they wanted to take their time and admire as much as possible. George was very fond of them, so he was content to take a leisurely walk as well.

'You see the sign over there?' pointed George. 'Two miles left, so we are about halfway. Are the two of you still managing okay? You aren't feeling tired?'

'We are managing fine thank you, George. We do walk around our neighborhood quite a bit lately, but perhaps we should stop and enjoy the food we brought along,' Charles said. 'There is a bench over there we can use. Another beautiful view.' A brook ran about ten feet in front of the bench. The trickling sound of water made the spot especially tranquil.

Joanna began removing various compact containers from the rucksack while Charles removed a large thermos filled with hot tea and poured it into three plastic cups.

'Wasn't the thermos hot on your back?' asked George.

'No, it was fine. No problem at all. What are you assembling there, dear?' asked Charles.

'We have fresh scones with strawberry or apricot jam. I also have some cream and if you want to go the savory route, there is grated cheese,' Joanna said.

George could feel his stomach weighing him down before he had even taken a bite from one of the scones.

'Mmm. These are delicious, Joanna. Thank you so much for making the effort.'

'It's only a pleasure. A pleasure indeed.'

'You know,' George took a moment to formulate the thought, 'I don't know why I'm so lucky to have the two of you in my life. You are both extremely special people.'

Joanna and Charles thanked him profusely. The affection in the air was almost palpable.

CHAPTER SIXTY-FIVE

'Okay kids, but just one scoop each,' said Lila.

'Yeay!' squealed Julia and Noah.

'Coming right up. One scoop of chocolate ice cream with sprinkles,' said George. He tended to not eat much ice cream, but always had a supply in case Lila popped around with the kids. 'Would you like some?'

'I'm fine thanks,' said Lila.

George went to his kitchen and grabbed the ice cream scoop, white chocolate sprinkles and chocolate ice cream. He scooped the ice cream into two bowls and added a tiny amount of sprinkles on top before carefully handing the bowls to Julia and Noah.

'What do you say kids?' asked Lila.

'Thank you, Uncle George,' they said.

'If you ask nicely, I'm sure Uncle George will let you watch a little TV, but unfortunately we aren't staying long.'

'Please, Uncle George,' they pleaded.

George switched the television on and chose a suitable cartoon for them to watch, then returned to talk to Lila.

'What brings you guys around?' asked George.

'I'm visiting one of my customers who I have become friendly with.

She is in the hospital. Since we were in the area, I thought I'd make it more of an outing for Julia and Noah. They are probably going to get very fidgety at the hospital so this will hopefully pacify them.'

'Isn't the ice cream just going to make them more hyper?'

'Probably, but then it'll give me a reason to not stay too long. You know I don't like hospitals.'

'I'm sorry to hear about your friend. What is wrong with her?'

'Triple bypass surgery.'

'Ouch.'

'Apparently, she has been having a lot of chest pains lately. She is lucky to have been diagnosed before she had a heart attack. She might even have to have a pacemaker if she doesn't regulate in the next few days.'

'I can't even imagine what that must feel like, although I suppose after a while it must feel normal. How old is she?'

'Around mid to late forties I think.'

'That is extremely young for a triple bypass. Is she overweight or a smoker?' asked George.

'You are fucking telling me. It makes me think about my health and taking better care of it. She doesn't take care of herself properly. She smokes and doesn't exercise in any way and is on the chubby side. She has three teenage kids who must be very worried about her.'

'Well, I hope the surgery helps and she takes better care of herself.'

'Talking about not feeling great,' said Lila, 'how are you doing? Have you felt light-headed again?'

'I haven't had that sensation again. I've been running and also went for a hike with Joanna and Charles yesterday. I have had a niggly headache though, but nothing I can't handle.'

'I can't say I'm surprised. This Beatrice situation has brought a lot of anxiety into your life. How are Joanna and Charles? I haven't seen them in ages.'

'They are well. They still have a spring in their step despite what they've been through- and their age.'

'I'm happy to hear they are doing well, but back to you. Maybe don't overdo the exercise at the moment considering the headaches.'

'Yes, Mom,' mocked George. 'I've been doing fine. Beatrice is just weighing on my mind. The headaches have only been sporadic and, yes you are right, my stress levels have definitely been high.'

'I take it you haven't spoken to her yet.'

'No. She hasn't been around since I saw you.'

'It must be so frustrating. What is that bitch up to?'

'I do still have a small shred of hope she isn't up to anything malicious so please don't speak about her that way.'

'I'm telling you now, her intentions are not good.'

'Possibly. Just calm down,' said George.

'I'm just frustrated she is doing this to you. Is it normal for her to not keep in touch with you like this?'

'No. We usually contact each other practically every day. This isn't normal. Whenever I call her, there is no answer and my messages remain unanswered. Not that I was planning to discuss this on the phone.'

'Weird. She isn't on to us, is she?'

'It's possible she saw me following her when I wanted to see where she was staying. The rest she couldn't know.'

'Fuck. What are the chances she would think that you just happened to be walking there innocently?'

'None. It would have been far too much of a coincidence. I mean I had to rush to keep up with her initially and there isn't a plausible reason for me to be walking in the vicinity. It's also possible she didn't like the way I behaved the last time I saw her, although I wasn't behaving that oddly that she wouldn't want to speak to me again. If she does suspect something, it's because she saw me following her.'

'What are you going to do?'

'I don't know. There isn't much I can do at the moment. I've left a few messages. If I don't hear from her in the next couple of days, I'll message again.'

'Man. Don't let it get to you, George. You'll get through this.'

'I know.'

'You shouldn't ignore the headaches or light-headedness though. Go and see your doctor to be sure. He might decide to put you on a calming medication or something. You never know, you might have a deficiency or some shit. Maybe you are low on iron or vitamins. For all you know, Beatrice could be drugging you.'

'Drugging me?' George laughed, 'I'm fine. Really.'

'George,' Lila said, 'you need to check it out. Look at my friend. If she hadn't gone to the doctor, she wouldn't have realized she needed a triple bypass.'

'Okay, fine. If it makes you happy, I'll go to my doctor.'

George didn't want to get into an argument.

'Thanks. It's always best to play it safe.'

'You're probably right. As usual.'

Lila looked at her watch. 'Kids! Time to go. Say goodbye to Uncle George- we have to go visit Mommy's friend to see if she needs a mechanical heart.'

CHAPTER SIXTY-SIX

George peered at his reflection in the mirror to ensure he looked presentable.

'You look good, sir, there is no need to adjust anything,' said a student from the film and media department. 'We just need a few more minutes and then we'll be ready to film.

'Okay, thank you, Trevor.'

George was used to attending classes with a collared shirt with his sleeves rolled up during these hot summer months. Wearing a suit for the purposes of filming was making him hot and bothered. The university had, at last, started creating online courses to acquire global studentship. The institute had been sluggish off the mark in this regard as many of the lecturers had been requesting a movement into online courses for a few years. The university had decided to commence with its trial testing. One of the requirements for the lecturers chosen to present was formal clothing, hence George's suit. The subjects that were being trialed were philosophy, agriculture, web development and strategic management.

George had been chosen to represent the Philosophy Department due to his easy-going nature. He scored highly in both peer review as well as student review. He was well versed in the subject matter and had an ability to think out of the box, which his peers greatly valued. In converse, when lecturing he could talk effortlessly and keep the topics interesting which his students appreciated. He avoided technical jargon, especially with his first-year students, in order to be more relatable and easier to follow. Some of the subject matter became quite complex and he had always felt keeping the topics uncomplicated and bolstering it with ample practical examples was the best approach. He also liked chatting about ancillary topics that were not in the course material. Being as interesting as possible was key in his mind.

However, this was a different medium and with it a different landscape. George was required to be much more to the point. He was in two minds if this was the best approach since he knew what he was going to say was not going to be as interesting as his usual lectures because he was forced to focus on the crux of the subject matter rather than expanding thought. This was because he had to retain the attention of students signing up for the courses. Their attention spans would be less because they would have more distractions in their homes or wherever they were watching. There was also the possibility they would only be watching in short bursts of fifteen to twenty minutes. Therefore, each mini-video needed to be concise as possible. George hoped the next step of evolution for online courses would be more interactive and laid-back so that he would eventually be able to revert to his more natural style of lecturing.

George was used to lecturing freely without notes or aids because he had been teaching for multiple years. However, with this medium, he was asked to use cue cards in order to follow a stricter path. While he found the process somewhat awkward, almost as if he was a recently qualified lecturer again, he did enjoy participating in new, innovative forms of education. The world was changing in immeasurable ways and he didn't want to be left behind. He couldn't help but wonder what the next step in the evolution of education would be.

'Sir, we are ready for you.'

CHAPTER SIXTY-SEVEN

'Beatrice, what are you doing here?' said George in surprise as he stood at his doorway.

'Phew, it's been hectic, George,' said Beatrice as she blew long strands of hair out of her face.

'I've been trying to contact you and you haven't responded. What happened?' asked George as he stepped aside to let her in. Beatrice hugged and kissed him before entering.

'My phone was stolen. I haven't been able to contact anyone and I've been flying so I wasn't able to replace it. Now I've lost all my contact numbers. That is why I was unable to tell you I was arriving today.'

'Didn't you backup your phone numbers?'

'No, it doesn't look like I updated the recent ones, or at least they didn't transfer onto the new phone. Talk about feeling lost. I tried calling your university yesterday, but you weren't in your office at the time so I decided to just arrive unannounced.'

'So, you aren't mad with me?' asked George.

'Mad with you? Why would I be mad with you?'

'I don't know. You didn't respond so I thought you were avoiding me.'

'Why would I be avoiding you? Things are great between us, aren't they?' Beatrice asked.

'Wow. I must admit that this has thrown me. I was somewhat off the last time we were together and you noticed so I thought maybe you didn't take kindly to it.' George decided to hold back on the rest for now. He wanted to play this out to see where the conversation went.

'George. We aren't perfect people. You were burnt out. I'm not a child. I understand sometimes you aren't going to be entirely yourself. It's fine. You don't need to be so pessimistic. Relax.'

'I'm just glad you haven't been avoiding me.' George was still clinging onto the hope there was a reasonable explanation for the lies and that their relationship could continue to blossom. He was relieved to hear she hadn't been avoiding him. It was at least a step in the right direction.

'Are you free today? I'm so sorry for arriving unannounced like this. I hate being as unorganized as this.'

'Sure, I'm free. I was planning on doing a little work, but I'll just shift it to tomorrow. Can I get you something to drink?'

'I'd love a coffee. I feel like I'm still in a different time zone,' said Beatrice, half yawning.

'I think I'll join you.'

The two sat and chatted for a while. Beatrice confirmed her phone number was still the same, but it had only been reactivated the day before, therefore any messages and missed calls sent before yesterday were not received. He gave her his contact details once more. George could see the conversation wasn't going in the direction he wanted it to so he commenced with the line of questioning he had been dreading for some time now.

'Is there anything you want to tell me?' asked George.

'Not particularly. Nothing interesting has happened over the last few days other than the theft. That is a strange question. Why? It almost sounds like there is something you expect me to want to ask.'

'It's just that I know very little about you. We hardly ever talk about your life. I know nothing about your friends or if there isn't more you want to know about my life,' George replied.

'I see. There isn't much to say. I've moved around my whole life so

I've never formed roots anywhere. It's been this way ever since I was a child. The downside is that any friends I do make, I don't keep because I tend not to keep contact once I've moved on. Plus, I'm a workaholic so I don't get much time to relax. Having said that, my work colleagues are nice. We work well together and we do have fun at some of the more interesting cities.'

George realized he had to ask a more direct question or she would continue to have an explanation for all his vague queries. 'I called your airline, Beatrice.'

'Oh. Why did you do that? Is this because I wasn't responding because my phone was stolen?'

George didn't answer the question. He thought her conclusion was a reasonable explanation and it could help justify his reason for calling. By not answering, it implied that it was the reason, without him lying directly to her. Instead, he said: 'They didn't know who you were, Beatrice.'

'Okay... Why would they? It's a large organization.'

'No, I don't mean they don't know you personally. They looked you up on their system and you aren't listed on their database.'

'It was probably a mistake of some kind.'

'Mistake? So, they pay your salary, but they don't have you on their database?' George asked.

'Wait. How did you even get them to check their database? They aren't allowed to confirm any personal information. What are you suggesting? Were you spying on me?' Beatrice had become defensive. Her voice was becoming sterner by the second.

'Don't try to shift the blame onto me. Do you work there Beatrice?' George too had become stern.

The directness of the question threw Beatrice, fracturing her defenses. 'How can you accuse me of such a thing? When did you call my company?'

'It doesn't matter when I called them.'

'You were spying on me. How could you do that? I thought we trusted one another. What have I done that would give you a reason to doubt me?' Beatrice began to cry. 'How could you do this to me? To us?'

George was struggling to hold it together. Seeing her like this made him feel guilty and sorrowful. He wanted to reach out and hug her. He realized, though, that to get to the truth he couldn't hold back. 'Is Beatrice even your real name?' The question was a bombshell that even made George flinch.

'What?' The tears poured down her face. 'How could you ask such a question? Just because of some admin issue, you think I'm lying about my name? About everything?'

'They have no record of anyone named Beatrice. I also googled you to no avail. I couldn't find a single reference to you, a photo of you, or any link to an airline.'

'What are you talking about? Companies don't disclose details about their staff online and, as I said, I'm a workaholic. I don't have the time or anything worth posting on social media. I don't even have any social media accounts, at least none in my real name. I had some random accounts in the past which I haven't used in years.'

'Where are you staying? I followed you the other day and ended up in the commercial district. There are no hotels out that way. Are you even from out of town?'

Beatrice didn't respond. She just cried.

'Do you want to know what I think? I don't think you are an air hostess. I doubt your name is Beatrice and I think you live here.'

Beatrice continued to shed tears, but eventually, with strain, found her voice, 'How... could you say... that? What is wrong... with you? Would I... lie about that?'

'You are married, aren't you? I'm a fling of some kind you don't want anyone to find out about. That is why you don't like being in public with me and why your availability is so erratic.'

'I... can't believe, you could think that. You are not well. Are you insane? How could you do and think these things? To think I loved you. Now I realize I don't even know you. I can't deal with this.'

Beatrice grabbed her handbag and stormed out. George remained silent. He felt jarred by his line of questioning. Yet questions remained unanswered- he knew she was keeping information from him. He found himself almost being more confused than before he confronted her.

What a mess he was in. George had left purgatory and was following Beatrice ever closer to his own personal hell.

CHAPTER SIXTY-EIGHT

The next day, after the dust had settled and George had time to think about the confrontation with Beatrice, he decided he would give Lila a call to let her know what had happened. As difficult as waiting was, he first wanted to get through his workday before calling. He needed the argument to saturate more before sharing what happened. He found himself struggling to focus for large parts of the day and even forgot what he wanted to say on two occasions during lectures. He brushed off the absentmindedness and the lectures continued uninhibited with the students not seeming to notice.

George was relieved to finally arrive home. He was mostly a social drinker, but if today didn't warrant some harder alcohol, he didn't know what would. He poured himself a neat bourbon and dialed Lila's number.

'Hi, George,' she answered.

'Hi, Lila.'

'You at home?'

'Yes, I just got home,' said George. He could hear Julia and Noah arguing in the background. 'You won't believe who came to visit me last night.'

'Beatrice?'

'Yes.'

'Really! Did you confront her? What was her excuse for not responding? Is she married or stalking you? Sorry. I'm asking too many questions. What happened?'

'Beatrice said she lost her phone and hasn't been able to contact anyone, nor does she know my phone number by heart. She tried calling me at work, but had no luck.'

'Convenient,' said Lila.

'That's the thing though. In isolation, her reasoning is perfectly reasonable explanation. The problem is when I look at the sum of all these plausible oddities, they appear to be implausible. My intuition keeps telling me she is deceiving me in some way.'

'How did she seem?'

'She seemed normal. There wasn't a hint of negativity in her disposition. I don't think she saw me following her. Either that or she is a brilliant actress. She was just as warm and loving as she usually is.'

'Okay…'

'She carried on as if everything was normal which admittedly threw me off balance a bit.'

'You did confront her right?' asked Lila.

'I'm getting there. I confronted her about the supposed company she works at not having a record of her. She was quite taken aback when I said it. She wasn't expecting it because I have never been confrontational with her. I'm not sure if it was the shock of me finding out or the surprise I went as far as to enquire about her from the airline.'

'She admitted she doesn't work there?'

'No. She was quite defensive at first, but then she just broke down crying. It made me feel exceptionally awful seeing her so hurt. Especially since it was by my hand.'

'What did she say?'

'She said there must have been an admin issue of some kind. Then she started attacking me slightly because that was the only way left to defend herself. Then, I told her I followed her… no wait… before that I mentioned there was no sign of her existence online.'

'How did she react to that question?'

'She just said she doesn't have any social media accounts in her name.'

'I guess that isn't uncommon.'

'At the same time, I asked her if Beatrice was even her real name. The question didn't go down well. She became a bit of a mess when I asked. It wasn't easy to watch. Then, I raised the fact that I followed her that evening. Maybe there wasn't even a point in mentioning it because by that stage she was barely responding.'

'I'm proud of you George. The experience couldn't have been easy for you.'

'It wasn't and I don't feel proud of myself. I can't get the image of her crying out of my head.'

'I'm sorry to hear it's been so difficult. Did she say anything else that would explain what has been happening?'

'That's where it ended. She burst out before I could ask her further questions. I'm no closer to figuring out what her secret is. I haven't heard from her since. She must be livid at me.'

'Stay strong. Just remember you aren't the one lying about their life. It's one thing to hold back on telling your boyfriend certain facts about yourself, but to blatantly lie about fundamental parts of your life is not fucking cool. You guys have been seeing each other for months now. That bitch shouldn't be feeling she can't trust you with things at this stage. What do you plan on doing now?'

'Nothing. What more can I do?'

'Have you considered going to the police?'

'Police? To what end? She hasn't harmed me in any way. They'll just laugh at me. My girlfriend lied to me. Big deal.'

'But we don't know if there is something more fucking sinister at play here.'

'I know. It's possible, but I don't have any proof of that so it's being overly dramatic.'

'Have you considered getting a private investigator?'

'I hadn't thought of it. Do we even have one in town?'

'I have no idea. No wait, I remember a few years ago, one of my customers getting a private investigator to check if her husband was having an affair.'

'Was he?'

'Not exactly. His mistress ended up being red meat. She was forcing her vegan lifestyle on him and he couldn't take it. So, he was going out to eat burgers on the quiet. She must have picked up he was uneasy about keeping something from her, but she never considered it was fucking meat. Hahaha. Makes me fucking laugh every time I think about it. Sorry.'

'A private investigator actually doesn't sound like such an awful idea. Why did I not think of that? Damn it. I should have done tried an investigator before confronting her. Then I could have confronted her with concrete information and deductions.'

'Don't beat yourself up. You are a trusting person by nature and that isn't a bad thing. Fuck it. Sorry, George, I have to go. These kids are going to go all kung fu on one another if I don't break them up.'

'No problem, Lila. I just wanted to let you know what happened.'

'Thanks. Take care of yourself. And don't forget to make a doctor's appointment if you haven't already.'

'I will. Bye.'

'Bye.'

George continued drinking a few more glasses of bourbon for the next couple of hours, letting his thoughts stew for longer in his head. Tomorrow's hangover was going to be rough for him. To hell with it, he thought. His toilet seat would have to comfort him back to health.

CHAPTER SIXTY-NINE

George stood before the door on which a sign read Rex- Private Investigator. He couldn't believe he was doing this. He had lived such a normal, uncomplicated life up until now. He had booked an appointment for that morning and wasn't going to back down now. He looked at his watch. The investigator was waiting for him. George knocked on the door and entered.

The two men greeted one another and the investigator ushered George to a worn chair before sitting opposite him. George half expected the private investigator to be wearing a beige trench coat and hat with a saxophone playing in the background. Childhood memories of television stereotypes must still subtly be imprinted in his mind in certain instances, he thought. The man sitting opposite him was, in fact, dressed in denim shorts, casual striped polo shirt and sandals.

'Go ahead,' said investigator Rex, reaching for his note pad.

'Where to start?' began George. 'I have a girlfriend who is lying to me. I believe she is living another life that she won't admit to.'

'What made you believe this was the case?'

'She is avoidant of being seen in public and she always excuses to not meet my sister. We have been seeing each other for months and my sister has still not managed to meet her. I realize that it sounds petty but it's my sister that triggered my line of questioning as to whether something untoward was happening.'

'Go on.'

'I did some basic investigating of my own. I googled her but couldn't find anything about her. I'm not even sure if she has told me her real name. After confronting her about it, she did say she has some accounts she hasn't used in a while, but they aren't in her real name.'

'Don't worry about that. Everyone leaves an online trail of some kind. I'll do some more advanced deep dive searches to see what I find. Did you do anything else?'

'I called the airline company she works for to try and find out her itinerary.'

'They gave you that information?' the investigator asked.

'Not exactly. I made up a story about trying to arrange a marriage proposal party. The idea was to see if she was available on a day she said she wasn't. It was more of a confirmation than a question.'

'What did you find?'

'They didn't even have a record of her. According to the lady I spoke to, she doesn't work in any of their departments.'

'Interesting. Anything else?'

'I followed her on one occasion to see where she is staying. I, unfortunately, lost track of her and ended up in an area where there are no hotels or any form of accommodation really. Therefore, I think she maybe doesn't even live out of town. Which, according to her, she does.'

'Very good. Anything else?'

'No. I did confront her, but she didn't admit to lying or having an alternate life.'

'That's fine. I'm going to need a few specific details from you, but this seems pretty straight forward. Do you have a photo of your girlfriend?'

'No...' said George. 'We usually spend time in my apartment so for the most part there hasn't been an occasion to take photos. I hadn't even realized I don't have photos of her, but then again I'm not particularly one for taking photos.'

'That is going to make this investigation harder, but it isn't the end of the world. Hopefully, she wasn't dishonest about her name. Are there any details about her that are likely to be true?'

'She is an orphan. When she described the experience, it seemed genuine to me. I don't recall if she mentioned the name of her orphanage. I don't think so.'

'This detail could be useful. It will help narrow down the search. What is her plausible age range?'

'She is in her early thirties, possibly late twenties, but I doubt it.'

'Have you seen any of her credit cards, driver's license et cetera?'

'No. Sorry.'

'Is there anything further you want to add?'

'I don't think so.'

Before parting, George gave the investigator Beatrice's full name, the name of the airline company where she said she worked, the street address where he was able to follow her to as well as the address of the park where they first met and, finally, a physical description of her. The investigator disclosed what his hourly rate was and the likely amount of hours he would spend on the case to which George agreed. George made an advance payment for eight hours which was the minimum rate to commence an investigation.

They shook hands and the investigator confirmed that if they were lucky, he should be able to verify within a few days whether she was living a double life. The quick turnaround time took some of the weight off George's shoulders.

CHAPTER SEVENTY

George sat patiently in the waiting area of his doctor's practice. He felt that Lila was overreacting, but it was better to be prudent than not. He felt physically fine, but he had to confess the sleepless nights he was having, due to Beatrice, was taking a toll on him. Even so, he wanted to avoid taking pain killers for his headaches and rather let his immune system rejuvenate him. George had, however, succumbed to the need for a medical boost on the odd occasion. He leisurely paged through a recent car magazine which rested on the coffee table. The latest Porsche 911 had been released and was receiving rave reviews for its handling, but disapproval for its obstinate design philosophy. He couldn't help but wonder why people like him took an interest in automobiles they couldn't afford. The psyche of wanting what one can't have is a strange beast. He was busy reading the specs of the monstrous top-of-the-line model when the receptionist advised him the doctor was ready.

'Good afternoon, George. Good to see you again,' he said, shaking George's hand.

'Good to see you too, doctor.'

'Please take a seat. How can I be of assistance? I haven't seen you in a while. You look well.'

George took a seat on one of the chairs adjacent to his doctor's desk. His desk, walls and cabinets were overburdened with the latest medical reading material and promotional medicine ornaments. The room looked like organized chaos. There was, however, one open area on his desk, around his keyboard and mouse, which was accompanied by a large photo of the doctor's family.

'I do feel well. I took up running a few months ago and am feeling ten years younger. Not to mention twenty pounds lighter.'

'I noticed. Good for you, but you have to try and be regimental about it otherwise it will all unravel very quickly. What seems to be the problem?'

'I've been having regular headaches of late which is quite unusual for me. Historically, I hardly ever have headaches.'

'How regularly are they occurring?' asked his doctor.

'About once or twice a day. I sometimes take a mild pain killer and then it takes the edge off. I also felt quite light-headed the one day, but it passed shortly afterward.'

'Has there been a particular time of the day when these have occurred?'

'No. Not specifically.'

'Are you under any stress?'

'Yes. I've been having relationship issues that have resulted in quite a lot of stress.'

'Any issues with your eyesight of late or undue strain?'

'No. I can't say I've noticed.'

'How have you been sleeping?'

'I've had the odd restless night because of an overactive mind but, other than that, it has been fine.'

'Please lie down on the examination bed, George so I can inspect you.'

George lay down on the bed for the doctor to check his blood pressure and a few other routine precursory procedures.

'Your blood pressure is fine. I tend to agree with you. Your problem is probably stress but, to be safe, I'm going to draw some blood to see if you have any deficiencies.'

'Is drawing blood really necessary?' asked George.

RUBEN DA SILVA

'In all likelihood, further testing isn't necessary, but the fact you are having the headaches so frequently means I prefer leaning on the side of caution and sometimes the solution can be found where you least expect it.'

After drawing blood, his doctor escorted George back to the desk.

'I'm going to prescribe a relaxant to calm you down a bit. Take them twice a day for two weeks and then as needed thereafter. I'm also going to prescribe a pain killer which you can take when needed. My receptionist will send the blood to the diagnostics lab. She will call you in the next day or two if there are any concerns or if you need to return for another examination. Try not to stress though. I know relationship issues can be difficult, but it's important to stay positive.'

'Thank you, doctor.'

CHAPTER SEVENTY-ONE

Two weeks later, George found himself back at the doctor's office despite the blood tests coming back clean. He had been taking the relaxant medication twice a day and the pain killers on the odd occasion.

'Welcome back, George. Please take a seat.'

'Thank you, doctor.'

'How have you been feeling, George?' asked his doctor.

'I've been taking the medication for the past couple of weeks like you prescribed, but I can't say I've noticed a significant difference in the way I'm feeling. I'm still getting the headaches just as often. Maybe they are not as severe, but it's hard to say. Perhaps it's too early to notice a difference.'

'Don't stress about it. The medication I prescribed usually takes a while before the benefits are noticed. Please continue taking them.'

'Don't worry. I'll definitely continue. I think I might be feeling slightly calmer already which has been helpful.'

'That's positive to hear. I've taken a look at your blood test analyses and they came back with very pleasing results. This, at least, mitigates many of the possible reasons for you feeling the way you have been. The fact that you started running has certainly helped your general well-being. Your cholesterol levels are normal. Blood sugar levels are good as well as glucose. Iron levels are normal and, for what it's worth, you have no sexually transmitted diseases.'

'That's positive to hear,' said George.

'Yes, all very positive results. Yet we still need to determine what your problem is. I'm going to suggest you see a specialist to investigate further. Perhaps some scans at a hospital will enlighten us as to what the problem is. I know a neurologist who is one of the best in her field. Unfortunately, we don't have a neurology unit in town so it will require a bit of a drive, but I'm confident she will be able to ascertain what the problem is.'

'Oh, okay. A neurologist sounds serious.'

'It's nothing to be concerned about. We'll just be consulting with someone more specialized. You might even find you just need to see a psychologist to alleviate the baggage you are carrying.'

'I wonder if a psychologist is all I need?'

'Let's see what the neurologist diagnoses, but perhaps a psychologist is something to consider thereafter.'

CHAPTER SEVENTY-TWO

'What is knowledge?' asked George.

'Knowing factual information,' responded one of the students.

'Correct, but having information is not satisfactory. One needs to filter through the good and the bad to determine, as you put it, what is factual. From a philosophical perspective, one needs to decipher what is useful and what is useless.

'It's therefore important to determine the components of knowledge in order to obtain a better understanding of what knowledge is and therefore access whether we have the levels of understanding at our disposal that we think we have.

'This leads us to epistemology. Epistemology, as you may remember, is regarded as one of the four main branches of philosophy, alongside logic, ethics and metaphysics. Epistemology is the field of philosophy concerned with the nature of knowledge as well as its validity and scope when distinguishing between fact and opinion. Philosophy has broken knowledge down into two types. These are propositional knowledge and ability knowledge.

'Propositional knowledge is knowledge articulated by a declarative sentence. Simply put, it's a statement that can either be true or false.

For example, we are all here now in class. Either the statement is true or false. Contrastingly, if I were to state you must all stand up now, the statement is not propositional because it isn't either true or false.'

A student put up his hand and asked, 'But professor, if scientific knowledge is constantly changing and revising what was known before, how do we determine what is factual and what isn't? Everyone used to think the sun revolved around the earth until they realized it didn't. Therefore, scientific fact can be refuted.'

'That is a fair question. We shall wrap back round to your assessment shortly,' said George.

'Let's look, though, at ability knowledge- this is knowledge derived based on facts we know. For example, knowing how to walk, eat or speak.

'Knowledge requires three components. These are belief, truth and justification. This is known as the tripartite account of knowledge. It's important to note that a true belief is not sufficient, but justification is also required. For example, Mars, the planet of war, was regarded as a hot and barren planet. I assume this was because the planet is a reddish-orange color. Mars is, however, further away from the sun than the earth is, therefore the assumption it was brutally hot was unfounded because the planet is in reality colder than earth. Scientists have for quite some time believed Mars contained water, in part because photographs of the surface showed what appeared to be erosion as a result of rivers and other possible bodies of liquid. This was, however, merely a theory until more recent ice deposits were discovered. This breakthrough resulted in true belief becoming a justified true belief and therefore knowledge. Theorizing there was water on Mars wasn't knowledge.

'A justified true belief in something forms the cornerstone of what philosophy can interpret as knowledge and can be dated back as far as Plato in ancient Greece. However, knowledge does not require certainty and knowledge can be obtained via luck. For example, Alexander Fleming learning that mold could impact bacteria and the resulting birth of penicillin.

'There is more to knowing than simply determining a fact correctly. In other words, there is more to knowing than having a true belief.'

A student in the front row was furiously writing down notes as George went through his lecture.

'This leads us to the Gettier problem. Edmund Gettier proved that a justified true belief does not automatically result in knowledge. One can have a justified true belief about something and can be correct based purely by coincidence. For example, you visit your doctor's new office in residential area X and therefore you believe he lives in area X. You have a justified true belief this is his house because his office clearly is only a portion of the residential building's floor space, as well as the fact that the home is located near to his old office. There was, however, a misunderstanding and this is, in fact, his father's house and the father wanted to rent out an available room. Coincidently, your doctor lives a few houses down and your doctor does live in area X. Therefore, in this case, you were merely lucky that your belief is true because it was a coincidence that he also lived in area X.

'If this is the case, what needs to be added to justified true belief to result in knowledge? Unfortunately, it isn't obvious that you can merely add another component to the justified true belief account of knowledge to solve this problem.

'This, in turn, leads to an insightful conclusion. It's therefore not entirely obvious what knowledge is. Do any of you recall the movie *The Truman Show*? In it, a young Jim Carrey is living in an artificial town and unbeknown, to him, he was the star of a reality television show. His whole reality is not what he thought it was and therefore, his knowledge of the world wasn't factual. Therefore, determining what is factual is not always as clear-cut as it may appear.'

CHAPTER SEVENTY-THREE

George found himself in one of his favorite places, the local record store. The shop sold new vinyls as well as second-hand ones. He still thoroughly enjoyed browsing through the second-hand section searching for an unappreciated gem. It was like an Easter egg hunt for him. The whole tactile experience and not knowing what lay behind the vinyl in front of him evoked joyful memories of being a teenager searching for music to buy. Music had been a coping mechanism for George when he was a teenager. It had enabled him to be transported out of his consciousness into a more carefree environment, one where he had not lost his parents.

Having an older sibling had helped tremendously as he had access to all of Lila's music. Also, Lila had had much cooler friends than George and with it came a plethora of new underground music that blew young George's mind away. It was only in his adult years that George began listening to more music of his parents' generation and not merely his own. Financial restrictions closed a lot of doors for Lila and George in their youth, but music always had alleyways to access the next room. With Lila having a large network of friends, many CDs were exchanged and copied. Even though they were unable to afford to buy more than a few CDs, Lila had dozens of copied albums. They were also not against sneaking into concerts if an artist or band was performing that they wanted to see.

Much had changed since then. George was now financially comfortable yet the music industry had lost much of its traditional sources of income. George, therefore, always felt obliged to buy vinyls for all the albums he loved. It was his way of helping the arts.

'Hi, Ben.'

'Hi, George.'

'Have you received any new stock of late?' George asked the store owner.

'You're in luck,' said Ben, 'we got back from a record convention about two weeks ago. They must have had a few hundred thousand records.'

'A few hundred thousand! That's crazy.'

'Yeah, man. So, we managed to get about three thousand second-hand vinyls to replenish our stock. Take a look. You're going to have a field day.'

George didn't need to be told twice. He moved over to the vinyl area and began trawling through the plastic delicacies in search of hidden treasure. On occasion, he stopped to inspect the cardboard packaging for damage or scratches on the vinyl itself. Ben had done an admirable job of ensuring that they had, for the most part, only bought second-hand albums that were in excellent shape.

After an hour of foraging, George settled on The Verve's *Urban Hymns*, Lead Belly's *Goodnight Irene*, Billie Holiday's *Greatest Hits*, and Edith Piaf's *Platinum Collection*.

George drove home extremely pleased with his findings. He couldn't wait to sample his purchases.

CHAPTER SEVENTY-FOUR

George once again found himself seated in a waiting room. Unfortunately, because there wasn't a neurologist in town, he had to drive to the city where he had travelled to for his book signing, the city he once called home when he first met Isabella. Lila joined him for the trip to support him in case the results weren't palatable. Despite his doctor saying the need for a specialist was precautionary, both he and Lila wanted to prepare for a worst-case scenario. Neither was pessimistic by nature, but it concerned them that the medication George's doctor had prescribed hadn't worked up until.

George had texted Beatrice the night before to let her know what was happening. Despite all that had or hadn't happened, he also wanted her at his side. Beatrice replied back while he was asleep and so he only saw in the morning that she had responded. Beatrice was tremendously supportive and, regardless of the way he had treated her, she had indicated she still loved him and wanted to be there for him. Her text had given him much comfort and relief. For George, Beatrice's compassion, above all else, was her most endearing trait.

George had decided not to tell Lila that Beatrice was going to join them. He didn't want to have an argument about her for most of the drive. Lila still considered Beatrice to be untrustworthy. He wanted to avoid stress, but he did realize that having them in the same room was going to be awkward.

Doctor Grant, the neurologist, walked into the waiting room and greeted George and Lila before escorting them to her office. Doctor Grant was a slender lady in her sixties who exuded composure and appeared to be exceedingly astute.

'Thank you both for making your way here. I do apologize you had to travel so far,' said Doctor Grant.

'It's no problem, doctor. The distance isn't as tiresome as it sounds. It was a pleasant drive. Thank you for fitting us into your schedule,' said George.

'We enjoyed the drive here- we get along very well,' said Lila. She tended to be lost for what to say when she had to watch her language in a formal environment. George knew she was not likely to say much in front of the neurologist, but she might raise some points that he might forget to mention.

'That's good to hear,' said Doctor Grant. 'I have a brief write-up from your doctor. I see you are struggling with consistent headaches and they haven't diminished with medication.'

'Yes, that is correct. My doctor prescribed a calming medication about three weeks ago, but I can't say it helped my headaches. She also prescribed a pain killer, but it didn't solve the problem and only took some of the edge off.' George replayed his doctor's visit in detail. Lila was dismayed to hear that George's headaches were more severe than she had realized. She was relieved to be there to support him, but also to obtain a first-hand account of what was happening.

Doctor Grant ran a few basic diagnostics with George before sending him for an MRI. She didn't want to discuss possible causes and diagnoses before analyzing the results of a far more thorough test. If the diagnostics did not shine any light onto the problem, she would consider the next most suitable form of assessment.

Lila accompanied him to the diagnostic rooms. Thankfully, there wasn't a queue, with only one person ahead of them, an elderly lady who entered the MRI room as they arrived. About twenty minutes later it was George's turn.

'That was effortless,' said George when he returned.

'I'm glad. Hospitals are so advanced these days. At least we know we are in the best possible place to get you right,' Lila said. 'Why didn't you tell me the headaches were bothering you so much?'

'I didn't see the need to worry you more than you necessary.'

'I'd prefer it if you didn't keep issues like this from me. You know I always have your back.'

'Fair enough.'

They sauntered to the cafeteria and nibbled at a cheese and tomato toasted sandwich to kill time because Doctor Grant was only available again in three hours. George told Lila that Beatrice might be joining them. Lila didn't want to argue or bring any negative conversation to their already delicate situation. She merely agreed it would be nice of Beatrice to join them. George could read his sister well enough to know she wasn't being sincere, but he appreciated her non-combative approach nonetheless.

The next three hours crept forward lethargically due to the lack of distraction as well as the influence of trepidation. When it was at last time, they returned to the neurologist's office. They were both thankful the waiting was over. They sat at her desk once more to hear the results of the MRI.

Doctor Grant had already removed the slides from their envelope and was giving them another once over to see if there was anything she had missed.

'I've taken a look at your MRI results,' Doctor Grant began, 'and I believe I have found the cause of your problem. I'm extremely sorry to tell you this, but there is a mass on your temporal lobe. The reason for your headaches is a brain tumor.'

CHAPTER SEVENTY-FIVE

The room fell silent. The information was difficult for George and Lila to process. Their uncharacteristically pessimistic approach had not been pessimistic enough. Even though George knew there was a possibility the results could be dire, he had pushed such thoughts to the back of his mind and had focused on being strong. This outcome was, however, worse than any that had for a moment crossed his mind. He felt like a balloon deflating at an uncomfortable rate.

George remained silent. He felt a stabbing sensation in his chest, yet at the same time felt numb all over. Time moved at a snail's pace when they sat for lunch, but now it felt dormant. Not a tear had left his eyes nor did his voice falter. He remained resolute. The same could be said for Lila who also persisted to be brave, but she was hanging on by a thread.

The slow passage of time continued to wrap itself around George, but he couldn't ascertain if it was the shock of the event or if the tumor was flexing its muscles. He wondered if acknowledgment of its existence enhanced the tumor's influence and whether this was the beginning of the end.

There was a knock at the door to the neurologist's office which snapped George out of his stupor. A moment later Beatrice entered the room and with it, he felt his lungs expand as he no longer drowned in the passage of time. Beatrice realized she was late and could tell by the mood in the room that the diagnostics had not yielded favorable results. In fact, despite Doctor Grant not yet having gone through the potential procedures that could be done, the mood portrayed one of a death-bed scene.

George rose to embrace her and Beatrice hugged him tightly. His voice had become emotional. 'Thank you for coming, Beatrice. It's so good to see you. I feel far more relaxed with you here.'

'I would never let you down in your moment of need. I'm here for you George,' said Beatrice. 'I'm sorry I'm late.'

'It doesn't matter. What matters is that you are here. The prognosis isn't great. The doctor here tells…' George stopped mid-sentence. He noticed Lila was crying. She wasn't merely crying, but weeping. Her face had become contorted with sorrow. 'It's okay, Lila. We will get through this.'

'What are you doing George?' Lila spluttered.

'Oh, I'm sorry, Lila. I'd like you to meet Beatrice.'

Lila began weeping even more profusely, her wailing become shriller. She managed with much anguish to say, 'George, there isn't anybody there.'

CHAPTER SEVENTY-SIX

'Nobody here? What do you mean? Beatrice, please don't take offense. My sister, Lila, is obviously very emotional.'

Beatrice stared compassionately at Lila and, in return, received a blank look back from Lila. There was silence in the room for a few seconds.

'Beatrice,' said George, 'aren't you going to greet my sister?' Beatrice turned to George but said nothing. She merely shook her head.

George felt the floor slide out from under him as the realization of what Lila had said dawned on him. 'She isn't here?' George asked Lila and Doctor Grant.

'No George. I'm afraid the person you are referring to is not real. The tumor is causing you to hallucinate. These sensations are one of the potential symptoms of a tumor such as yours.'

George sat back down again. He bent forward and his head sank. Lila leaned over from the chair next to his and cradled his head. She had stopped crying, but her tears were still flowing and as they glided down her face, they dropped and ran along George's hair.

'What does this mean, doctor?' asked George after he raised his head. His eyes were also watery now.

'It indicates you might have been experiencing more of these symptoms than you had realized. If you are having hallucinations, it could signify that some of your memories did not occur the way you remember then. In fact, people or objects might not have been present as you just experienced.'

'Are you saying it's possible this person I have been seeing has never existed at all? That she has been a figment of my imagination this whole time?'

'It's unlikely that all your interactions haven't been real, but it's possible. Your tumor is in a temporo-occipital region which tends to result in more complex hallucinations although I must admit I'm surprised by the degree of hallucination you just experienced. Do you have any reason to believe that encounters with this person have all been illusions?'

George took a moment to ponder the question.

'Yes, I suppose so. This person, Beatrice, has behaved strangely in certain respects. Now that I think about it, I don't know if I have ever seen her interact with another person. It's almost as if my mind created an unverifiable character who could easily slip in and out of reality without me realizing she wasn't real. She seemed so real. As real as you are to me now.'

George was dumbfounded.

'Sometimes the hallucinations can be vivid and believable,' said the doctor.

'It's ironic that I could always sense something was off. I thought she was being deceitful or had an ulterior motive which resulted in her keeping aspects of her life from me.'

'In a sense she was,' Doctor Grant said.

'I can't believe this. It makes me feel like my whole life has been fake. I don't know how to process all of this. It's all so surreal. It's as if I'm dreaming.'

'That is quite understandable. This is serious and impactful news you are receiving. Time is of the essence. Judging from the results of the MRI, as well as the vividness and complexity of your hallucination, the tumor is in an advanced state. We need to operate as a matter of urgency before you regress further.'

'This is a lot to deal with at the moment, doctor.'

'You don't need to make any decisions now, but we need to discuss the way forward.'

'What does this surgery entail, doctor?' asked Lila, eventually finding her tongue.

'Full removal of the tumor from his temporal lobe is the only approach I would advise.'

'What is the likelihood of success, doctor?' Lila asked.

'As I have already stated, regrettably we are in an advanced stage and the tumor is an awkward position. We shall perform a biopsy beforehand to confirm this but, with hallucinations this advanced and still occurring, the tumor cannot be dormant. The operation would have about a seventy percent chance of success. However, if damage occurs to the temporal lobe when removing the tumor, it could result in visual agnosia, which involves degradation in the identification of familiar objects. It's also possible to suffer from prosopagnosia, which is an impairment in the recognition of faces and distinction of facial features. You could also suffer from a disturbance of language comprehension or an impaired long-term memory. '

Doctor Grant paused, then continued. 'I apologize for my frankness, but I feel it's important to not sugarcoat such an important situation. On the positive side, the odds of you walking away healthy are quite high and I think it's important to focus on the constructive.'

George and Lila looked at one another in dismay.

Turning back towards Doctor Grant, George said, 'All this time I've been trying to understand the absence of evidence she left in her wake when I should have been ascertaining the evidence of absence.'

CHAPTER SEVENTY-SEVEN

'You coming in?' asked Lila as George pulled up at her house.

'I suppose so. I'm feeling lost at the moment so the company will be nice and, besides, I don't know what to do. It isn't going to be easy telling Joe.'

'It'll be okay. Maybe I should make a pot of green tea. How does that sound?'

'Some tea sounds perfect. Thanks, Lila.' George placed his hand on hers as she was about to climb out of the car. 'Thanks for all your support.' Once more Lila burst out crying. She had been resolute on the drive back home, but his kind words were enough to push her over the edge. George unbuckled his safety belt and lent over to comfort her. He wasn't used to seeing her like this. She had remained steadfast during the death of their parents, but now the possibility of also losing her brother was too much for her. It was as if all the accumulated pain from their youth was unraveling.

Once she had composed herself, they walked into her noisy, energetic home. George found it surreal to see the kids playing with their father without a care in the world as if nothing was wrong. Life waits for no man- it continues uninhibitedly, George realized.

They all greeted one another before Lila went to the kitchen to start the kettle and tell the kids to continue playing in their room. She returned before the kettle began to whistle. Lila didn't want to keep Joe waiting.

'Joe, we have something to tell you,' she said. 'Maybe you should take a seat.'

'That doesn't sound positive.' The apprehensive expression on Joe's face heightened. He took a moment and sat in one of the chairs in the living area.

'I don't know how to say this,' said Lila.

'I have a brain tumor,' George said.

'What? A brain tumor? How?' asked Joe.

'There is no how or why. There merely is,' George said.

'But they can remove it, right Georgie?'

'They can, but there are risks involved with the procedure.'

'What kind of risks?'

'The neurologist expects a seventy percent chance of success. Apart from death, if I survive, I could suffer from visual recognition issues, struggle with language or have issues with my long-term memory.'

'And if you don't do the surgery?'

'The tumor is advanced. I'd only have a few months to live. Maybe a year.'

Joe couldn't contain himself and began to sob. His deep tones bellowed through the house. George had never seen Joe being emotional before, let alone cry. He was a man's man and seeing the hulking frame of his brother-in-law shaking with sorrow was excruciating for George. He was surprised at how jarring the impact was. In a way, it was worse than his own pain.

The noise of Julia and Noah's playing ended abruptly, but they did not come out to see what the commotion was about.

Joe began to compose himself. 'What are you going to do?'

'What do you mean, what is he going to do? He is going to have the fucking surgery. Right, George?' Lila yelled.

'I haven't decided yet. This is an important decision. I think I should take a couple of days to think about it. Doctor Grant did say I could take a few days to figure this out.'

'What is there to think about? You'll die if you don't get that shit out of your head.'

'I could also die if I do take it out. Also, I need to consider what life could be afterward with all the complications that could take place.'

George could already tell it was going to be dreadful to tell others about his affliction and the choice he had to make. The next couple of weeks were going to be an avalanche of unpleasantness.

CHAPTER SEVENTY-EIGHT

C limbing like a sloth into his bed, George let out a large breath. It had been a long day. One of the worst days he had ever had and, for someone as adept to hardship as he had been, that was saying something. It had been arduous being around Lila and Joe in such circumstances. He wondered if he was cursed. He lost his parents at a young age, then he lost his wife at the beginning of their marriage and now he stood to die in his early forties. Life could be malicious. He couldn't blame some people for just wanting to hibernate under a blanket. A dark, isolated cavern sounded welcoming to him right now. However, he always had a high fortitude. It wouldn't be easy waking up tomorrow, but he would not likely lie in a bed of hopelessness. He would face reality in all its cruelness to push beyond the negativity.

George could already tell it was going to be a long, restless night. His mind was still racing furiously. Thoughts and memories bubbled in and out of his consciousness. George couldn't help but appreciate the ironic humor of his brain running at such an optimal level even though it had a faulty valve in its engine room.

What was he going to do, he wondered? If anything were to go wrong, how would he cope without all of his faculties? He was a scholar. Any issues with language or recognition would be catastrophic for his career and he knew he wasn't cut out for any other vocation, especially ones allowing for limited cognitive function. Thankfully, he had income protection insurance and the book's sales had given him a decent nest egg therefore, financially speaking, he should be alright. Having said that, he had no idea how his future finances would change if the operation did not go well.

Then there was the fact that Lila and Joe might have to take care of him. The last result he wanted was to become a burden on them and potentially on Julia and Noah in the long term. Despair was beginning to fester more rigorously in his mind. He needed to redirect his train of thought.

George realized his chances of coming out of this with a clean bill of health were quite probable. Many people would not think twice about a seventy percent success rate. However, success for most people was the opposite for George. The consequence of having his tumor removed was that Beatrice would be wiped from his life, never to be experienced again. After all these years, she had made his life worth living again. In the end, she wasn't having an affair with him or anyone else. She had been true to him all along. He had been carrying her with him all this time.

George then realized Beatrice was, in fact, a causal loop. She was the cause of his happiness as well as his potential pending death. To remove his demise meant the end of his peaceful life and to let his peaceful life breathe, meant it would, in turn, suffocate. The tumor had ironically brought joy to his life. His intuition had put doubt in his mind which had made him stress and resulted in him seeking medical attention, which in turn divulged the root of everything. If he hadn't fallen for Beatrice, then he wouldn't have discovered the tumor. Without Beatrice, there would have been no tumor but, without the tumor, there would have been no Beatrice.

CHAPTER SEVENTY-NINE

'Thanks for meeting me,' said George as he shook Mr. Yang's hand and hugged Rose. He had invited them to a small nook of a coffee shop down the road from his apartment. He needed to get out to ease his cabin fever and this was the most appropriate location he could think of that was convenient for them to socialize. The owners were a retired Spanish couple who had converted their secluded back yard into a makeshift coffee shop on weekends for some additional income. They only catered for five petite tables that were segregated by large shrubs which created a maze-like effect, with each table being secluded. This made it a perfect venue for fresh lovers, yet dichotomized by its appropriateness for the private revelation of bad news.

'What a beautiful coffee shop. We have never been here before,' said Rose. 'I love the way the creepers climb up onto the rafters and create a canopy. It's so nice and cool here.'

'Very nice,' said Mr. Yang, adding his own two cents. He pressed a switch on the post next to him which illuminated an orange bulb above them that signified the heralding for a waiter. As each table was surrounded by plants, the owners had fitted the orange bulbs as a way to monitor tables without constantly interrupting their guests. 'Waiter,' he said, 'can we have some menus, please?'

'Certainly, sir,' replied one of the owners.

'You okay?' asked George as the waiter went to fetch menus.

'Stupid drivers on the road here. They think they own the road. One nearly made me have an accident.'

'You do tend to drive quite recklessly,' said Rose. 'In any case, he is exaggerating. He had to swerve to miss the other car, but the likelihood of us having an accident was slim.'

'Only because I'm a great driver. If I wasn't, we would be calling a tow truck right now.'

'Yes, dear. Any particular reason why you invited us here, George?' asked Rose.

'There is, but let's order something first.'

The owner returned with the menus. George and Mr. Yang ordered an English breakfast while Rose decided on an omelet. Twenty minutes later, they were served their meals accompanied by two coffees and an orange juice.

'Mmm... tasty,' said Mr. Yang. 'Old people sure know how to cook.'

'That is slightly offensive, Yang,' said George.

'What? I was complimenting them. I hope Rose's food tastes this good in twenty years.'

Rose gave Mr. Yang a stern look. A response wasn't warranted. The couple was used to giving each other a hard time. In fact, in a strange way, the banter helped keep their marriage strong.

The three continued to enjoy their meals and socialize. Only once they had finished eating did George begin to share what had been happening. 'I invited you here this morning because I've been struggling with headaches lately.'

'That's lousy,' Rose said, 'you should have it checked out.'

'You stressed George?' asked Mr. Yang. 'It's probably the whole Beatrice thing.'

'Actually, I have already been to see a doctor about it and Beatrice is the cause of the problem, but not in the way you think.'

'Oh. What did the doctor say? How is Beatrice to blame?' asked Rose. Her tone implied her interested and concerned.

'I was on medication for stress because of her, but I wasn't sure if it was helping. I also went for blood tests, but the results came back clean so I was referred to a neurologist. She performed a few further tests, including an MRI. I have a brain tumor.'

'What! Are you serious, George? I don't believe it- a brain tumor,' said Mr. Yang. He was feeling guilty about his somewhat self-centered behavior up until now because he hadn't realized his friend was gravely ill.

Rose rested her hand on George's. 'Are you coping okay George? What did the neurologist say?'

Both their faces portrayed how concerned they were for their friend. They were shocked by the news because George looked so healthy and the thought of his dire health situation was hard to perceive and deal with.

'I'm afraid it's terminal unless operated on.'

'Fuck! I mean, that's terrible news,' said Mr. Yang.

'She has booked me for the operation in two weeks. I have until the end of this week to confirm if I want to move forward with it.'

'What are your choices? Is there even anything to consider?' asked Rose.

'There are only two choices. Don't operate, in which case I won't make it beyond another year, but at least I go out on my own terms. If I have the operation, there is a seventy percent chance of success which is reasonably favorable odds. If it goes wrong, I could have issues with my speech or memory. I could also suffer from visual recognition issues. I wouldn't be able to take care of myself so I'd have to stay with my sister or go to a caring facility of some kind. I don't even want to think about what life would be like in those circumstances. That is assuming I survive the operation.'

'Fuck me! Sorry,' said Mr. Yang.

'Wait, but what does your girlfriend have to do with this?' asked Rose 'You said she was the cause of your problem.'

'There are several symptoms with a tumor like this. To be quite honest, I don't even know exactly which ones I'm suffering from. Hell, I don't even know what is real some of the time.'

'What do you mean you don't know what is real?' Rose asked.

'I'm suffering from hallucinations. The neurologist said they are unusually complex ones. In my case, they are so realistic I can't distinguish them from reality. It's difficult to say when I've been hallucinating. Beatrice. She is..,' George's voice broke, '...she is a hallucination. I think she has been one this whole time.'

'Fuck me sideways,' blurted Mr. Yang.

Rose gasped and raised her hand to her mouth. Fighting back the tears, she placed her hand once more on George's and asked, 'A hallucination this whole time? How do you know?'

'She arrived while the neurologist was running through the diagnosis. She was there in the room with us. As real as she has always been, but I was the only one that could see her. I was completely floored when Lila told me Beatrice wasn't there and, with that disclosure, all of the oddities I was trying to figure out about Beatrice fell into place. On the positive side, she wasn't cheating on me or a stalker. She was just a person I fell in love with. Nothing more and nothing less. It's quite paradoxical. The greatest thing that has happened to me in years turns out to also be the worst.'

CHAPTER EIGHTY

Joanna and Charles climbed steadily up the stairs. They held on to the balustrade to summit the four flights. George was expecting them and was waiting at the top. Lila had phoned them to explain what was happening and they, in turn, had immediately texted George to find out if they could visit him. It had been several years since they had been to his apartment because of the distressing memories of Isabella the apartment evoked. George's health overrode any unpleasant recollections they may have had as it solidified their composure.

They greeted one another emotionally as Joanna and Charles each gave George long affectionate hugs.

'Please come in. Thank you for coming.'

'We are sorry our visit is under these circumstances, George,' said Charles.

'What can you do? That's life. Can I offer you something to drink? I was about to put the kettle on.'

'We'd love a cup of tea, if possible,' said Joanna.

'I'll have the same then.'

They all stood in the kitchen while George made tea for them.

'This place brings back a lot of memories,' said Joanna.

'I'm sure. I haven't changed much. There hasn't been a need and I can't say I've been motivated to do so.'

'Your apartment is a comfortable space. There is no need to alter anything, except maybe adding a garden.'

'Adding a garden on the fourth floor could be challenging, but yes, I'm comfortable here.'

They sat in the living area and drank their refreshment while George ran through how he had been feeling, going to his doctor and neurologist as well as the diagnosis and likelihood of success. George had felt uncomfortable mentioning Beatrice to his in-laws in the past, but now that he knew she wasn't corporeal, he realized it was inappropriate to mention her to them. It would be best for him to leave them thinking their daughter was the only love of his life. Muddying the water served no purpose.

'On the positive side, at least your chances of the operation succeeding are high,' said Joana.

'Yes, that is true. The neurologist has given me a few days to think about how to proceed, but has made a place holder booking for an operation in two weeks.'

'Two weeks is quite a long wait, isn't it?' asked Charles.

'It's quite long, but Doctor Grant is fully booked for the rest of the month or two so, from her perspective, two weeks is in fact soon.'

'I take it you have decided to go ahead and have the operation. Surgery is worth the risk surely?' asked Joanna.

'It isn't an easy decision, but yes I'm probably going to have the operation.' George hadn't made up his mind yet, but because he had chosen to not elaborate on everything, he decided it would be simpler to reinforce their thoughts on the matter for the time being.

'I can't believe it was just the other day you took us for that hike and here you are with a very serious condition,' said Joanna.

'The whole situation is quite surreal, isn't it?' responded George.

'You're telling me. Thank you again for taking us,' said Joanna.

'Yes, it was a wonderful outing for us,' added Charles.

'It was my pleasure taking you. I can't believe we haven't ever done it in the past. I guess Isabella wasn't an outdoors type of person, so I wasn't hiking as much when we were married.'

They decided to move onto more uplifting topics of conversation. The distraction helped George and they stayed for some time after he made more tea for all of them. Eventually, it was time to leave so they thanked George once more for the hike while remaining supportive and resolute for him when they said their goodbyes.

CHAPTER EIGHTY-ONE

George was deep in thought when his cellular phone rang. He reached out to see who it was, but didn't recognize the number.

'Hello. George speaking.'

'Hi George, it's private investigator Rex here. I've performed a deep dive on the individual you requested.'

George was interested in the PI's outcomes despite Doctor Grant's revelations about Beatrice. 'That is great news. You were quite quick. What did you find out?'

'I'm sorry to tell you this, but not much. The woman is a bit of a ghost. I couldn't find any evidence of her. On the online side, I couldn't uncover anything concrete. No banking records. No ID number either. I haven't been able to obtain a photo of her which means querying people at the locations you specified was a waste of time.'

'I see. What does this mean?'

'Well, she is clearly using an alias of some kind. I tried variations of her name- just searching under her first name and under her surname, but no luck. Any individuals with the same name grossly deviate in terms of age or race. I also didn't have any success following the orphan lead. So, I'm afraid I have hit a bit of a roadblock. I'm going to need you to acquire a photo of her or look at her credit cards when she isn't looking. I need more information to continue the investigation.'

'I see. Well, that is unfortunate. We actually broke up and I haven't seen her since.' George saw no sense in continuing the investigation, therefore he wanted to respond in a decisive dead end.

'Okay. Does that mean you want me to end the investigation?'

'Yes, please. I don't see the need to continue.'

'Very well. I'll stop then. Since I didn't uncover anything, I'm offering you a twenty-five percent discount on the agreed cost.'

'Thank you. I appreciate that.'

'Should I email the invoice to the same email address you gave me before?'

'Yes, please.'

'Have a great day further. Should you want me to reopen the investigation or need assistance with another matter, you know where to find me.'

'Thank you very much. Goodbye.'

George had already concluded that Beatrice had never been real. At least now the investigation put any uncertainty to bed.

George couldn't determine if he was pleased with the news. If the investigator had found something, then he would most certainty have gambled on the odds of a successful operation. Now, with Beatrice being unequivocally intertwined with the tumor, it made his decision much harder. Her love had made him feel alive again and going back to an existence without her now seemed dismal.

George wondered when he'd see her again and if she would be different to the woman he had fallen in love with. Perhaps it would be like an evaporating illusion when one realizes they are dreaming. Would he continue to fall down the rabbit hole of delusion?

CHAPTER EIGHTY-TWO

'Hi, Isabella. It's me again- to wake you from your slumber. It's another beautiful day. You would have loved this summer. I remember how you hated the cold. You always wanted to cuddle in the winter.'

George fidgeted, then continued 'It's always peaceful here, but I suppose the quietness is to be expected from a cemetery.

'Anyway, I'm here to tell you I have a brain tumor. Quite a serious one. I have a crucial decision to make. I might end up lying next to you in the near future. If I don't operate, I won't have more than a year to live. If I do operate, there is a possibility I would join you even sooner. I never imagined that my time would come so soon.

'As it turns out, Beatrice has been a hallucination this whole time. She is a symptom of the tumor. Just my luck I finally find someone to move on with and it ends up being smoke and mirrors of my own accord.

'Maybe she is a blessing, a gift to ease my suffering in my last days. These are the types of bizarre thoughts that are running through my mind of late.

'I don't know what more to say. I hate these one-sided conversations.'

CHAPTER EIGHTY-THREE

'I was wondering if and when I was going to see you again,' said George, as he stepped aside to let Beatrice in.

'I'm so apologetic you have to go through this, George. It must be so hard for you at the moment.'

'To say the rug has been swept out from under me is an understatement. Other than the headaches, I feel absolutely fine. I still went for a run yesterday morning and didn't have any side effects. It's hard to comprehend I'm so ill.'

Beatrice hugged George. Neither said a word, but they held each other tightly for several seconds.

George broke the silence first: 'I'm sorry I accused you of lying to me.'

'You could tell something was off about me and you assumed the most plausible solutions to the problem you could think of. I understand. I still love you.'

George choked up. 'I still love you. Does this mean I'm in love with myself?'

Beatrice couldn't help but laugh. 'I guess you could interpret it that way. They say love begins at home, but you take it to another level.'

'How do you function? How much of you do I control?'

'Don't ask me questions like that. I don't know how this works. I'm just a passenger of sorts. I sure could use a cup of coffee though.'

'I do feel a bit sluggish. Maybe that is why you are asking for coffee? Maybe my body needs caffeine and my subconscious is asking for it through you? Wait, what happens to the coffee I make for you if you aren't physically here?'

'Maybe you drink both or maybe, in reality, you only make one cup. Stop over-analyzing everything. Let's just relax and chat.'

'You are probably right. We might as well just enjoy the time we have together.' With that thought, all the trauma from the past few days slowly eroded away, just by being with Beatrice and looking into her face. Her presence still intoxicated his being and was the perfect cure to numb the pain.

'My coffee?' asked Beatrice.

'Oh yes, let me put the kettle on.'

'You know, I think you should consider writing another book.'

'Really? Why?'

'Because it makes you happy. It fulfills you. Writing is also a distraction for you. I'm sure the creativity and applying your mind will do you good.'

'It isn't that simple though. I can't just sit at my laptop and start churning out pages if I don't have a premise in mind and know the broad strokes of what I want to do beforehand.'

'You haven't thought of another premise since the last book?' asked Beatrice.

'No, I can't say I have. It wasn't my intention to write another book so I haven't been brainstorming ideas. I suppose I could create a sequel to the first book, but I hadn't structured the first one with this in mind.'

'You could write about completely different subject matter.'

'Such as?'

'Such as what you are going through now.'

'That could work. Stories about trauma can be quite popular. A lot of people appreciate melancholy chronicles. I could turn this whole ordeal into a story. Let me think about it. Thanks for the suggestion.'

'What is going to bug you later is whose idea was it- mine or yours.'

George handed Beatrice her cup of coffee and pondered the question. He went to fetch a notepad from a drawer and started scribbling ideas in it. Beatrice didn't say anything further and let him have space to think.

'How far back do you think I should go? I suppose you would have to be in it as well. You definitely make the story more... interesting.'

'I would hope I'm in it,' said Beatrice, 'I'm the fascinating part of the story after all. Are you thinking of making it autobiographical or fiction?'

'I'm not sure yet. There are many pros and cons to either option I need to weigh up.'

'If you go with fictional, I'd like to be more elegant. Like an old-school movie actress.'

'More elegant? What are you talking about? You are perfect as you are. Would you really want me to base you on someone else?'

'Not base me on someone else. Merely tweak me to be more like... Audrey Hepburn.'

'You've watched too many movies. I prefer you just the way you are.'

Beatrice leaned over and gently kissed him on the lips.

CHAPTER EIGHTY-FOUR

'Morning, Julia.'
'Morning, Uncle George. My mommy and daddy are in the kitchen making breakfast.'

George gave Julia a generous hug and then strolled through to the kitchen. The barrage of aromas made his stomach growl. 'It smells scrumptious in here.'

'Hi, bro.'

'Hi, Georgie!'

Lila wiped her hands on a hand towel and hugged her brother. Joe felt the gesture of a nod of his head was sufficient considering that he was frying sausages and didn't want them to burn.

'You guys are going all out by the looks of it. Sausages, eggs tomato, pancakes. Is that a loaf of bread baking in the oven?'

'More like a loaf of bread warming up in the oven, but we'll keep that to ourselves. How have you been, George?' asked Lila.

'All things considered, I'm well. I feel pretty normal.'

'That's good to hear. It's important to maintain a positive outlook.'

'Exactly. These sausages are going to be delicious because I'm positive they will be,' said Joe.

'That's not how it works dumbass,' scolded Lila. 'What am I ever going to do with this man, George?'

'You chose him,' said her brother.

'And a fine choice it was,' Joe said.

'Julia, please help me set the table,' said Lila.

George assisted Julia with the cutlery. A few moments later they were sitting around the small kitchen table to eat breakfast. George managed to squeeze himself in, but the table didn't really have space for an extra person. This meant the food congregated like a steep hill in the middle.

It was the simple moments like these which they all enjoyed. They were all chatty, with the children often clamoring for center stage. It was a wonderful distraction for George. With the laughter and trivial conversation, he almost forgot what was happening in the recesses of his mind. He decided to reserve more morbid conversations for after breakfast. Lila and Joe also appeared to be ignoring the elephant in the room.

An hour later, after George and Lila went back for seconds and Joe for thirds, the children became restless and scrambled to their rooms to play.

'I can't believe we finished all of the food. The buttons on my shorts feel like they are going to snap,' said George.

'With my husband around, there are never leftovers.'

'What can I say, I told you I was positive the food was going to be delicious,' Joe said as he leaned back and expanded his stomach.'

'You sure can eat, Joe.'

'It's a skill- one I'm very pleased I have because it's so rewarding.'

'Pity you couldn't have more productive skills than eating,' said Lila.

'Talking about productivity, I've decided to write another book.'

'Really? That's great news. What are you planning on writing about?' asked Lila.

'I'm thinking about my circumstances, the brain tumor and everything that it will entail.'

'So, a biography?'

'I'm not sure if I want it to be an autobiography yet. If I make it fictional it enables me to be more flexible with events and people. You must remember, I don't even know what hallucinations I've had other than Beatrice. Perhaps there have been other people or events I've experienced that also weren't real. I need to be in control of this as much as I can.'

'Wait,' interrupted Joe, 'are you sure Beatrice has been a hallucination this whole time? I thought we weren't sure about that yet?'

'I forget to tell you both. The private investigator I hired couldn't find any trace of Beatrice. She never did exist. Not in a tangible sense anyway. That must have been why I was doubting who she was and thought she was hiding something from me. My subconscious might have known what was going on this whole time and was trying to alert me.'

'I'm sorry it turned out this way, Georgie. It sucks that she wasn't ever real. My heart breaks to think about the whole thing.'

'Not at all. In a way, I'm glad she wasn't a real person.'

'Why?' asked Joe.

'At least this way my memories of her are positive. She never cheated on me. In an odd way, she is dependent on me and always only wanted to be with me.'

'Have you seen her since the trip to the hospital?' asked Lila.

'I saw her again last night. We chatted for a couple of hours about what is happening.'

That news was hard for Lila and Joe to swallow. They realized he wasn't well, but hearing he had had another hallucination the previous day reiterated how grave his condition was.

'Wasn't it weird? Knowing she was there but not?' asked Lila.

'In a strange way, it was liberating. We still had a normal conversation, except one with more of an insight as to what was happening. In fact, she was the one who suggested I write a book.'

'I'm not going to lie, bro, that is really fucking weird considering you know she isn't real.'

'I suppose our interaction was a little more on the strange side, but we still seemed to have a normal conversation, just as we did before. That must sound very bizarre to the two of you.'

'Look on the positive side, Lila,' said Joe. 'At least he is being productive and writing will be a diversion for him. I think it's a really good idea irrespective of who came up with it.'

'I suppose so. It's still weird though. You might not be able to write for the next couple of weeks though. Major surgery is going to take a lot out of you.'

'I didn't say I was going to have the surgery,' said George.

CHAPTER EIGHTY-FIVE

'You are joking, right? You are going to have the operation, right?' Lila asked.

'No. I've decided to not have the surgery.'

'What do you mean, not have the surgery?' Lila was starting to become anxious, resulting in high-pitched vocals. 'Having no surgery is a death sentence!'

'I realize that, but I have still decided to not remove the tumor.'

'Are you sure you know what you are doing, Georgie? You might not be in the best frame of mind.' Joe was also becoming more concerned.

'I'd like to think I still have full control of my mind. Just because I'm seeing hallucinations doesn't mean my reasoning is impeded.'

'I'm not so fucking sure about that,' yelled Lila. 'Why in the fucking world are you not going to have the surgery? You know we'll do whatever is needed to help you. We need you in our lives.'

'For one thing, if the surgery goes wrong, it goes horribly wrong. Our lives could become dramatically difficult overnight.'

'We realize that, but isn't it worth the fucking risk? Joe and I have discussed it and we are willing to help you deal with the consequences of the risk. In all likelihood, removing the tumor will be safe. If it isn't, we'll manage it. You can either come live with us or if we can't provide you with the care you need, we'll hire a professional carer to take care of you. Either way, we'll manage it together. Like a family.'

'I don't expect you to understand, but if I remove the tumor, I remove Beatrice.'

'So what, she isn't fucking real!'

Her riposte was enough to push George over the edge. 'Not real! To you maybe but, to me, she is as real as the two of you are now! She has made me happier in the last few months than I have been in years. Now I look forward to waking up in the morning. Do you want me to go back to my previous hopeless existence?'

'Hopeless! What the fuck are you talking about? We've had plenty of great times before Beatrice showed up.'

'I know and I'm grateful. I really am. I love spending time with you guys, but it isn't enough. I need more. I can't live through your lives. I need one of my own. A happy one and, if the cost of that happiness means that I have to curtail my life, so be it.'

'I don't believe this! You are thinking of ending your life so you can spend a few more months with your imaginary friend! Joe, doesn't that sound crazy to you?'

'Georgie, you don't even know what quality of life you will have for the next few months. What if you go completely wacko in the next few weeks? You'll give up decades of your life just to spend what could be weeks with her. You don't even know if you'll see her again,' said Joe.

'He doesn't know if he'll imagine her again, not see her again.' Lila tried to add salt to the wound, but it didn't have the impact she desired. Instead, George appeared to be steadfast in his decision.

'There is no reason to believe I won't continue to see her. Please hear me out. In your best-case scenario where the operation goes perfectly, I lose her by default. I can't go back to a life without her.'

'But, George,' said Lila, as tears began to form, 'she isn't real.'

'Does it matter? What is reality anyway? She makes me happy. I'd gladly have six months with her instead of sixty years without her.'

CHAPTER EIGHTY-SIX

'Thank you all for being here today. I apologize I haven't been able to attend lectures for the past week and a half. A sincere thank you to Professor Daedalus for covering for me during this time.'

With the assistance of other faculty members, George had managed to take a few days off to gather himself and decide what was required. Now that he had chosen Beatrice, it meant the end to his lecturing career. He remained physically and mentally able for the time being, but for how long he was unsure. His condition would no doubt reach a stage where he would become incoherent. The chances of the tumor merely taking his last breath without mental degradation was not likely. He didn't want his students to be privy to his ruin and had therefore decided to exit in a dignified manner while he still could.

George was standing on the stage in the university's main hall, looking out onto roughly a five hundred-strong crowd. The audience was made up of his students, faculty members and senior university representatives.

'Most of you don't know why you were invited here today. I felt it was only right for you to hear directly from me and the only way to do so was to have you all gathered here at the same time. I certainly don't want a broken telephone effect occurring on campus because you didn't hear what is happening directly from me.'

The crowd began to murmur. It had picked up on the negative connotations being emphasized by George's tone and choice of words.

'It's with great regret I tell you I shall no longer be lecturing at this fine institution, an institution, I have called home for the past sixteen years, an institution, I have been extremely proud to have been a part of.'

The murmuring began to increase.

'It's with further sorrow I tell you the reason for my departure. Regrettably, I'm suffering from a terminal brain tumor- one that the doctor feels limits me to about another year.'

A few gasps could be heard from the crowd. This was heart-wrenching news for many students as he was their favorite lecturer. If he had looked closely, George would have seen that quite a few of the eyes staring back at him were beginning to tear up. George had gathered that this would be the case. Therefore, he addressed the crowd as if it was one entity rather than the individuals it was made up of. By not focusing on any individuals, no one was able to trigger any emotions he was trying to contain.

'I can't say for how much of the year I would be able to perform my job properly. Therefore we are working towards making the adjustment for all of you as seamless yet as expedient as possible. A replacement position will be advertised from this afternoon and interviewing will commence as soon as we can.

'I do apologize to everyone that may be affected by this upheaval, but Professor Daedalus and I are trying to make the process as painless as possible. I would also like to sincerely thank Professor Daedalus, not only for his assistance over the past two weeks, but also for his mentoring over the past twelve years. I have learned so much from you and am eternally grateful for your support, professor.

'But now the time has come for me to move on. Such is the nature of life. I have no regrets. From the moment we take our first breath, so the grains of our hourglasses begin to fall. What matters is that as the last few grains end their journey, you are satisfied with how you managed the passage of time. Life is hard and many aspects are out of our control. Life will inevitably keep finding ways to overburden you. Sometimes we let these events get us down, but in the greater scheme of things they are inconsequential and it's important to try and remember this when you are struggling. Focus on being able to keep your head up high. Keep to your moral compass as best you can because life can take everything away from you, but it can't take away your honor. I feel the need to repeat this point. Life can take everything away from you, but it can't take away your honor. Always try to be honorable. It will invariably be the harder road to travel, but it's the more spiritually rewarding road.

'Having sleepless nights just to make a quick buck isn't worth it. Society tends to regard success by how much wealth you can accumulate. In reality, it's measured by how happy you are. Focus on doing activities and being around people that make you happy. Don't always follow the path traditionally taken because these were designed for the masses and you are an individual with needs and likes of your own. Living a life to impress others will never fulfill you.

'It might not always seem this way, but the ordeals you may be dealing with at the moment aren't always as awful as they appear, especially to those of you who are students. The responsibilities of being an adult are fast approaching and they can make life monotonous and arduous. Don't be in a rush to grow up. Innocence and naivety might seem like outdated commodities, but holding on to them for as long as possible will provide more joy than turning your back on them.

'Many of you fantasize about your future careers and how grand they will become. Some of you might even make your fantasies a reality. A successful career can be wonderful. It can bring you great pride and not having anxiety over financial matters is a state worth striving for. However, it's all meaningless if you are unable to share it with someone. Ensure you surround yourself with people you love because they will provide far more meaningful joy than any career can provide. Life is meant to be shared. This might sound like a simple enough task to achieve, but being able to put your loved ones before your career will be a conflict you shall continuously encounter and is one only the bravest manage to navigate successfully.

'Follow your dreams when you can. They are the essence of your inspiration. Enter careers that interest you because performing tasks that don't spark your creativity will erode your soul if you chose to do them in high volumes.

'Be good to those around you. No one is better than you and you are no better than anyone else. No single characteristic defines one's worth. Helping those in need will bring far more joy than buying yet another object for yourself. Charity must begin with yourself but, once you are on your feet, there are few ways to nourish your soul than the act of helping another individual.

'Don't be extravagant. There is no need for it as you shall just remain in the financial rat race you are in now. Buying a more expensive car than the one you already have, merely for the sake of it, isn't worth the financial stress it may induce. Rather invest the money or, if possible, donate it to those in need. Always ensure you have some money set aside for a rainy day because storms will often be on the horizon.

'I realize this is going to sound contrary to what I just stated but, at the same time, don't remain frugal. Treat yourself on occasion without being extravagant. You'll work hard for your money and sometimes you'll need to treat yourself and remember it's worth all the energy you give to your careers.

'While you are young, take risks. As you get older it will be harder and harder to do so. You might fall and hurt your head, but climb right back up and do it again. On at least one occasion, the risk will bear reward and will more than compensate for all the other failed attempts. The only thing worse than a failed attempt is not knowing if you would have succeeded had you tried.

'I thank you.'

CHAPTER EIGHTY-SEVEN

'I'm not sure how the next few months are going to go, but for what it's worth, I'm glad I'll be spending them with you,' said George.

'I feel the same way,' Beatrice said.

'I'm just sorry this has to be so hard on Lila, Joe and the kids. She has been so good to me over the years and here I am turning my back on her. She doesn't deserve it. She has been so selfless that it tears me up seeing her like this. Sometimes you have to do what is best for you though.'

'Are you sure this is what you want to do. You are forfeiting the rest of your life for me.'

'As I told Lila, I'd gladly spend the next few months with you than the next few decades without you. I can't go back to living the life I used to live. I didn't realize how empty and aimless my existence was until I met you.'

'She will understand, if not now, then in time,' said Beatrice. 'She is going to need your support to get there though. She wants what is best for you. I'm sure you will still get to spend plenty of time with them. There are still many joyful days ahead.'

'It's agonizing that I won't get to see Julia and Noah grow up. They are great kids. I wonder what they will grow up to be one day and who they'll marry?'

'That is the cycle of life. Many facets are not in our control.'

'Alas, that is what makes living it so special. The fragility of it all is beautiful.'

'Let's see where the future takes us,' said Beatrice. 'Who knows, maybe the hallucinations will become much more fantastical and we could end up on Mars or somewhere equally spectacular. Wouldn't that be exciting?'

'I'm glad you are finding this amusing, but perhaps you shouldn't be taking my terminal illness as light-hearted as you are.'

'Oh, come on, think of all the wonderful things we might see. Maybe we could end up in a *Blade Runner* type future.'

'Call me pessimistic, but we are more likely to end up in a horror film.'

'That could be exciting, too.'

'You know, I don't think I've ever told you how much I appreciate your optimism and playful nature. You are special. Tangible or not, being with you is wonderful.'

'If we are going to take this ride together, we might as well try to enjoy it.'

'You might have a point there. Living on Mars or in a *Blade Runner* future does sound intriguing.'

'Of course I have a point. Since we are in the space of giving compliments, I still haven't thanked you for the choice you made. It was a very brave decision. It couldn't have been easy choosing me over the rest of your life.'

'It wasn't easy. Most people would probably think I'm crazy and perhaps that the tumor made me think irrationally.'

'Which basically means that I made you think irrationally?'

'In a sense but, be that as it may, I love you. I couldn't go back to a life without you. Beatrice, you are my life.'

A WORD FROM THE AUTHOR

Thank you for reading my novel. It is immensely satisfying to be able to publish this story, especially since it was merely a concept I played with for many years, with no intention of writing. A few years ago, I concluded that it was worth putting to paper and needed to test myself creatively.

The concept was practically fully formed before I began writing, but even I was surprised at how ideas began to correlate and how sometimes unintentional bread crumbs to the conclusion arose. It was also gratifying to see how seamlessly the introductory philosophy course I took added depth to the story. Despite this, I'm sure I left a lot on the table, although in certain respects, this was intentional.

Should you have any queries or feedback, I'm more than willing to hear from you. My email address is ruben.da.silva.author@gmail.com.

If you enjoyed the novel, I would appreciate it if you were to leave a review rating on amazon.com for Absence of Evidence. It helps create awareness for the novel. Thank you.

ABOUT THE AUTHOR

Ruben da Silva resides in Cape Town, South Africa. Ruben, a one-time author, is a chartered accountant by education and profession. He wrote his debut novel as a means of balancing his life. Ruben, a creative person by nature, is also a part-time painter. Ruben's greatest passion is music, which he ensured played a part in his novel, not merely in terms of the main character but also in the writing process. His novel heavily stemmed from his thoughts on life and the philosophical ramifications thereof.

www.ingramcontent.com/pod-product-compliance
Lightning Source LLC
Chambersburg PA
CBHW020726210626
46807CB00016B/212